THE DARK SIDE OF THE MOUNTAIN

BONNIE S. JOHNSTON

D1430703

SOUL MATE PUBLISHING

New York

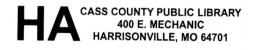

HA CASS COUNTY PUBLIC LIBRARY
400 E. MECHANIC
HARRISONVILLE, MO 64701

0 0022 0482110 8

THE DARK SIDE OF THE MOUNTAIN

Copyright©2014

BONNIE S. JOHNSTON

Cover Design by Leah Suttle

This book is a work of fiction. The names, characters, places, and incidents are the products of the author's imagination or are used fictitiously. Any resemblance to actual events, business establishments, locales, or persons, living or dead, is entirely coincidental.

All rights reserved. No part of this publication may be reproduced, stored in a retrieval system, or transmitted in any form or by any means (electronic, mechanical, photocopying, recording, or otherwise) without the prior written permission of both the copyright owner and the publisher. The only exception is brief quotations in printed reviews.

The scanning, uploading, and distribution of this book via the Internet or via any other means without the permission of the publisher is illegal and punishable by law. Please purchase only authorized electronic editions, and do not participate in or encourage electronic piracy of copyrighted materials.

Your support of the author's rights is appreciated.

Published in the United States of America by
Soul Mate Publishing
P.O. Box 24
Macedon, New York, 14502

ISBN: 978-1-61935-865-2

ebook ISBN: 978-1-61935-619-1

www.SoulMatePublishing.com

The publisher does not have any control over and does not assume any responsibility for author or third-party websites or their content.

To my granddaughters

Sydney Grace and

Addison Norine Johnston

With love

Author's Notes

Over thirty years ago I learned that two frontier forts were captured and burned by the Shawnee and Delaware Indians during the French and Indian War. These forts lay in what is now West Virginia between the South Fork and South Branch of the Potomac River. As many as forty people were killed and at least seventeen captured and marched to Indian villages on the Ohio River. It is upon these factual events that this novel is based.

Firsthand sources for these events are rare, and the few accounts in existence were written long after the actual events. Internet sites and various books have provided me with family traditions and court records, but the accounts vary. It is not known exactly who died at the hands of the Delaware Chief Killbuck or who was captured by the war party.

I have combined the facts available and speculations in order to tell the remarkable story of Anna Margaretha Mallow who was captured at the Fort Seybert along with her five children. The novel is a work of fiction, and the dialogue and descriptions of the characters are based on the author's imagination. Since no records exist regarding Anna's captivity and return, characters have been invented to tell that portion of her story.

I am indebted to my husband, Frank Miller, who has patiently supported and helped me in this endeavor. I am also grateful for the encouragement of Patricia Cruise, a former colleague, Beverly Swanson, Robin Hill, David and Carol Sollars and other members of my family. It is my hope that readers will gain perspective about the difficulties and tragedies that confronted immigrants before the American Revolution.

Chapter 1

September 15, 1749

Anna

My name is Anna Margaretha Mallow, and I am nervously excited after weeks of unrest. I was christened Anna Margaretha but much prefer the shorter Anna. My husband Michael holds me tightly as our ship glides with the tide toward the port of Philadelphia. We dream of a good life ahead, and we dream of our own land where we can raise our children without fear of armies tramping down our crops or leaders constantly changing. I hope to have many children and live to see my grandchildren and perhaps great-grandchildren. My unborn child kicks in excitement knowing the opportunities that lie ahead of us.

I was torn with the leaving of our homeland and my family who did not want us to go, especially since I was four months pregnant. My mother pleaded with me to wait until after our child was born. She feared she would never see my unborn babe if we sailed to this new land, and I feared she spoke the truth. But my husband Michael's parents were encouraging because his brother George was making arrangements to come with his wife. Our homeland has been beset with problems and armies destroying our farms. Boundary lines were changed. Our troubles seemed endless, so we sought an alternative.

It is just after dawn and will be hours until we dock, and I reflect on how we arrived at this point. When I was a little girl, I imagined meeting a handsome man who would take me away from a life of poverty and drudgery. I watched my mother work so hard, raising seven children, all destined to be poor, and I do not want to be poor. I was only twelve when I caught a glimpse of a tall, dark-haired man entering the church in front of us. My heart stopped, and I often saw his image in my childish dreams. The years passed, and he paid little attention to me until I turned sixteen, and then he watched until he found the nerve to ask my father if he could court me. My father was only too pleased at the possibility of relieving himself of his oldest daughter, and I was consumed with pleasure.

It must have been fate, God's will. How fortunate I am to be a Mallow; the name goes back for so many generations. How proud I am to be a part of this old, prominent family. I married Michael, and my mother grieved. She feared for Michael's ambition, for the prospect we might leave Griesbach and venture to a new world. My poor father never voiced his fear, but he had too many mouths to feed. One less daughter made things easier.

After weeks of ocean voyage, I now stand, my swollen belly pressed against the ship's rail, awaiting sight of the port of Philadelphia, finally, after all this time. The salty smell of the sea surrounds us. The sun begins to warm my face, and the soft breeze blows strands of hair over my eyes. The main sail has just been lowered allowing the early sunlight to spread across the wooden deck in bright splashes of light.

Nine weeks has it taken us to get here from that dirty English port of Cowes where many German families spent endless days, awaiting passage. Cowes was a horrible, ugly port city where we were surrounded by hordes of immigrants, mostly Germans like us, some lacking funds but begging for passage money. It was necessary to guard our supplies for fear of the rampant theft. We had to wait in Cowes until the ship's captain thought the vessel was full, full of people and full of cargo. We waited five days until *this happened and were forced to dip into our precious provisions during this agonizing time.*

Many poor souls simply could not afford the passage money. I saw one desperate father thrust his son and what funds he had into the arms of a young couple, begging they take the child with them. The couple did so, much to the joy of the child's poor parents. Knowing they would never see the child again, I am still haunted by their tormented faces as we pulled away from the dock.

Our trip has been horrific. We were packed into the bowels of the ship as tightly as one could imagine since there were over five hundred of us on a ship that could carry half that number in comfort. Michael and I were thrust with people we did not know, all of us with one thing in common - hope for a better life. The voyage was a trial. It was more difficult than I ever imagined, but Michael had warned of the difficulties and hardships. We were cramped with other families below deck with only a board and blankets for our rest. We tried to secure a curtain from the rafters for privacy, to little avail, but we managed. The days when the pots were not emptied were unbearable; the smell was overwhelming. The food, hard biscuits full of bugs, sustained us when we did not receive the promised broth with meat three times a week. We brought fruit, but it was depleted before we left England where we were detained while cargo was loaded. Many of our contract provisions went unfulfilled, but there was nothing we could do.

It took us over two months to sail to this land, and I often lost track of the days, mostly miserable days. Shipboard, there was never a silent moment what with children crying, women complaining and weeping, and husbands' shouting. Sickness prevailed: dysentery, constipation, sores and boils, scurvy and the like. Besides the stench of so many unwashed bodies, we also endured lice, vomiting and seasickness, not to mention deaths. How many people died

I do not know. I watched as several shrouded bodies were dropped into the sea, families watching, distraught and grieving. I was overcome with emotion when I saw their tormented, tear-stained faces.

We also endured storms, the likes of which I have never known, never having been aboard a ship on the open sea. The winds screamed, and the ship rolled and creaked as it traveled ghost-like through a curtain of black rain. We clung to whatever we could find and prayed. How we prayed during those times. How sick and miserable we were, thinking the storm would never end, and we would all die.

The nausea has long ceased. I feel good but worry that my diet is not sufficient for my unborn child. People were good to us, one in particular, Sarah Goodale, who, with her husband, sailed with us from Cowes. Others shared what they had, and observing my pregnancy, provided items of nourishment, extra milk from the cow and occasional dried fruit.

Now, as we stand at the rail, awaiting sight of the harbor, I feel secure and hopeful. Michael told me it would be so. I must stop daydreaming. It will not be long now . . .

Three hours later, as the sun hung high in the clear, blue sky, the docking of the *Phoenix* had been completed, and the medical inspections began. Anna followed her husband closely as they were pushed into a line of nervous immigrants soon to be prodded and pinched by British medical authorities and questioned by German interpreters. She began to feel nauseous as smells of unwashed bodies and urine began to overwhelm her. Hearing a woman's cries, Anna turned toward the sound but the crush of people obscured her view. Michael grabbed her arm and pulled her forward. "Anna, you must stay close to me."

"But I heard a scream," she whispered.

"You will no doubt hear many screams. That woman was too weak to climb the steps to the deck, and she will be forced to remain below as will others, I fear."

"But why won't someone help her?"

"She is ill, and the British will not allow her to infect others. She will probably be sent back to England,"

"No, they can't do that. She survived the voyage and could be helped."

"It is just the way it is. Others will be sent home, some for as little as tongue discoloration."

Anna bit her lip and clutched Michael's arm as tightly as she could as they moved forward. Soon Michael was briefly examined, pronounced fit and pushed forward while Anna found herself facing a beady-eyed inspector dressed in a black topcoat.

"Stick out your tongue, Madam," ordered the interpreter who stood next to him.

Her face became pale, and nausea rose in her throat when she watched the inspector's claw-like hand move close to her face, and she feared she would be deemed unfit and sent to the dismal hold below. Before she could recover and do as she was told, the inspector dropped his hand and shoved her past him. She realized that he was afraid she might vomit. Michael grabbed her arm and pulled her through the crowd to an area near the railing, hoping both could breathe some fresh air.

Anna and her husband were confined to the top deck until all had been inspected. Seated on Michael's heavy bag, containing his precious tools, Anna felt her eyes fill with tears as she stared at the worn and soiled wood planks. She could not shut out the sounds of screaming and crying of those who did not pass the inspection or manage to climb to the top deck. Noting her discomfort, Michael tenderly squeezed her shoulders. "My dear wife, I know this has been a difficult trip for you. We agreed this move was for our unborn children. You are strong and will soon forget this awful voyage. The bad memories will fade."

Anna looked up at her swarthy, dark husband, curls protruding from his wide-brimmed hat. "I know you are right, but I am afraid." Memories competed with sounds, clouding her mind. She struggled to compose herself.

"There is nothing to fear. This is a bright, new land with opportunity."

"I cannot forget my family and our neighbors. I still see the sad looks on their faces when we left the village. We will never see them again, I know." She looked down at her hands and quickly pulled her sleeves over her chipped nails and rough palms. Suddenly ashamed, she did not want others to see evidence of her station in life.

"My Papa. He said nothing, nothing at all. Mama, Mama was so sad."

"I know, sweetheart, but my father gave us his blessing, and George and his wife will soon follow us here. You will have family."

"Oh, I know you are right, but I am so tired today. I don't know where we will stay tonight. I don't know where we are going. I don't know where our child will be born, surely not on the ground in the wilderness."

"Look over there." Michael pulled her on her feet and pointed to the crowded dock. Standing on her toes, she was barely able to see a few well-dressed men, shouting in German, and offering a variety of services as they waited for the passengers to disembark. "We will find lodging with one of them tonight. That is what they do – provide lodging for immigrants like us. They also indenture children of the poor souls who don't have enough money to leave this ship."

Anna was puzzled. "I have no idea what indentured means."

"It's simple. These wealthy Germans who live in Philadelphia give the poor immigrants money for their passage, and, in return, acquire their children for slave labor for a period of years."

"How cruel. It is unnatural to separate families. Didn't the immigrants sign a contract like we did? Surely, they knew how much their fare would be." She was suddenly consumed by a sense of injustice.

"You forget, my dear. Most of those you see on this ship cannot read or write. They would sign x's on anything to get away from the life we all led. Nothing is going to change there. But we are here, here in this new land. In just a few days we will have our own farm, I promise you."

Anna was hardly comforted by her husband's words, but she remained silent. It was much too exhausting and noisy to attempt further conversation. She was unable to shut out the sounds and felt as if she would be swallowed up by the sea of brown and gray that engulfed her. She concentrated on smoothing the wrinkles out of her worn, drab dress and tucking strands of hair under her dull, white cap.

Hours later, Anna, Michael and the tired, frustrated passengers who had passed medical inspection were led by the ship's captain and a justice of the court across the rickety gangplank onto the wooden dock toward the nearby courthouse for the all-important oath of allegiance to King George II. Her husband's arm in her grasp, Anna was surrounded by hundreds of wide-eyed immigrants of all ages as they crowded into a large room while an interpreter shouted for silence and explained the procedure. She understood that they were required to swear allegiance and sign their names, or their marks, and, in return, would be eligible for land warrants and eventual naturalization. Anna watched her husband sign his name in perfect German script and felt pride that he did not scratch an x as many men did.

The procedure completed, Anna and Michael joined the relieved immigrants who were scarcely aware of what they agreed to and marched back to the ship for final accounting.

Anna was tired, and her back ached. Michael supported her and tried to provide assurance, but she could barely stand, let alone contain her frustrations. However, she managed to hold back her tears and concentrate on walking down the muddy path to the ship.

As the sun began to settle behind the city, Michael finally paid their full fares and was granted permission to leave the ship. Anna felt tremendous relief but became aware that others were not so fortunate and huddled with Philadelphia citizens, signing indenture agreements in order to disembark. She watched as several children were torn from their parents and forcibly taken in hand by strange men.

"It is so unfair. Those poor children. I cannot watch any more of this." She turned away and wiped tears from her eyes with the sleeve of her worn gown,

For the second time today, shadowed by large buildings and warehouses, Anna, Michael and other immigrants crowded and pushed their way along well-traveled cobblestone path up a rise to the city itself, a thriving port town full of strange smells, sounds and people. Anna hiked up her heavy, wool skirts, avoiding the mud holes, and carried her treasure box and a bag. The smell of spoiled fish accosted her nostrils, but she lacked a free hand to cover her nose. She could barely contain her nausea as she tried to dismiss the strange odors surrounding her.

Diverting her attention, she noted the three and four storied buildings and watched people of all colors, including black men and women whom, she learned later, were owned by residents. She also observed dark, native people dressed in unfamiliar garb and gawked in surprise at their bare chests and strange weaponry. She heard unfamiliar languages in addition to German, French and English and was full of questions but silenced by her frowning husband. She watched several immigrants in threadbare coats speak with waiting residents who were only too happy to provide lodging and assistance for exorbitant funds.

Shortly, Michael made arrangements for the night with a German-speaking gentleman who introduced himself as Herr Mecklenburg. Anna understood that he and his wife regularly supplied rooms for German immigrants and suspected that they supplemented their income handsomely by doing so. She listened quietly while he described the accommodations and price. When the transaction was completed, she became aware that Mecklenburg looked at her with sympathy. She wondered if it were because of her advanced pregnancy or the fact that she was an immigrant. Suddenly embarrassed by her worn, drab clothes, she lowered her eyes. Seeing her discomfort, Mecklenburg smiled. "Frau Mallow, you will soon have the food and rest you need. Follow me."

Anna trudged behind her husband as they followed Mecklenburg and threaded their way down a street that led away from the crowded dock. Mecklenburg carried Anna's small bag while she clutched a small box holding her two treasures, a small mirror from her grandmother and a pair of candle holders, a gift from her aunt. During the long voyage, Anna had often looked at herself in the small mirror. When she became aware that her thick dark hair had lost its luster and her oval face had become thin and pale from the voyage, she had put the mirror away and decided she did not want reminders of her condition.

Breathing quickly but unable to keep silent any longer, Anna tugged at her husband's arm. "How do we get to our land? Where will we find our route? How long will it take? And what about the naked savages we saw on the streets?"

"Be patient. All will work out. Tomorrow we will hire a guide to show us the way. Do not concern yourself with the natives because they are harmless, poor people. The British are in control here. You need only concern yourself with our child. I will take care of the rest."

Briefly annoyed at her husband's tone, Anna ceased her questioning and concentrated on walking and trying to make sense of the many new sights that confronted her. She was exhausted and hungry, and the slanting rays of the sun failed to comfort her.

In less than an hour, the weary couple followed Mecklenburg into a three-story brick house where they were greeted by a well-dressed Frau Mecklenburg who instructed a servant to provide water and a chamber pot for their needs. Smiling at her tired lodgers, she then ushered them to a small room on the second floor.

"You poor dears. You need a good night's rest. Now wash up and join us for a good supper."

When Anna saw the large feather bed, she forgot the uncertainty of her future and looked forward to sleeping under the colorful quilt spread over the bed. Today had been the longest day of her life, and she would be glad when it was over.

"Frau Mecklenburg," she exclaimed and could not suppress a brilliant smile. "We are so grateful for your hospitality. I cannot tell you what a bed will mean for me, for us. It has been months, four at least, since I slept on a real bed. And to sit on a chair at a table for supper."

Seeing her husband frown, Anna ceased speaking and thought, "He does not want me to talk too much." She lowered her eyes from Frau Mecklenburg's pleasant gaze and turned her attention to her belongings and the welcome pitcher of water that would allow her to remove some of the grime from her body.

She knew, however, that Michael was pleased with their accommodations and would discuss their destination, the Tulpehocken Valley, the German settlement in Pennsylvania, with the Mecklenburgs at supper. She had many questions herself, but she knew that she would not ask them for fear of irritating Michael. Perhaps she would learn more about the natives, a subject Michael had already dismissed. "Please cease your worry about natives. You have enough to think about. Our child will occupy your time. I will handle the rest."

September 17, 1749

Anna

It is a warm, dry morning, but we do not mind as we have finally secured our warrant from the land office and have purchased a wagon, supplies and horses for our journey to Tulpehocken, the German settlement. The land is not free as some thought. We will eventually have to pay for it. It has been a difficult two days, but we are finally on our way after spending two nights with a German family who greatly overcharged us for the stay. We had no choice and were fortunate to have a roof over our heads.

Our two-day stay with the Mecklenburgs left me with many questions. Arriving late, we were served supper, fresh breads, cheeses and stew, by a silent, dark young woman, black hair hidden beneath a tightly secured scarf, large gold earrings falling from her earlobes. She said nothing but sullenly performed duties as prescribed by her mistress. Michael told me later she was a slave, born in Africa and forced to come to America by her own people who sold her to a slaver. I have heard little of such things.

I saw such hate, such anger in her dark face. I felt pity for her but could not look directly into her penetrating eyes when she briefly glared at me. I wonder if the Mecklenburgs see her anger? If we should ever be in a position to own slaves, I would hope we would treat them kindly and gain their respect. It is not God's will, I think, for people to be enslaved."

We have been warned that the roads are poor and that mosquitoes are still unbearable in the swampy land that we will pass through. Our journey will be very difficult I fear, but we are prepared and travel with three other families and our guide. We know that we will have to erect a shelter on our land, when we find it, while the cabin is being built. I am afraid that I will be no help since I am cumbersome, so I hope it stays warm and dry and that others will aid us.

Our meager possessions are safe in my small bag behind me, and Michael's tools are in a large bag under the wagon seat. My treasures are safe on my lap. I shall try to enjoy this beautiful, warm day and pray the good weather continues.

Michael is so excited and speaks German with those traveling with us, Germans also. I watch these determined men trying to share their enthusiasm and hope for the future, but sometimes I am afraid, of what I do not know. Perhaps it is just the tremendous change we have made. I could cry when I think that I will never see my parents or siblings again, but I must try not to think of that and concentrate on the child who moves within me. I pray the birth will not take place in the open.

This country is so big and so wild, nothing like what we left behind. I hear stories that the native people are not pleased with our coming. Others have assured me that we will not be harmed, that these wild-looking people will not accost us. I saw several while we were in Philadelphia. They looked poor and harmless to me. Some begged for bread, and some hawked their wares, baskets, furs and such. Michael told me not to worry and not to look at them. He is confident and fears nothing. I shall trust him in all things.

I am thankful we are with other Germans, and I do not have to learn English. I fear my education is lacking although my mother taught me to read. I can write German script, but not very well, not like Michael. We have no books to read, just a German Bible. Maybe I will not have to learn English, at least not for a while, I hope.

Chapter 2

October 19, 1749

Enchanted by the valley, Anna marveled at the primal trees and the lush green meadows surrounding neatly, cleared acres of slightly rolling land. The land was fresh and new, not worn, dusty and ancient like the area from which she came. She was subtly aware of freshness in the air, and somehow the sky seemed bluer, crisper, the clouds whiter, and the streams clearer. She was pleased that her child would be born in this new land and, fortunately, under a secure roof.

Anna gave birth to their first child on this bright, windy day in October. The child entered the world in a comfortable cabin on the frontier of the colony of Pennsylvania while the nervous father remained outside, smoking a pipe and pacing, hoping all would end well. When Anna's cries ceased, a young girl sprinted out of the cabin door, shouting, "Herr Mallow. The baby is here. She is here. Come see."

Dropping his pipe on the ground, Michael caught the child by her arm. "A girl you say? I have a daughter?"

"Ya, ya," she squealed as she led him toward the cabin door. The two entered the warm room and soon observed the female child, a small, fine-featured infant, swaddled and tucked in next to her tired mother. Michael smiled at his wife. "Thank God you are both well." He turned to a woman hovering over his wife and child. "We could not have managed without you, Anna Maria. Was the birthing difficult?"

"No, Herr Mallow. Frau Mallow will give you many fine children." She patted Anna on her arm. Anna's eyes slowly closed, and before she fell asleep, she heard her husband say, "We shall call this child Anna Maria, after you Frau Moser."

Anna's last memory before she slept was of the day she met Anna Maria, the day their wagon slowly passed the neat, well cared for cabin and lane. She recalled how tired and despondent she was as Michael drove the old wagon toward their unseen claim when they were startled by a woman running toward them. Anna turned toward the figure as Michael stopped the wagon.

"Hello. You are newcomers to our valley, no?"

"Ya." Michael nodded as he scrutinized the woman before him. "It is good you speak German. My name is Michael, Michael Mallow, and this is my wife Anna Margaretha. We have spent over a week to get here from Philadelphia after a long voyage from Griesbach. Our claim is not too far from here if my map is correct. Could we trouble you for a cup of water from your well? As you can see, my wife is in need of refreshment."

"Of course, Herr Mallow. We cannot allow a fine young couple to live without a roof over their heads. Your babe will be born in comfort, not on the cold ground."

"Your husband? He will not mind?"

"No. We have watched immigrants come and go for the decade we have lived here. We all came here for the same reasons. Our village was not far from Griesbach, and my husband Adam brought me here where we have happily settled and are raising our three children. You will find this valley hospitable and profitable. We have aided many during these years, and I know a good man when I see one."

Overcome with emotion, Anna immediately warmed to this stout, pleasant woman who reminded her of her family back home. As the image faded, a smile spread across her face as she drifted into a deep sleep within the security of a warm cabin, her first child cradled in her arms.

October 29, 1749

Anna

Our first child, our tiny daughter, has just been christened in the Lutheran Church. Sweet Anna Maria Moser stood as her sponsor, and I was very grateful for all of her help. I had hoped our new friends, Jacob and Maria Seybert, would still be here to participate. I was distressed when they left as we had only known each other for three weeks, a short time to become friends. We are only just beginning our life here, but the Seyberts are moving on. They have been here eleven years, carving out a farm in this area. But three years ago reports came of an even finer valley south of us, just waiting for the plow. I cannot understand why they wanted to leave. Their lives were good here. I can only hope Michael does not uproot us before a decade passes. Seyberts are not the only ones who are entranced by thoughts of a more plentiful land, where game is so abundant, it can be shot on your doorstep, and land can be had by the stroke of a pen or the building of a cabin. It scares me.

The Seyberts, like us, were punished by the harsh times in the Palatine area. Jacob's mother Hannah, widowed in 1732, was left with four children. It was difficult for a widow to survive, but she was fortunate to find Henry Lorenz and marry him.

Jacob avoided military service but knew it could come anytime, and he might be dragged off to serve some nobleman who desired more territory. His mother was overwhelmed by taxes, taxes on anything and everything. None of them could expect any relief in their positions so, without dissent, their families agreed to the voyage with hope of a better life.

Encountering the same difficulties as we did, Jacob, his brothers, sisters Elizabeth and Catherine, and parents traveled almost three hundred miles to the coast to secure passage for all of them to England. They left in April and did not arrive until September 1738, after five months of treacherous and tiring travel over rivers and oceans. I hope Michael does not decide to follow them to that place called Virginia. The thought of moving again makes me ill.

After the christening of the Mallow baby, the Mallows and Mosers departed the small church, and, braving the chilly wind and blowing leaves, a harbinger of the winter to come, walked to their waiting wagon. Michael steadied his wife who carried their newborn close to her breast. Leaves had fallen, and the path was covered in bright splashes of red, orange and yellow. Anna handed the baby to Michael and climbed up to the seat where Michael joined her, and the two couples returned to the Moser farm where they would remain for several more weeks while their cabin was being completed.

Anna thoroughly enjoyed their hosts and their lively offspring. Several years older than their guests, the Mosers had produced three lovely children, small versions of themselves. Anna had laughed when she watched their oldest daughter, Anna Barbara, now ten, follow and copy her mother in all things, often repeating her mother's remarks, hands on her hips, and head nodding in agreement. Their eight-year-old son, called Adam, mimicked his father, strutting around the cabin, thumbs tucked into his belt, complaining about weather, wild animals or Indians. The youngest daughter, fascinated by the new baby, spent much of her day, rocking an imaginary child while humming a German lullaby.

Feeling guilty occasionally, Anna also knew that not all immigrants were able to stay in warm cabins; some lived in lean-tos, and some lacked funds to purchase bare necessities and were soon forced to return to the city, their dreams unfulfilled.

Arriving at the crowded Moser cabin, Anna concentrated on her new baby and suppressed her questions and fears about the future. She had been surprised, however, that the valley was so remote, so unsettled in comparison to the area from which she had come.

She had asked Adam, "If there is trouble, who will protect us in this valley?"

Adam echoed her husband. "Do not worry about our security. Our valley is safe. You must concern yourself with your family now."

"Yes, I must think of our daughter, and all will be well."

Since leaving Philadelphia, she no longer feared the natives and substituted that fear with one of the wild animals that seemed to surround them. She heard unfamiliar cries at night and knew Adam kept a loaded musket by the door to fend off unwelcome prey, wild animals or Indians, she knew not which and did not want to know.

January 1, 1750

It was New Year's Day in the Tulpehocken Valley although few celebrated since most were confined inside their cabins while a heavy snowstorm blanketed the valley. Tulpehocken Creek was frozen over, and the wind moaned as it pushed against the cabin door. However, Anna was content and happy in their newly completed cabin despite the biting cold and swirling snow, which occasionally drifted through cracks in the log walls. Michael sat on a stool, carefully cleaning his flintlock, a mass of dark curls tied at the nape of his neck, while Anna rocked two-month-old Mary, as she was now called, and relished the warmth of the fire and the smell of the burning wood. She closed her eyes, a faint smile on her face, as she snuggled under the quilt and allowed pleasant memories to flow through her mind.

For Anna, it had been a whirlwind three months with a newborn and a new cabin. Life spread before her like an open book, and the valley was generous in supplying for their needs. She marveled at the generosity of their neighbors, and their larder now held potatoes, onions and dried apples. Mosers had sent over a barrel of salted pork, enough to last the winter.

Anna cuddled her sleeping baby while she relished in the warmth of her fur covering. Smiling contentedly, she thought of Michael's big bay gelding, resting safely in Moser's barn along with their first cow expecting a calf in the spring. She savored the memory of the horse's soft nose and gentle, large brown eyes and the day that Michael proudly paraded him in front of her.

"Oh, a beautiful horse, our horse."

"Yes, my love. And he will not be the last. You will see." Michael grinned.

Adapting readily to frontier life, Michael enjoyed the hunt and had recently bagged a large bear from which he would tan a bearskin for Anna's warmth. There was no shortage of meat, and venison was plentiful along with wild turkeys and rabbits.

As a lock of thick, black hair partially covered his forehead, Michael sang a German song as he worked by the fire, using his native tongue as did their neighbors. He looked at his relaxed wife and child. "You must practice your English, my dear."

"I know, but you are so much better at pronouncing English words." She did not open her eyes, and the faint smile remained on her face.

He laughed. "I'm afraid I will always sound like a German, but our children, they must learn the language. You must be able to help them."

"I know you are right, but not tonight." She found the language difficult and could not produce proper English sounds, but she knew she would have to master the language. In the meantime, she would not worry about it. She was too tired to think of such things on this cold evening.

She had managed to block memories of her family and the village where she had grown up and rarely thought of the neatly arranged, thatched houses, the vineyards, and the colorful gardens. However, she constantly prayed for her family, but doubted that their lives had improved. Although Michael was not in the least devout, he joined Anna in thanking God for their good fortune. All was comfortable and well in her new world, wilderness though it was. She looked forward to a warm, cozy winter with her family, safe in this valley, surrounded by like-minded Germans who had little knowledge of the conflict between the British and the French over control of this newly settled continent. She kept her eyes closed, relished the warmth and thought of sleep.

July 1, 1750

Anna

It is so warm today; the air is so heavy that I can hardly breathe. I am sitting, without shoes or stockings, on a log in front of our cabin. My toes play in the loose dirt, and my gown is pulled up to my knees while I attempt to keep cool. My Mary is crawling now, trying to reach anything that moves in front of her. She wants to put all things into her mouth, and it is hard to prevent her from eating dirt. She is such a good child though, and Michael adores her. He lights up when he comes home after his day's labor.

We are finally settled, and I can look out on one cleared acre, planted now with corn. The little green stalks are now plain to be seen, perhaps as high as my knees. The cow and her young calf enjoy the still-green grass although I fear the sun may dry it out this month. Our barn is progressing well with the help of our wonderful neighbors. It is a good life. I just hope I can enjoy Mary for a while longer and not become pregnant for at least another year. I will nurse her as long as I can, of course. The women tell me that will prevent conception. I wonder . . .

It is pleasant to be outside despite the heat. My chores are done for the day, and I await Michael's return from the field where he is burning stumps. I can see smoke rising in the distance. I have prepared rabbit stew, which simmers over the cabin fire. Of course, the cabin is too warm, but we can eat outside perhaps. If this breeze continues, we can keep windows and the cabin door open for some relief from the heat but not from these pesky flies.

I am glad we are here, settled, and all is well. I miss my family but suppress the memories as much as I can. I miss female companionship because there are things I will not discuss with Michael. But I try to think of the future, our lives here in this new land.

Our cabin is but one room, but that will suffice. I can stand in the fireplace opening for it is six feet tall. There is a mill several miles from us, so I have access to flour and cornmeal. I have all the hooks and shelves necessary for baking and cooking. I am a good cook because my mother taught me well. I want to be a good wife and mother. And how I love my black-eyed, strong husband. What more could I ask for?

January 1, 1751

Winter had arrived with a vengeance in early November and had not relented. Anna, despite a quiet, pleasant summer, had become restless, attributing it to melancholy over the loss of her family or loneliness during the long days while Michael labored outside. She looked forward to Sundays at church when she was able to see her neighbors and catch up on local news, not that there was much to learn.

"What is wrong with you?" Michael often asked during the days when her face exhibited a perpetual look of sadness.

"I miss having someone to talk to sometimes, but it will pass."

"You can talk to me, you know,", but she could not put her thoughts into words.

Anna suspected that Anna Maria Moser, having spent a rare day at the Mallow cabin the week before, was well aware of her unspoken remorse at having left her family. It was not surprising, she thought, that Anna Maria invited them to a gathering on the first day of the new year.

"You need to visit neighbors more often instead of staying alone in this cabin, day after day. I will plan a celebration on the first day of January, weather permitting. You must join us."

"Of course we will, but I will have to ask Michael."

"You tell that handsome husband of yours it is high time to show you and your daughter to our neighbors. I will take no excuse for a no."

On the day of the celebration, feeling better than she had in weeks, Anna dressed herself in her drab, brown gown over her worn shift. She tied a crisp white apron around her slim waist and pinned her black tresses under her white cap. Wishing she had a new gown, she carefully tucked in obstinate strands of hair and pinched her cheeks. Looking into her mirror, she was shocked at the dark circles appearing under her eyes and hoped no one would notice.

"Michael, do I look all right? Am I pale?"

"You look fine, my dear. Both you and our daughter are beautiful. There is no need to worry." Anna remained unconvinced because Michael rarely commented on her appearance. Besides, she was tired of being told not to worry. She could worry if she wanted to, she thought.

By noon, Anna, Michael and Mary had joined their neighbors and gathered in the small, cramped Moser cabin for a day of festivities and feasting. The room was filled with happy children and chattering adults who conversed over one another. After a meal of venison, wild turkey, potatoes, turnips, apples and corn bread, the immigrants rested in satisfaction, enjoying their neighbors' company despite the overly warm cabin. Orange shadows from the flaming wood illuminated portions of their faces in rapid movement while voices overlapped in a pleasant hum. Anna leaned next to Michael as they both sat on a bench near the fire, young Mary resting at their feet.

Anna tensed, and her smile faded quickly when Adam Moser abruptly stood up, faced the group, and motioned for silence. "Hear me, neighbors. I have news, news of Jacob and Maria and Virginia." She dreaded that word 'Virginia' and fear spread throughout her body.

Waving a piece of paper, Moser began to read portions of the letter he had recently received from Jacob Seybert, written in Seybert's scrawling German script. "Friend Adam, Maria and I send our warmest regards, dearest friends. We miss all of you, and none here can take your places in our hearts. We will thrive in this new land, and our claim will be productive once we finish clearing it. Other Germans have located here, but the area was first settled three years ago by Irishman Roger Dyer and his family."

Anna listened with a bitter taste in her mouth as laughter filled the cabin while Moser continued to read Seybert's description of Roger Dyer who had moved to escape the German immigrants who, he believed, would overwhelm his family with German ways. "Dyer cannot escape us after all because two of his daughters married Germans."

While her eyes burned from the smoke-filled room, Anna tried to suppress her fears. She did not understand the reason for Seyberts move nor did she want to hear more about the

Virginia land. She wondered how could they possibly be better off than they were in the Tulpehocken Valley. After all, there were no churches, no close towns, few close neighbors, and endless land to clear. There was certainly no military protection, not that there was much here, but it just felt safer in the settled Tulpehocken Valley. Finally, bristling with unspoken anger, Anna breathed a sigh of relief when little Mary became restless, and the conversation lulled.

When Anna and Michael reluctantly took their leave, darkness had settled over the valley, but the moon helped light the way as small clouds chased each other across the moonlit sky. The sorrel mare plodded over the hard-packed bridle path as she pulled the wagon toward the Mallow cabin. Anna held her young daughter wrapped in a bearskin on her lap. Shivering from the bitter cold of this New Year's Day, Anna leaned against her husband. "Ah, husband. What a lovely day we had." She hoped he had forgotten about Virginia and would not bring the subject up.

"Aye, that it was, my love." He patted her arm. "Seybert seems to be doing well in the South Branch Valley, it seems."

"Perhaps so, but I don't understand why they moved. Do you?"

"Yes, they left for profit, for more land in this beautiful new world we live in."

"Didn't they do well enough here?" She knew the dreaded word would soon come up.

"Of course, they did. They just wanted more, and Virginia offers cheap land. Even the Virginia governor is encouraging settlement on the frontier. The British King wants the entire territory, all the way to the Mississippi River, I think. Soon there will be British soldiers and militia to protect even remote areas like the South Branch Valley."

"I still do not understand why there was not enough land for Seyberts here. Besides, I hear it is dangerous on the frontier." She could not bring herself to say the word.

"Why not strive for more? There is much to be had in this new land, for the taking. People are moving constantly westward. One must be first to secure the best land because, someday, sooner than you think, the opportunities will be lost."

"No, I think not. There is too much land. No one knows how far it extends. I hear it goes on for a thousand miles, clear to the ocean in the west."

"The French and the Spanish claim the western lands."

"What of the native people, the savages? Did they sell it, the land I mean?"

"Some of it they did, but there are some tribes who say the land is still theirs."

"What about the South Branch land?"

"Virginia is secure, at least the portion where Seyberts settled. The great tribe called the Iroquois sold the land to the British years ago. But it is true that the claims of the Virginia Colony stretch way beyond the South Branch Valley in the county of Augusta. There are no boundary lines because Virginia wants as much land as it can claim. The French occupy the Mississippi Valley, so there is conflict, of course. But I do not think the eastern part of Virginia will see trouble."

"Ah, then the Seyberts do not have to worry about the savages."

"I do not think they do although Jacob says some of the natives still live in the area but do not bother them. Seyberts are safe. It is a good place, I think."

"For their sakes I hope so. Now, I do not want to think about a place where there is little of civilization and few people. I pray you are not influenced by Jacob's glowing report. I doubt that his wife Maria is quite as enthusiastic."

"I think she is, for, after all, she has her entire family with her."

"I do not wish to complain, but I fear this land in some ways. How much will be sacrificed for land ownership and settlement? Those who pave the way for others may lose much. There is danger, I fear, and I do not want to be subjected to such danger. You say the natives want the land back. There are no churches or schools, and I do not want our children to be illiterate. At least the church can provide what we cannot. You told me how important it will be for our children to read and write, English, no doubt. You are educated, and I want the same for our children. I want them to know more than I do." She still could not bring herself to say 'Virginia'.

"Have no fear. It takes people like us to carve out this new land. Yes, it is hard, but the rewards for our children will be great. The natives will be pushed back for they cannot withstand our numbers. You may think it is wrong for us to take their land, but their way of life will soon be finished. They are too small in number and too backward. It may take years, but it will happen. You worry too much."

Feeling a chill, Anna sighed and snuggled deeper into the heavy fur, and the couple spoke no more of the Colony of Virginia but proceeded silently along the dark bridle path lined with towering dark shapes as they made their way to their new home.

June 1, 1751

Anna was pleased that the quiet Tulpehocken Valley now teemed with German settlers who had carved out their neatly arranged, productive farms from the wilderness. Two Lutheran churches had been built, and the industrious Germans prospered and saw their numbers increase.

Anna and Michael worked hard and succeeded beyond their expectations. Furthermore, their land increased in value, their livestock increased in numbers, and they began to forget the problems from which they fled. Anna regularly thanked

God for their success and pushed unpleasant thoughts into the recesses of her mind, hoping they would not reappear.

Early this morning Anna kneaded bread dough before her children woke and mused about that unknown land, Virginia. She knew that the nature and ambition of her husband and other German immigrants kept them susceptible to reports of more and better land to the southwest in the Colony of Virginia, a huge area, largely unsettled beyond the eastern portion.

Deep in her thoughts, Anna was abruptly startled when Michael reached around her waist, placing his large hands over her protruding belly. "Is this my son, sweetheart? Do you carry a male child this time?"

Leaning back against him, she laughed. "You wish. Perhaps I shall have only daughters, you know."

"Just one son is all I ask." He chuckled and released her, frowning at his hands now covered in flour residue.

Anna was glad they had a child to discuss. Perhaps she would not have to listen to Michael's thoughts about Virginia and the land speculators. Anna hated these men who had bought thousands of acres and continued to entice Pennsylvania and Maryland settlers with cheap prices.

"Lying opportunists," she called them. "I do not believe a thing they say. They just want to take our money."

Michael brushed off the flour from his hands. "Adam had another letter from Jacob Seybert. The area is quickly being settled."

Anna's mood immediately soured. "I do not want to speak of Virginia. You always tell me not to think about things. Well, I will not think about Virginia. Anna Maria told me. . ."

"You listen too much to the women."

"You underestimate me. We have moved here, and I know what we went through. Do you really think I want to move all over again? We have been here only two years. We are having another child in the fall. Do you think I do not see your ears prick up when that word Virginia is mentioned? There. I said the word I hate."

"Now, sweetheart, there is no need to worry. I said nothing of moving." Anna, hoping the conversation would cease, returned to her kneading and molded the dough into loaves. Somehow, she doubted that he was telling her the truth. Virginia was seducing her husband like a lover, but she hoped the problem would be resolved when her second child came in the fall. In the meantime, she would avoid the topic as much as she could.

October 6, 1751

Within the Mallow cabin on this chilly October morning, two-year-old Mary whimpered softly as she was firmly held by formidable Anna Maria Moser, her namesake. Anna was being delivered of her second child under the capable hands of neighbor women. Abruptly, Anna's screaming ceased, silence ensued, and then the faint cry of a newborn child could be heard above the wind. Anna Maria smiled at her namesake. "It is fine, little one. The child has arrived."

Michael stood quietly along the side of the cabin, smoking his pipe, looking at the brilliant blue sky. After a short time, a female emerged from the cabin. "You have a son, a fine son."

He rushed toward the door, but she held him back. "Wait, you must know. He has a defect, a small one but. . ."

"What is it woman? For God's sakes tell me." A startled look spread across his face.

"He has a harelip, a small defect."

"Let me in. I shall see it myself." Michael pushed by her through the cabin door.

And so Michael met his first son, to be named Johann Adam, after Anna Marie's husband whom Michael greatly admired. Leaning over the bed and examining his tiny son's disfigurement, he briefly frowned but quickly smiled when he saw his wife's questioning look. Anna's fear faded when she saw her husband smile, and she knew he would not fault her for the tiny disfigurement. Both observed their swaddled newborn with his black eyes and a few dark curls on the top of his head.

"You have presented me with a son, my love. He is beautiful like his mother."

Young Mary followed her father to observe her new brother. She, too, smiled and gently touched the baby's face, her fingers lingering on his lip. Anna watched them both and then turned to Anna Maria. "We are so thankful for your help. We could not ask for better neighbors."

Anna watched Michael walk with Anna Maria to the cabin door as she took her leave. The late afternoon sun had fled behind a few dark clouds, and the wind had picked up. The pleasant October day began to take on an ominous change while black clouds on the western horizon threatened to engulf the valley with their fury. Anna ignored the weather and turned to her swaddled baby while Mary climbed into the bed next to her mother.

Michael quickly returned to his wife after Anna Maria had mounted her waiting horse for the short ride back to her family. "I hope the storm waits until she gets home." He then turned his attention to his wife and new son. Soon, Anna dozed, and for the remainder of the evening images drifted in and out of her mind, as her new son lay swaddled at her side and Mary rested silently on the bed.

January 1, 1752

The snow is deep outside our cabin, but I do not mind. It is comforting to be inside in this warmth while our fire roars, my babies sleep silently, and all is well. Michael is restless as he often is when we are cooped up inside. He is so proud of our cabin, our new barn, and, of course, his new son, Johann Adam.

But, there is always a but, I have received sad news of my family from my sister, written many months ago, but not arriving until December. My poor father died a year ago, Christmas Day in fact. He was sickly and downtrodden before our voyage. I still see the sadness, the emptiness in his eyes, as we said good-bye that final day. We were not close those last few years after Michael entered my life. I thought it was because I was no longer his little girl, but perhaps he had given up, even then, after working so hard for so little.

My mother soon followed, dying four months later of a sudden, unnamed illness which left her bedridden and unable to move for weeks before God Almighty took her, a blessing, her children by her side. My sister said she died with my letters on her bed table, worn pieces of paper from being read so many times. Thankfully, she died knowing I was fine and the mother of two, thriving in the new world. She was at peace, I hope.

I pray for my family, sisters and brothers, nieces and nephews all. May God protect them from the unrest they encounter; nothing has improved in my homeland.

As I hoped, I have not had to learn English although I have picked up words and phrases because there are English traders and a few English settlers among us. There are also Quakers, but I do not know much about them. They believe in peace and want to aid the natives and teach them our ways, but I think they are arrogant to believe our ways are the only ways. I will resolve to learn English. I must, eventually, because English is the language of this new country, and my children will need to learn it. In the meantime, I teach Anna Maria, my Mary, German words. She is a quick study and will have no trouble with English.

Several of our neighbors have sold their farms and

moved south, some to Maryland, and many farther to Virginia and the so-called South Branch area. Unscrupulous men continue to come to our valley to entice us to move where land is cheap and opportunities abundant. I am even more skeptical. We are fine here and have no need to move.

December 31, 1752

Time passed quickly for Anna and Michael, and they prospered. Anna was happy, happier than she had ever been in her life. As long as the subject did not come up, she successfully managed to hide her apprehension of Virginia. With neighbors' help, their land began to be cleared, corn planted and harvested, and livestock housed in a new barn. Anna's herb garden bordered the southern exposure of the cabin and amply supplied parsley, basil, onions and dill for cooking. She had learned to scour catnip and mint in the forest for additions for teas as well as medicinal purposes. Bundles of tied herbs now hung from the rafters near the fireplace.

Although Anna was comfortable with neighbors and the Lutheran Church, she was often overcome with loneliness. Her life was defined by chores, but she rarely complained. She was well aware that it was helpful to be busy and had no trouble in that regard. She had taken her husband's advice.

"Don't worry," echoed in her ears, and she did not.

Today, the uncharitable winter cold brought sleet, wind, and snow that swirled outside the cabin as Anna, Michael and their two little ones sought warmth from the roaring fire. It was dark; whether day or night was difficult to determine. Anna rocked slowly while she concentrated on her knitting and tried to ignore the wind biting at the door. The children were asleep, Adam in his cradle, and Mary on her small trundle bed. Michael surveyed the scene and finally spoke softly to his wife. "I want to sell our farm and move to Virginia." Her suppressed fear suddenly emerged in full force.

Anna was silent. "Did you hear me?" He stared at her, his eyes wide and wary.

"Ah," she murmured as she dropped her knitting. "I was afraid of this. Too much nonsense about the bounties of Virginia. I do not want to go. I like it here with friends, our church. We are settled here, and I have no desire to move again. None at all."

"Hear me out. The land in Virginia is more fertile. We can have as much land as we want. We can sell our farm here for a profit, a tidy sum. Others have gone. The Seyberts thrive there, I hear."

"I do not think I can endure a long trip and the building of another cabin. It is so hard and not necessary." Her eyes were downcast, full of moisture.

"I already have a buyer in the spring." He lowered his eyes.

"You do? You did not tell me. How could you do that without my consent or knowledge?"

"Anna, please. It is what we must do. It is a good move, I promise you. Have we not made good decisions so far? You will have your school and your church. Our children will have great opportunities."

Containing her rising anger, Anna refused to look at her somber husband, and instead, returned to her knitting, a look of sadness upon her face, and she said nothing. She was suddenly anguished and afraid.

"I cannot fight him," she thought. "I should, but I cannot. Help me, God," and she silently prayed.

Michael won the battle as Anna knew he would. The family would move to the South Branch area of Virginia located in the large county of Augusta. Although Anna did not want to uproot her young family, she agreed to go, finally, after much cajoling, arguing, and tears. Deep within her, she feared the move, but she tried to dismiss her misgivings. She was no match for her forceful husband.

Chapter 3

April 1, 1753

On a dreary day in April 1753, Anna, Michael and two small children began the arduous journey, over one hundred and eighty miles, from the Tulpehocken Valley in Pennsylvania through Maryland and south to the waiting lands of frontier Virginia.

Although she had refused to discuss the details until she could stand it no longer, Anna had finally asked, "Please tell me how we will get to this promised land you are taking us to?"

Michael had patiently explained their route and drawn a rough map. "We will take the Great Wagon Road from Lancaster to Hagerstown and then toward Roanoke. The road is an old Indian trail used by settlers moving to the frontier and the Shenandoah Valley of Virginia. It is well-traveled and safe, I hear."

"I certainly hope there will be others traveling with us. I probably will be unable to help you know. There will be two children to care for." She had little faith in the aid of others.

"Do not worry, my dear. We will be fine."

Now, as she climbed into the crowded wagon this morning, she scowled. "If I hear him say not to worry one more time, I will scream."

Having no knowledge of the country beyond the Tulpehocken Valley, she had no idea what the Great Wagon Road meant. She knew that the road wound south through the Virginia towns of Winchester and New Market where they would take a western cutoff leading across the mountains to the South Branch Valley.

"How will we cross the mountains to the South Branch Valley?"

"I told you there is a cutoff leading to the Dyer Settlement close to Seyberts."

"What condition is it in? Can we drive the wagon over the mountains?"

"Of course, we can. How do you think Seyberts got to their land? Now, stop your questioning and prepare. I am anxious to start our journey."

The packing completed, Michael helped Anna and the children settle in the wagon, and then he tied the cow and the bay gelding to the back of the old vehicle. He checked the hitching apparatus, making certain the harnesses on the horses were secure.

Anna watched her husband and recognized the determination etched on his face. She knew he was excited to be moving for new opportunities, but she was not, no matter how hard she tried. She was carrying a child again, and two young children would add to the difficulty, but Michael seemed not to notice.

As their journey began, she looked back sadly at the cabin and clearing that she would never see again. She remembered Anna Moser's last words. "My dear friend, I hate to see you leave us. It breaks my heart, for you, for your two little ones. I know you have no choice. Your husband is strong, forceful. You must trust his judgment and support him, no matter how difficult it is. Pray God, it will be a good decision for you all. Remember, you are a strong woman." But Anna feared that she was not, and a veil of self-doubt fell upon her.

The wagon had barely moved when Anna remembered. "Where are my seeds, the seeds Anna Maria gave me? I cannot leave without them."

"They are in a bag behind you." Michael was irritated and pointed to a small bag wedged behind the seat. She breathed a sigh of relief because she had learned the importance of herb gardens and knew no doctor would appear in remote Virginia.

Anna watched until dust and haze eventually merged the scene into the horizon. Only then did she turn forward in the wagon seat to watch the swishing tails of the two horses laboring to pull the heavy vehicle along the rough road. Young Adam remained dozing in her arms while Mary squirmed between her parents, being cautioned by her father to try to stay still. Anna wiped the tears forming in her eyes, and so their journey began.

Michael seemed to sense her displeasure. "Stop fretting. We are embracing new opportunities. Do you not feel well?"

"I am fine." Sadness remained etched on her face.

He patted her arm. "We are headed to Seyberts. They will house us while our cabin is built. You will be comfortable with them. It will only take a few weeks to get there, and we will find lodging on our way."

"And what if we don't find any lodging?"

"We will make do. After all, we can sleep under our wagon if we have to."

Anna closed her eyes and refrained from commenting. The journey was underway, and she could do nothing to change it. She could not clear her mind from worry and was angry with herself for allowing Michael to force the move.

"What is wrong with me," she wondered. "Anna Maria refused such a move, and I did not."

May 15, 1753

Anna
Once again, I have deferred to my husband, and so we have moved. I did not wish this move, but I am a loyal wife so I agreed in the end; to what purpose I do not know. I love Michael and trust him, but what if he is wrong . . . this time? What if this move is not a good one? Only time will tell.

We are lodging with Jacob and Maria Seybert and their delightful children as we wait for our cabin to become livable. We will live a mile from Seyberts, but that is not overly far, so we shall visit, of course. I have seen our claim and doubt that it is as fertile as our Pennsylvania acres, for it is not level. There is no doubt that the Irishman Dyer took the best land, but then he was here first.

On our trip here we saw several Indians and a few wigwams, more like huts, I thought. I was surprised, but Jacob tells us they are friendly, and we should not fear them. Today, two came to the Seybert's cabin to borrow a kettle. Jacob did not hesitate to give them one, knowing it would be returned along with a payment of meat of some kind. He said they are always honest in this regard. He has no fear of these natives who live near us.

Never having seen an Indian this closely before, I watched their blank, unsmiling faces. They spoke English and were respectful, but there was something unsettling about these men, their chests bare, and their tomahawks and knives stuck in their belts. They had no hair on their heads except for a small patch of long strands to which they attached a feather. A chill ran up my spine as I searched their black eyes for some sign of warmth. There was none. I suspect they hate us for we are taking their lands and hunting grounds. I wonder if I should fear these men? Jacob says not, but I think he may be wrong.

Michael has explained to me that the great northern Iroquois tribe had sold all of this land to the British nine years ago. But the Delaware Indians, those I saw, still say this land is theirs and was not the Iroquois to sell. So they have stayed where they have lived for decades. I think they must be very bitter and want to stop the advance of the settlers. However, they speak English and trade for goods.

I am carrying my third child and expect the birth late

*this summer. It is good, for we will be settled before my time
comes. Maria has promised to assist at the delivery, and I
am grateful for her help. I have just become settled with two
children but will have to learn to handle one more.*

*Our trip here was difficult. Several times the wagon
wheels became stuck in the mud. The road, if you could call it
that, was very rough and full of ruts and mud holes. Michael
managed, and others headed our way aided us. The trip over
the mountains to this valley was the worst. Most settlers gave
up on wagons and traveled by pack horses. We managed to
arrive, wagon intact, but could not have done so without the
help of the few men traveling along the same trail.*

*It took weeks until we arrived at Seyberts, bruised, tired,
and hungry from our travel. Fortunately, my pregnancy was
not so advanced to cause me severe discomfort. Adam has
the sniffles and has been coughing, but Maria has given
him tea, and he seems better today. My sweet Mary hovers
over her brother and comforts him with her cheerfulness.
She protects him, perhaps because of his disfigurement,
minor, but of concern for her.*

*And what of this new land? I recognize its beauty and
ruggedness. I know that others thrive here, but I still fear the
undertaking. I already miss our former cabin, our neighbors,
the peace we had in Pennsylvania. I alternate between being
angry and happy at the same time. There is nothing I can do. It
is done . . . the move I mean. I shall pray it was the right move.*

June 18, 1753

Anna, holding Mary's hand, and Michael, Adam in his
arms, stood in front of their newly completed cabin that was
almost swallowed up by the dense, dark green foliage that
dwarfed it. Anna saw little difference between this cabin and
the one they had left in Pennsylvania. The rolling land of

South Fork Mountain made for a rugged and beautiful view, but it seemed to her that the land would be less productive than their acres in Pennsylvania. She had not grasped the need to move, and it made no sense to her still. But, she was here, so she might as well make the best of it.

"Is it done? Can we move in soon?" She tried to sound pleased.

"It is nearly ready, but it needs your touch to make it home, of course. And you can plant your garden there," and Michael pointed to a spot along the side of the cabin. "We will move in this week once our furniture is completed. Come, look at the fireplace. It is huge and will warm us and provide all the necessities of cooking and heating. We will have a fruit cellar in back, and I will begin to clear the land. Seyberts will house our livestock while we construct a barn."

Arms spread wide, Anna stood in the large fireplace opening, marveling at the hooks and racks. She visualized cords of wood stacked by the cabin and a roaring fire within. She imagined additions, such as the one Roger Dyer, the Irishman, had added over the decade he had been in the South Fork Valley, and she thought of the future. For now though, the cabin would do and hold the four of them. She tried very hard to hide her frustration and concentrate on the future her husband foresaw for them.

"Come. I want to show you something." And so she followed her husband, holding her son, out of the cabin and walked behind the structure.

"See, a spring, a spring that bubbles and flows to the creek bed below." Straining to see what he meant, Anna observed a trickle of clear water, playfully winding its way down a slight hill into the brook.

"We will have a spring house, a place to get water and to cool milk and cream. See. We will build the structure here."

And he pointed to the spot where the water emerged from the weeds and made its way along its course.

"Hum," she thought as she tried not to think about the desirable flat land on both sides of the South Fork River, the land belonging to the Dyer family.

July 4, 1753

Profusely sweating, Anna, after a restless night, awoke to the sounds of dawn early on what promised to be a very hot July day. She rose so as not to wake Michael or her two slumbering children and walked to the cabin door. Opening it as quietly as possible, she stepped outside, breathing in the humid warm air and stretching her aching back, feeling the child adjust within her. She stepped gingerly off the porch steps and walked behind the cabin to the close-by spring where she filled a bucket with cool water to splash upon her arms and face.

As she bent over the bucket, she heard a soft sound behind her. Abruptly turning around, she stood face to face with bare-chested, pox-scared Indian, long earrings dangling from his large lobes and silver bracelets adorning both arms. He was older than she, but tan and firm and solid of build. Sensing her surprise and apprehension, he picked up the bucket while motioning her to proceed back to the cabin door. She followed his instructions and walked behind him to the front of the cabin as he set the bucket beside her and stared with piercing, black eyes.

"Biscuits. Do you have bread?"

"Yes I believe I do. Are you hungry?"

The Indian patted his stomach. "Yes, hungry for bread."

She passed him and entered the cabin while he remained a short distance from the door. Returning with a napkin containing three biscuits, she handed them to him, and he hungrily devoured first one, then another. "Thank you, Killbuck thanks you." The two stared at each other in silence for several seconds before Anna lowered her eyes.

Then, with a sly grin emerging on his face as he swallowed the last bite of the biscuit, the Indian chief Killbuck turned around and walked into the forest beyond the clearing of the Mallow cabin. Taunted by the smell, he thoroughly enjoyed the lingering taste of bread, white man's bread, such a delight, one of the good things the whites offered. He and two warriors had spent several weeks wandering the hills and valleys around the South Branch area to assess the strength and number of white population. His clan would soon disappear from this valley to join their brothers the Shawnee in eastern Pennsylvania and Ohio, but he wanted one more pleasant tour of the land he so loved and hated to leave.

These whites, he thought, have no idea what will come. The woman, the pregnant one he had just visited, would come to fear him, not look at him with pity and disgust. She may have given him biscuits, but she simply wanted to rid herself of his presence. He could have killed her in an instant, of course. It was tempting, but he would wait, wait for the move to be complete and the alliance with the French to be sealed. Then it would begin, and the whites would scatter to the East in terror while their cabins burned and their children died.

As part of his campaign for vengeance, Killbuck envisioned the flaming frontier, the smoking ruins, the scalped bodies, and the cleansing of the earth of these hated usurpers. And he saw his people returning to the life they loved, the land they protected, the game increasing and thriving.

Anna did not look at the departing Indian but took the bucket into the cabin. She briefly shuddered at the thought of the savage who stood within a foot of her. She feared him, his look, his black eyes, and could not get his image out of her mind. He hates us she thought. He could have killed me but did not. And she had a premonition of fear, which did not subside for several days.

Before Anna shut the cabin door, Michael was up, standing in front of her. "I heard a voice, a man. Who was it?" and he rushed past her to open the door.

Anna grabbed his arm. "Stop. An Indian. It was an Indian. He meant me no harm."

Fire in his eyes, Michael shoved past her, but she grabbed him again. "No, he is gone. I gave him biscuits."

"Why did you not wake me? I'll be damned if a savage can walk up to my front door. Damn him. I'll kill him."

"No. Stop. He is gone. No harm done. He was just hungry."

"You're wrong. You're wrong. He was scouting us to see our weaknesses. They are unpredictable, these savages. Do not trust them." He put his hands on her shoulders and looked at her, face bloodshot with anger. "Do not talk to them. Get me." Pushing her aside roughly, he grabbed his rifle and slammed the door as he went in a fruitless search of the foe.

Anna stood in fear for several moments before she realized Michael would never find the savage who would have disappeared into the forest by now, and she waited in silence knowing her angry husband would soon return, and the children would wake at his voice.

September 15, 1753

Anna
My time has come. It is not so bad, and Maria is again by my side. Michael has left our cabin as usual, though I would like him close. If we have a daughter, I want to call her Sarah after the kind woman on the ship, the one who helped me so much while I was indisposed. I can still see her

face, her graying hair, her deep blue eyes, and her pleasant smile. I do not want to name a son after my father. It might be fitting, but I fear it might be a bad omen.

This will be my third child. It was predictable because the neighbor women and my mother have prepared me for a child every two years. Since birthing is easy for me, and I desire my husband, it is inevitable that I should bear a child regularly. Ah, that I could stop at three but still satisfy Michael. There are remedies, of course, but I will not think of that. It must be God's will.

The pains are coming regularly now, and I know it will not be long . . .

Anna gave birth to her third child, second son, in a newly constructed cabin on acres of mostly uncleared land in the frontier forest of Virginia. Michael examined his newborn son who closely resembled his older brother and allowed no input from his wife. "He shall be called Johann Michael. It is fitting he should have his father's name."

"What if I wanted a different name?" Anna thought, but was too exhausted to argue, and she had no alternative. She looked at Maria Seybert standing at her side and wondered if Maria could read her mind. She hoped not because she had no wish for Maria's sympathy. But Maria quickly smiled at the young parents and took her leave, pleased that the birth had gone well.

Chapter 4

May 1, 1754

"Michael, supper is on the table." Anna stood in the cabin doorway while she sought the familiar figure of her husband in the distance. She glimpsed him leaning on the split rail fence, gazing into the distance. She knew he was deep in thought or ignoring her call. Patiently waiting, she suspected he was thinking about his conversation with Jacob Seybert two days before.

Michael had returned home that day in a foul mood, and she saw anger on his flushed face. "Seybert says the French have control of the forks of the Ohio. British forces have been defeated, and the French will construct a fort there. Colonel Fry and Colonel Washington were to take the area, but they failed. Fry died and now Washington is in command. There will be trouble with the savages here. Some of them have aligned with the French."

Anna was not certain who Washington was, but recognized the distress in her husband's voice.

Becoming impatient, Anna called again, and this time Michael turned, waved, and jogged toward his waiting wife. When he had entered the cabin and taken his accustomed place at the narrow table, Anna decided to ask about the Indians who no longer appeared in their valley. "Where did they go, those savages who lived around here? And why did they leave so suddenly? I thought they were friendly and traded with us. But I guess I will not have to worry about your killing one who asks for food." She laughed and joined her family at the table.

Michael's voice rose in anger. "I told you then, and I will

tell you again. The Indians are dangerous and were watching us. There is a war going on now, you know. And we better hope the British win or we may not get title to our land. Besides, the local Indians probably left to join the French."

"I do not understand what all of this means. I am glad the savages are gone, and I can allow the children to play outside safely. I wish you would explain this situation to me. Has war been declared?"

"Since the British tried to take a French fort, I call it war whether it's official or not. The savages will support anyone who will promise them their land back. I fear it will be years until we get a clear title to this land, and we better hope that young George Washington is as good as the Redcoats think he is."

"Dear Lord, will these problems never end? What happened to our promised land? You assured me this was a good move. Do you still think so? And do not tell me to stop worrying. It seems to me there is plenty to worry about, not to mention our three little ones." She turned from her husband and concentrated on feeding young Michael.

"Stop it. We cannot know what the future holds. I do the best I can for all of us. This war will affect all the colonies, not just Virginia. I trust the British, and they will not allow us to remain unprotected. They want to control the entire continent, you know."

She ignored his remarks and continued feeding young Michael while Mary coaxed Adam to drink his cup of milk. She wanted no more of this conversation and refused to look at her somber husband. Although she had all she could handle with her three little ones, she suspected and now knew that there was danger ahead. What kind of danger she did not know. For some reason, she visualized Killbuck, and she shuddered.

July 17, 1755

The fires had been ignited, and the conflict continued with no end in sight. Anna awoke to an unpleasant, humid day, and a sour mood remained with her all morning. Michael had informed her that the British general Braddock had been defeated a week ago and killed by his own man.

"Dyer was right. The Redcoats do not know how to fight these Indians and French. Braddock would not let his men hide in trees like the savages, and so they were soundly defeated. Now, we all have to join the local militia."

She knew that Michael had no choice. "Tis not fair. I am carrying our fourth child, and you have to ride with a militia to protect us. This war just gets worse, and I do not want you gone."

"It is the law. All men over sixteen have been ordered to enlist, you know. George Washington's orders now that he is in command. You are not the only wife to deal with this. Now, there will be two hundred men in this county, Augusta County, to protect us."

"Well then, you'd better secure another flintlock because I want one here when you are gone. And you'd better teach me to shoot it, just in case."

"That I will do. That I will do. Now, I must return to weeding our corn crop. Call me if you need me." As he turned to leave the cabin, Anna followed at his heels until she stepped on the stoop where she sat to contemplate the situation, relishing the July sun. She wished she knew more of politics, but the war seemed so far away. She wished they were still in the Tulpehocken Valley where everyone spoke German. Here, she was forced to learn English but spoke it poorly. Feeling inadequate, she was irritated that Michael spoke English so well now, although his German accent refused to leave.

Anna glanced down at her hands, folded on her lap. Spreading out her fingers, she noticed that her skin was rough and red from exhausting hours of washing clothes in the large wooden bucket. Her body ached from the effort of scrubbing and wringing.

These thoughts made her tired, and she soon returned to the cabin to begin the endless washing, prepare supper and see that Mary still had her brothers in hand.

October 31, 1755

Today, after the successful birth of her fourth child, Anna could tell that Michael was elated, for another son had just entered the world. Now he had three sons in all, plus his first born Mary, sweet helpful child as she was. Without asking his wife for a name preference, Michael once again chose his name. "We shall call this one Johann George," named after Michael's brother who had followed them to the South Branch Valley.

"George he will be." Anna again succumbed to her husband's wishes, and she knew George would be pleased. Besides, it was pleasant to have family within a half a day's journey although they rarely visited.

Resting comfortably, Anna had time for reflection while Michael stoked the cabin's fire hoping to get more warmth. He turned toward her.

"Are you warm enough, my dear? I fear winter is coming early this year. The walnut crop is very heavy, a bad sign you know. And the wolves will take our shoats if I don't pen them up."

"I don't suppose it will be worse than last winter. We only lost one last year," she answered from the heavily quilted bed. Quickly forgetting about winter, wolves and hogs, she looked at her sleeping child and gently pushed a thin strand of dark hair from his pink forehead. "He looks like Michael you know." The unrelenting wind smothered her response as it pushed against the cabin walls.

Something about the baby triggered a memory of her mother. She closed her eyes to conjure up images of both her mother and her homeland. She remembered the neat hillsides, covered with lush vineyards, and recalled the majestic mountains along the Rhine River. She could still see the neat, thatched-roof houses of her neighbors and the beautiful flowers appearing every spring, bringing added color to her drab existence. On the other hand, she was aware that Michael was pragmatic, never for a minute looking back but rather focused on the present with dreams of the future. Anna savored her memories in silence because there was no one to share them with.

Anna's moments of reflection came occasionally with other women, the older Elizabeth Heavener in particular. Still slim and attractive, she was Jacob Seybert's sister who had married Nicholas Heavener, another German with whom Michael had become fast friends. With Elizabeth, Anna sometimes voiced her fears and her longing for her birth family, whom she knew she would never again see.

Elizabeth empathized. "We have no choice, you and I, you know. We are at the mercy of our husbands' wishes. I, too, miss the old country, but we are here and have children to consider. I love Nicholas with all my heart and have never said no to him. I hate his militia duty and fear his death because widows have difficult times. But what can we do? The only way to survive is to live day by day and hope for successes. Your Michael is a strong man and will protect you and your children. If you love him, you will have more children. That is just the way it is."

"I know, but it is also this war I worry about because I do not understand it. I fear the savages and know they have already raided farms and killed settlers."

"I worry too, but none of the Seyberts will run from this trouble, and that is what I am, a Seybert through and through. German stubbornness, as you know." A sad smile passed across Elizabeth's face.

Becoming warm, Anna suddenly woke from her dozing and, taking a minute to look at her sleeping son cradled upon her breast, hoped that the next one would wait several years. She turned her head from the bed towards the fire and the strong profile of her husband as he carefully stoked the now-roaring fire.

Suddenly, an unpleasant memory surfaced, and she recalled a conversation with Michael just three days before. He had repeated an argument that occurred when the militia convened at Seyberts. Roger Dyer warned, "We are in trouble here. There'll be no protection from them savages. The governor is a dimwit, and the British don't know a damn thing about fighting the red men. It's already started. Settlers have been murdered and farms burned. Many have left for the East."

Seybert disagreed. "Dyer, stop. British interests lie in protecting us. They want to control the Ohio Valley."

"Sweet Jesus, Seybert. You are much too optimistic, my friend. The British care nothing for us and think we are the dregs of society. Yes, they care for the land, but not us."

"We have permission to construct a fort near the river to protect us should the savages raid our valley."

"Ya think that's enough, Seybert? Think we can hold off a horde of savages? I don't want to see my family scalped."

Anna was silent for a moment until she thought of the danger. "Will Indian raiding parties increase in the spring?"

Michael's face exhibited determination mixed with fear. "I do not know, but we will need to be prepared. There will be Seybert's fort, you know. Now, you must not worry about the savages. It is too close to your time."

She had been unable to forget the conversation. It was late in the evening before she finally fell soundly asleep, the baby cuddled in her arms and Michael, pacing by the fire.

May 15, 1756

Anna

I am so frustrated and afraid. Sickness penetrates my belly constantly. People are leaving our valley for fear of the savages who have killed many these last two years. I watch my four babies with fear in my heart. So we will have to move to forts every time an Indian shows his face around here. How I hate our situation; one minute I see our progress and love our farm; the next, I see images of painted savages descending on our place, tomahawks in hand, blood everywhere. Sometimes, I cannot stand it.

Michael is often angry. He does not understand why soldiers do not come here to protect us. He is always mad at the governor, an idiot, he calls him. He fears for us of course, but will not consider moving east. He insists I practice my marksmanship and keep the children, as well as a rifle, in my sight at all times. What a difficult life. My oldest is not yet seven years old, yet she has become responsible for her four-and-one-half-year-old brother, Adam. She is old beyond her years and rarely smiles. How I wish I could guarantee her a pleasant, happy childhood. Michael Jr. and Georgie are too young to understand, Georgie barely crawling around the cabin floor. I pray God does not give me another child at this time. But I cannot refuse Michael. I do not want to.

My life has become routine, a struggle for survival to keep my children safe . . . to prepare them for their future. Our dreams are on hold, practically shattered by things beyond our control. And I can do nothing but my routine tasks. I have no time to teach my children anything except to be wary. There is no church to help me, and Michael is too busy tending the farm for our survival. The future looms as a blank slate.

I wish I could enjoy this wonderful spring day. The wildflowers are blooming, and our corn has been planted, now showing little green shoots protruding through the earth. The forest is a blend of greens, light and dark, and a cardinal nests in the old pine by the spring house. We wait for her eggs to hatch while she watches us warily. Ah, that I could take my children on walks through the forest to see the wonders of nature.

December 15, 1756

Forced inside by the onset of a wet, cold winter, Anna and her family remained within their cabin the entire day, wind and particles of snow filtering through the cabin walls. Try as he might, Michael could not prevent errant flakes from emerging triumphantly through the unhewn logs. "Damn it. I cannot stop this damnable snow from entering this cabin. The wind just blows it right through the logs." He tried unsuccessfully to plug an opening with a rag.

Anna watched his frustration. "We are warm enough. The children can sleep near the hearth, and we have plenty of furs and blankets."

But, as the flames danced in the dark, even the roaring fire could not maintain warmth. By evening, the four Mallow children, tired from being cooped up for several days, succumbed to sleep, rolled up in quilts and furs near the fire while Anna sat in a rocking chair and Michael paced back and forth, fretting about livestock and fearing he must hunt the next day regardless of inclement weather.

Anna was tired of his incessant movement. "Stop pacing. The weather will turn soon."

"We need meat, and I need to hunt. I cannot remain inside for another day. This damnable weather . . ."

"Stop. Come sit by the fire and enjoy our now quiet children, our babies. Are they not lovely?"

"Of course they are, and so are you, my Anna Margaretha." He stopped and placed his hands on her shoulders.

He leaned down and nibbled her ear while removing her cap with his hands. "Ah, your beautiful dark hair." He ran his fingers though her free tresses while kissing her on the neck. She leaned her head back and relished his kisses while taking his head in her hands. The familiar feeling of desire rose in her abdomen, and she stood up allowing herself to be gathered in Michael's strong arms, crushed against his hard body.

"Ah, my love," he murmured as he pulled her towards the low bed along the cabin wall. Throwing her down, he pulled the bearskin over them while attempting to unbutton her dress. She aided his effort, and both undressed quickly beneath the warm fur. She thought, "I cannot refuse. I do not want to refuse." And she responded to his kisses and pulled him to her, relishing the pleasure of his touch, his strong body, and his hard kisses, and, for the moment, forgot about both children and Indians.

August 29, 1757

Anna

It is so terribly hot, and I can barely move, cumbersome as I am with this child, my fifth . . . Oh, God, I hope it's my last. Four children in eight years has taken its toll. Will this heat never end? My clothes are wet and cling to my misshapen body. I can barely take care of Georgie and Michael, my little ones. Mary is such a help as the oldest, and Adam is no trouble. She takes care of that for me. I simply cannot get cool or comfortable and fear this will be a difficult birth unlike the others. The babe will come soon, sooner than I thought. It will be a girl I know, and I shall call her Sarah after the English woman from the ship. Michael may not approve, for he will prefer a family name, but Sarah she shall be . . . God willing.

I have taken a minute to sit and think, to try to get cool in the shade of our cabin while the children are briefly quiet. Sweat pours down my back, and I lift my skirts above my knees and observe my swollen ankles. I am not a pretty sight, I fear. I cannot even enjoy the view of our growing corn in front of me or the young calf who cavorts by our barn. I cannot look at my poor garden that has filled with weeds. I can only smell the hogs as they wallow in the mud in their pen by the barn.

The thought of Indians moves to the front of my mind although I try to suppress the images of nearly naked red men, their eyes unreadable but producing fear. It has not been long since poor Henry Lorenz, Jacob Seybert's stepfather, was savagely murdered in his own fields by one of them only two miles away. We have a new stockade under Seybert's command where we can fort should danger arise. The thought of packing up and moving to a small dirt enclave is depressing. I cannot bear to think of having to live for days, perhaps weeks, with neighbors, some of whom I do not like, and a horde of young children. There will be no quiet, just mass confusion. Perhaps, Jacob is a stronger man than I think and will be able to keep order.

As I sit, the pains begin. It is earlier than I thought. I squeeze my eyes shut and grasp my swollen belly, aware my time is close, and I will call for Michael and hope I do not pass out. I hope Maria gets here in time.

August 30, 1757

After Anna's long and painful labor on this hot, humid day, Sarah Christina Mallow entered the world with a soft cry. Maria, having spent the night at the Mallow cabin, held the whimpering baby and efficiently cleaned the child and handed her to her barely conscious mother. The child was tiny but managed to suck at her mother's breast and fall asleep as did her exhausted mother.

Shortly, Anna abruptly woke to the pleasant hum of familiar voices. "Ah, Michael, our daughter will be called Sarah, after Sarah Goodale, from the ship. I will never forget that kind woman's help when I thought we might die."

Michael frowned, but after a questioning look from Maria, he grinned in acceptance. "Well, my dear, you shall have your Sarah. I hope she will be as strong as that formidable Mistress Goodale."

Soon Adam and Mary entered the cabin, both smiling at seeing mother and child. Anna knew that fifteen-year-old Nicholas Seybert, Maria's oldest, had been entrusted to watch the two little boys and did so reluctantly since birthing excursions were not on the top of his list of activities. She smiled at Nicholas when he and the two little boys finally entered the cabin, and the boys lingered at the foot of the bed, not knowing what to make of the little bundle next to their mother.

Maria put her hand on Michael's shoulder. "I must leave now. It will be dark soon, and my family needs me." Anna thanked her as she turned to the door and stepped outside. Anna heard Nicholas say, "We must hurry mother. It is late." Anna's mind clouded with fear because she knew that it was dangerous to be out at dusk without a military escort. But she knew that Nicholas was nearly a man, and a very capable one at that. Jacob had taught his son well.

January 1, 1758

Anna

Today is the beginning of a new year. I have no idea what it might bring. The Indian threat is still with us and still more families have left, leaving no more than two hundred settlers in this county. We remain here, bolted in our warm cabin, while the wind wails outside. I doubt that the savages will bother us in this weather. I suspect they have enough problems finding food and feeding their own families. I pray this will be a better year but am not hopeful.

My Sarah, my four month old daughter, is so small and frail, unlike my other four robust children. I fear for her sometimes. It takes a healthy child to survive this existence of ours. I never thought we would have to endure this life that confronts me every day. I wish we could go back to Pennsylvania, even to the old country. Life is difficult, and I see no end to our problems.

Michael has become hardened, tough, and refuses any discussion of leaving. He has taught Adam and Mary to fire a rifle and has them on constant lookout for marauding savages. I have become an adequate marksman myself although I dislike guns.

Michael tells me the government will soon come to our aid and send soldiers to protect us. We just have to hold out awhile longer. What choice do I have anyway? I have nowhere to go, no family to run to. I would not leave my babies, and so we stay in this dangerous place, once called our promised land.

In the meantime, I wait for a change but see none. I have seen Seybert's stockade where I am afraid we will have to go in the spring. Maria says it is a safe place, and she is confident her husband can secure it until the soldiers come. Ah, she is a better wife than I, for I cannot stand much more of this. My nerves are raw, and I scream at my poor children. They are afraid, I know. Michael is, too, but will not admit it. He is so proud of our farm, his livestock, our cabin, and barn for which he has labored so hard. It is indeed a fine place, but what good is it if we cannot walk out our front door.

What kind of a life is it for my children? Shall they spend their days cooped up in a smoky, fortified cabin, fearing for their lives every second?

Anna was despondent like hundreds of wives in Pennsylvania, Maryland and Virginia. She felt the emptiness of dreams fading, the loss, and the presence of death. She had ceased pleading to return to Pennsylvania.

Michael's comments never varied. "We will not let them win or take our land by fear. We will survive here. Do not suggest leaving again."

Today, she had heard the familiar words and had to rid herself of worry and frustration, if only for a few precious minutes, so she sought the cabin window, threw open the shutters and stuck her head outside, breathing in fresh air, untainted by the smell of smoke. It was brief, but effective, relief, and she shut out sounds of her husband and children and embraced the cold, brisk air.

"Close those shutters. We do not know what is out there. You know better than to expose yourself to unseen danger."

She felt anger rising within her but obediently did as her husband demanded. Sometimes she feared her husband as much as the Indians, but she knew she was in Virginia to stay.

She feared that she could no longer protect her children, for events were beyond her control, but she learned to load a flintlock and shoot a target. She learned to look for evidence of Indians and to keep supplies handy, packed ready to go. She taught her children awareness, trying not to instill fear. She never let a child out of her sight and saw Indian shadows everywhere she looked. Hollow-eyed and pale, she often awoke at night in a cold sweat, hearing strange noises, only to have Michael try to reassure her that it was only her imagination. She feared every minute Michael was gone.

Sometimes she wished she were as strong as Maria who never seemed to have a moment of insecurity.

"Why do you not talk to me about the war? Do you think I do not know the danger we are in? I am stronger than you think despite my fears. I would die to protect my children." Shadows from the evening fire flickered on the sleeping faces of her children.

"I just want to protect you. There is no need to discuss the lurid details."

"Do you think I have not heard that Killbuck leads the raiding parties? Do you think I do not remember his hateful stare from a few years back?"

"I warned you then of his treachery, didn't I? Tis come to pass I am afraid."

"Maria remembers him from the years he lived here. She does not think he will hurt us because he knows some of us."

"For God's sake, do not believe what she says. Of course he will hurt us if he can. He hates all of us. He thinks we have stolen his land, the land of his ancestors. Why wouldn't he try to get it back? Now, he has the French to supply him with weapons and men."

Anna thought of Killbuck. Epitomizing the threat, his image often played in her mind, and she feared him, that strong, ugly, dark Indian who could have killed her but did not. Why? She did not know, but she feared him above all.

Anna remembered Hannah Lorenz's agony when her husband Henry was brought in last year, scalped and bloodied, dead from an Indian raid. She was visiting Seyberts on that fateful day when an Indian raiding party struck Jacob's mother's farm. That was the first evidence of scalping she had seen and would not forget. Poor Hannah had never been the same, and Anna mourned her descent into illness.

She had seen Jacob take firm command of the fort erected on his land where she knew they would be forced to go one of these days. Also, she had heard of children forcibly taken by the Indians to be added to their village clans. She could not imagine any of her little ones being taken to a savage village by terrifying men wielding tomahawks and hatchets.

Anna and Michael spent the remainder of the evening in silence. January would drag on, cold with miserable fury, matching the moods of the wary settlers who knew the weather would keep them safe, but dreading the appearance of spring when the Indians would return to exact revenge. Anna waited for the promised relief, British soldiers to protect them. The soldiers did not come, but spring began its ascent.

Chapter 5

March 11, 1758

Early on this bitterly cold evening, only those warriors who managed to sit close to the large fire enjoyed the warmth provided by the blazing and crackling wood. In a place of prominence sat a rugged Delaware chief listening to a young, regally dressed French marine officer from Fort Duquesne, who paced before the large group as though he were a king addressing the loyal subjects in the village of Sawtunk in Pennsylvania, the site of this war council.

"Brothers," he shouted. "Hear my words. Your French father has heard your cries for help. He knows the English have caused you much pain. They have taken the lands of your ancestors and your food supply, leaving your women and children hungry." Killbuck frowned as he listened.

The war chief was known for his cunning, intelligence and treachery. Strong of limb and thick in body, he was a force to be reckoned with. He thought, "I could crush this Frenchman with my bare hands."

He was well aware that he was scarred and ugly and considered by some to be an old man although he had seen but forty summers, and he prided himself on his fierce demeanor, enhanced by numerous deep wrinkles and penetrating, dark eyes. Covered by a red blanket slung over his right shoulder, Killbuck partially exposed his muscled arms and thick chest, knowing the imposing aspects of his powerful appearance often struck fear in the eyes of his beholders. He feared no one, especially these Frenchmen, but recognized the need for assets in his fight for the Indian way of life, now severely threatened by white settlers.

Motioning the young warrior White Otter to his side, Killbuck spoke quietly in his Delaware tongue. "Do you see these blue and gold toy soldiers parading in front of us, my brother? Do you think they speak the truth?"

Kneeling next to the older man, White Otter answered, "These Frenchmen. They speak of brotherhood, but I believe they are not our brothers. They desire us to do their killing for them. They give us gifts of ammunition and the demon rum. See how our warriors partake of their gifts."

"Ah, how we Indians love the burning sensation of their fire water. It will be our undoing, I fear. These French are clever, but we must be more clever. They, too, want control of the land. We must be our own masters, and we must stop the white men from crossing the eastern mountains."

Ignoring the droning of the French officer in his high pitched voice and the excitement of the warriors as they passed around jugs of rum, White Otter said, "I will do anything you ask of me. You are a wise war chief and the brother-in-law of our great Chief Netawatwees. We must protect the gift of land for your son who will be chief someday."

"Yes, if the spirits protect him."

It was then that Killbuck realized that the French officer was pointing to him. "Great Killbuck, war chief of the Delawares of the village of Sawtunk, we invite you to come to Fort Duquesne with your warriors when the moon is full, one month from now, for a great council. Many of our red brothers will join us. We will guide you in preparation for the great raids, raids that will push the English, who steal your lands, back to the big waters in the east."

Killbuck turned to a nearby French trader and said in Delaware, "Tell this damn Frenchman that I cannot understand his words, and you must translate for me."

The old trader chuckled. "Killbuck, you wily old devil. You understand French as well as I do, but I will translate." He repeated the Frenchman's words.

Killbuck grinned. "Tell the arrogant bastard that we are not his brothers, that we are self-sufficient and do not want his gifts. Tell him we will only come to Fort Duquesne to get ammunition. Tell him I know more about these settlers and the land than he will ever know. Tell him I will take many scalps and expect payment for them, and, someday, I will come for him and take his scalp."

Turning to acknowledge the French officer, the smiling trader spread his arms in greeting. "Killbuck thanks you from the depths of his heart. He and his people are grateful for the friendship and generosity of the French King and his children. He will be honored to attend the great council during the spring moon with his brothers, the French."

The young French officer was very pleased at the response and bowed in Killbuck's direction while the warriors laughed loudly at Killbuck's words. The officer continued, "We have knowledge of new forts in Virginia and they must be destroyed."

Barely able to contain his laughter, Killbuck stood up and nodded to the officer while his warriors lifted their tomahawks toward the East and chanted incoherent war cries. He then took White Otter's arm. "Be gone my brother. Seek out these new Virginia forts so that we will be knowledgeable when we raid the area during the next moon. May the Great Spirit be with you."

Quietly leaving the excited crowd, Killbuck watched White Otter and two dozen young warriors move some distance away where they had hidden their supplies and weapons, including war hatchets, scalping knives and tomahawks. Additionally, some owned rifles, secured at the defeat of General Braddock's forces in 1754. Since stealth was their advantage, these warriors packed lightly, carrying necessary items on their backs with blankets attached to their shoulders. They also carried dried meat and parched corn stuffed into pouches with extra moccasins and herbal remedies.

At Killbuck's orders and preparing to leave at first light, they would travel by foot, often more than twenty miles a day, over mountains, streams, and rugged pathways. Unencumbered by horses, they would be able to move silently through the forest, hiding and camping when necessary, attacking quickly and efficiently, and returning the way they had come, living off the land.

Killbuck observed the remaining warriors, drunk with rapture, but was greatly pleased with the way things were going and would anxiously await the return of White Otter.

He grinned at the old trader. "It is good to have loyal warriors, is it not?"

The trader nodded at the imposing chief and moved away to obtain his share of the rum. Fighting the urge to drink, Killbuck watched in disgust as the remaining warriors became senseless from the gift of the French. He knew there were many ways to defeat the Indians, and perhaps the French had chosen liquor as their method. However, he did not worry about his chosen few who knew the seriousness of their mission and would comply with honor.

March 15, 1758

Anna
We have lived here for almost five years on this beautiful rise where Michael has carved out twelve acres for planting from this dense forest. Our sturdy barn holds our stock in the winter months, and our corn crib has enough to last until fall harvest. Yesterday, our old mare birthed a fine colt, a

long-legged animal. My children are fine, all five; they thrive although sometimes I fear for Sarah, who seems frail. I am unable to enjoy our prosperity.

I am discontent and fear this war, the war I do not understand, the war that has us in its grasp. The friendly Indians, who used to live among us, have been gone for years but returned several years ago to kill settlers. Neighbors have been killed, and children have been taken as captives. What kind of life is this when I cannot leave my home without fear of attack? Michael's brother George took his family back over the mountains for safety, but Michael would not hear of our leaving what we have worked so hard to create.

Ah, what dreams we had when we arrived in this land so many years ago. How quickly time has passed. We have lived in fear of the Indians for over two years now. Some families have given up and left the area with no intention of returning as long as the Indians continue the raids into the colony. Even though two forts have been built for our protection, we are still very much afraid because no soldiers have come to garrison them. Although I suggested going back to Pennsylvania, Michael would hear none of it. He says we are here to stay, and our future lies in the land we are clearing.

Where are the soldiers, I wonder?

I try not to think of these things, for I am busy enough minding my five little ones. The chores never end, what with the cooking, sewing, weaving, and taking care of children and livestock.

I am thirty-two years old and still pretty when I dare to look in my small mirror. Five births have taken their toll, of course, but I am still slim and have no errant gray strands in my dark hair. Michael still desires me, and we often have the passion we had when we first married in the old country, but life is not the same.

We speak German, the two of us. I try to improve my English, and my children are learning it, but it is difficult. I cannot read English words and fear my reading of German is lacking. I read our Bible and miss the church. But, in the eyes of some of our neighbors, I am an uneducated German wife. I fear my children need more schooling than I can provide.

This weather matches my mood because it is such a windy, chilly day, with no sun, just heavy clouds hanging over the forest. Everything appears gray, dull, and uninviting, except for the warm fire and glowing embers within our cabin. It is unlikely the children will want to go outside, which is fine with me on this somber, cold day. Besides, it would be unwise to do so with Michael away.

I awakened this morning with a feeling of dread and a knot in my stomach. Michael told me last night that he would be gone this day with the militia. The group is meeting at the cabin of Philip Harper, five miles away, to discuss strategies for the protection of our families here on the South Fork. Michael says we must protect ourselves because the government has not yet answered our pleas.

Very early this morning Michael saddled and mounted his big, bay gelding for the trip and promised to return by dark. He cautioned me to keep the door bolted and the rifle loaded and handy. I watched him mount and handed him a pouch of johnny cakes for his trip. I watched him trot into the forest where he was immediately hidden from my view. Shivering from the cold wind, I stepped back inside and bolted the door, the pungent aroma of the damp forest with me.

Hours have passed, and I have completed my chores and fed my always-hungry, five children. I am still restless and do not like Michael's absence which occurs too often these days. I am constantly irritable and cross with the children, only to cover them with kisses after these incidents. The older two, Mary and Adam, know of the Indian threat and our quiet arguments, my begging to move back east until the Indian war is settled and Michael's refusing to consider it.

March 20, 1758

Anna woke early before her children stirred. Checking to see that Michael still slept, she quietly crept out of bed, grabbed her shawl and walked to the dying fire. Careful not to cause embers to fly out of the deep hearth, she stoked them until the flames began to rise and softly crackle. She then crossed the room, slipped on her worn leather shoes and opened the cabin door to locate a log to throw on the fire. She knew that Michael would be angry that she left the cabin, but she wanted him to sleep even though she could not.

She shivered from the cold and observed the frost that lay upon the dead grass and the barn roof. She knew the sun would emerge soon and dismantle the glistening crystals. She heard the noises of the hogs as they scoured for scraps in the hard earth. Locating a log next to the stoop, she managed to secure it with both hands and re-enter the cabin door.

When the fire burned sufficiently, she swung the kettle arm over the flames to heat the water. When it boiled, she would make tea and porridge for her family. In the meantime, she would have silence to think, to try to make sense of yesterday's events.

She sat with her eyes closed in front of the fire recalling every word of last night. They had been eating supper when they heard a knock on the cabin door, a most unusual occurrence for neighbors did not visit these days, especially after dusk.

Grabbing his rifle, Michael had unbolted the door only to see Jacob, who shivered in the cold. Relieved, Michael ushered him into the cabin. "To what do we owe this visit, Jacob?"

Removing his hat, Seybert spoke in a hushed voice as he looked at Anna and the now-quiet children seated at the table. "Mallow, we need to talk. Perhaps we should step outside."

"We will speak here. Anna should know whatever it is. And Mary is old enough to understand danger. The boys will pay scant attention."

"As you wish. My time is short for I must alert other neighbors who remain in our valley. We are in great danger. A tragedy occurred this morning. Our neighbors, Peter Moser and Nicholas Frank, were both murdered at Moser's farm by a war party."

"Sweet Jesus," Anna interrupted as she dropped the spoon she was holding.

"Be quiet, Anna, and allow Jacob to finish," Michael admonished.

"Frank was delivering corn to Moser who had run out. Pete's brother George and George's wife's kin, Philip and Adam Harper, were along to help. Pete's wife and the twins were gone. Good thing too. Seems he sent them north to her father's a week ago. Anyway, the men were just finishing some cheese and biscuits when Frank was shot dead. Then Pete was hit with a tomahawk and fell dead also. We think the men were sitting on a log near Moser's cabin . . ." He paused to clear his throat.

"Get on with it," Michael said impatiently.

"Yes, well, they had no warning. Then George was hit with a tomahawk, and the Harpers fled for their lives. They managed to run to their horses, mount and ride like the devil to Harper's cabin several miles away. The savages had hidden in the woods, probably since before dawn."

"So the savages are here now?" Anna said.

"No, we think they are on their way back to their villages on the Ohio River. Last night the Conrads disappeared. We think they captured Hannah and her children and are taking them back to their villages. Conrad returned from his fields at dusk to find an empty cabin. The savages must have been in a rush because they did not burn the cabin."

Michael, his face pale, turned from Jacob, glanced at his children still seated at the table, and looked at the fire.

Anna said, "Go on, Jacob. We must know."

"Well, the Harpers made it home, both bloody but wounds not life-threatening. Phillip's daughter Eve was hysterical. She insisted they go back to get George, her husband since last month. The rest of the Harper men and some neighbors took a wagon and rode back to Moser's, but they expected to find nothing but dead, scalped bodies. But they found George alive, just barely, and he was able to tell some of it. He was scalped but they did a poor job. Doubt that he will live long though. They brought him home to be tended to by his young wife. No doctor in these parts but they patched up George as best they could. Eve thinks he will live, but I don't think so, wounds too bad, too much blood lost."

Michael remained silent, grief etched across his pale face, but Anna could not.

"What should we do? What will you do? Your family?"

Before Jacob could respond, Michael spoke in a harsh, raspy voice. "We must summon the militia and go after these savages. The governor will not help us, so we must take care of this ourselves. Did anyone go after them?"

"We cannot ride off and leave our women and children in danger. The fort we built two years ago. We must use it now. You and your family must be ready to go there. The savages are long gone we think. A British spy stopped by Dyer's late today to give us a report. He did not know about Moser but he did know about a great council to be held at Ft. Duquesne in April. He said that he knows the Indians are meeting with the French at the full moon. Says this was probably an early scouting party who just happened upon settlers. The savages, they're mighty superstitious, you know, and will not return until after the great council. The French will supply them with guns and rum and encourage them to raid the colonies. He thinks we have four or five weeks before any of them Indian war parties return. We cannot know for certain, but I believe him. He has visited their villages and speaks their language."

"Well then, we must prepare. What is the condition of the fort?"

"I have checked it regularly, and the walls and blockhouse are secure. We need to supply it, though, because we have no idea how long we could be under siege when they do return."

"They will. You know they will. Pray God we have the time to prepare. I will not allow them to take this farm or my family."

Anna remained silent as she thought of the danger. She looked at her five children and watched Mary patiently attempt to feed baby Sarah. She looked at Jacob and saw the fear on his face and thought of Peter Moser and the last time she saw him. It was a week ago when Peter rode to their cabin to see Michael. He needed corn until his crop came in in September, but Michael had none to spare. She liked Peter perhaps because he was Adam Moser's cousin. She did not know Peter's brother George but knew he had married young Eve Harper, a slip of a girl Anna did not care for. Too flighty and young but would grow up fast, Anna thought, now that her husband was dying.

Jacob was not done. "The other fort, Upper Tract, will be garrisoned by the first of April. That's what the British spy also told us."

"I'll believe it when I see it. We've been promised that before, you know."

"Soldiers will come. Captain James Dunlap will be in command. You know him since he lives north of us in the Upper Tract Valley."

"How many men?"

"Don't know, but he can muster up to one hundred. Doubt he'll find that many though."

"My God. The frontier's a big place. Even a hundred men can't protect us. Those savages know the area better than we do, lived here for decades before us. That savage Killbuck probably leads them. We know that he has done so for several years now. Killed many. Wants his land back and rid of us." Michael's voice became shrill.

"We have two choices. Either leave or fort. That's it. I ain't leaving, nor are my kin either. I plan to take my mother Hannah to the fort. I plan to supply it. British gave me command, you know. I think we are safe for the time it will take the savages to go back to the Ohio River villages, get supplies from the French, and return to hurt us. Besides, those superstitious savages will not descend on us until after that council. They won't irritate the French or their gods."

Anna had heard enough. "Michael, let Jacob leave. He needs to warn the others."

"She's right. You must be on your way, and be careful."

The remainder of the evening passed in cold silence.

Now, the morning silence was pierced by a wail from the hungry baby, and Anna was soon consumed by her family's demands and put last night's conversation away in her mind and hoped it would stay there. Still grieving, she and her husband now silently completed the feeding of their children. Food had no appeal, and Anna could not swallow a morsel, but the morning passed quickly, and she had no time to reflect.

It was late evening when the Mallow children finally succumbed to sleep. Releasing her hair from her cap and covering her eyes, Anna quietly sobbed as she gave up any attempt to control her grief, grief she had successfully held in for several hours.

"Anna," comforted Michael as he placed his strong hands on her shoulders. "Stop your tears and listen to me. We cannot bring Peter and Nicholas back. It is terrible I know, but I will not listen to any more pleas to return east. Raids have occurred in Pennsylvania, you know. Many have been killed, and many taken captive. There is no safe place for us. We have to pray that this will pass, for there is nothing we can do, and there is no place for us to go. Pray to God that this will pass. I promise you it will."

Removing his hands, Anna looked up. "You cannot console me. This is no life for us, for our babies. I am angry it has come to this. I know, know that is too late to leave, and I shall have to endure. Endure I will, no matter what happens. You cannot assure me, nor can Maria, who thinks Jacob can protect us in his fort. I am sick of that talk. I am sick of the German stubbornness. Sick of it all. Those damnable savages intend to kill us. Not that I blame them, for we have taken their land for a handful of beads and a cask of rum." Anger filled her voice, a strange voice Michael had rarely heard.

Scowling, but with no answers, Michael turned away from his angry wife. Anna was tired of the discussion and felt an overwhelming urge to sleep. She dried her tears in haste and rose from her chair to prepare for bed, hoping tomorrow would be better.

April 1, 1758

Struggling through long and dreary days, Anna and Michael rarely spoke, and the children were unusually quiet despite their occasional fighting over objects and crying. On Michael's orders, Anna could not leave the cabin, which had become smoky, hot and oppressive. Her head constantly ached, and her eyes watered. For the first time since the ocean voyage, she put away her mirror, knowing that she no longer wanted to see her face for fear of what would stare back at her.

This morning Anna struggled through her endless chores and tried not to think at all. Michael had gone to check on their livestock and look for Indian signs as he did every morning. She fed the children, nursed the baby and made some biscuits, all without a conscious thought or remembrance.

At noon, thinking her ears were playing tricks on her, she ignored sounds of men and horses until she clearly heard Michael's loud voice. "Dunlap. By God you are here!"

Shocked out of her stupor, she ran to the cabin door, flung it open and stood in awe of the scene that confronted her. Men and horses lined the bridle path that led from their cabin as far as she could see. Rifles glistened in the April sun, and the horses' hooves echoed on the hard-packed path. She watched the lead horseman vault from his saddle and confront Michael, who stood a short distance from the door.

"Aye, Mallow. We are finally on our way to garrison the Upper Tract Fort." He spoke English and Michael responded in kind.

"What do you know? Any savages been spotted in our parts?" Anna heard her husband's heavy German accent.

"Naw, they ain't been seen around here since Moser's murder. Can you and your missus spare some refreshments for my men here?" Dunlap removed his hat.

"Ya, of course." Michael turned to his wife. "Have Adam help and get these men some water from the spring." She had not moved from the cabin door.

She turned to summon her young son but heard Michael continue, "Is this all you got, men I mean?"

"Yep, eighteen is all. Couldn't muster more I'm afraid, but we'll manage. Men are up for it. Your neighbor, William Woods, is over there," and Dunlap pointed to a neatly attired man who sat quietly on his lathered horse.

Anna stopped and waved at Woods who waved back, a smile on his handsome clean-shaven face. She had met him on several occasions and liked his Irish brogue and cheerful demeanor, a pleasant contrast to the sour Germans she usually saw. She also knew his wife Martha, two daughters and two sons and had never met such a handsome family.

Still smiling, she turned to collect tin cups so that she and Adam could distribute water from their spring to the thirsty, tired soldiers while Dunlap ordered his men to dismount. Both returned quickly, Adam filling cups from a bucket and she handing them to the men. She listened carefully and heard a chorus of "Thank ya, mam." She recognized several of the men but failed to recall their names. Most were simply strangers, and she did not return their appraising gazes. However, she had not experienced such excitement for months, perhaps years and was enjoying the commotion. As she watched the soldiers, she wondered if they had families or if they just hated Indians.

As she walked among the men, Michael continued to ask questions. "How can you patrol the entire valley with so few men?" Although she did not grasp all the words, she now knew enough English to follow the conversation.

Dunlap finished his water and wiped his mouth with his sleeve. "Mallow, we will do what we can. Our orders are to protect the valley and warn settlers if any remain. Do you know of any who are still in their cabins in the Upper Tract area?"

"Ya, I hear the Fulks and Elliots, two young couples, have claims and have chosen to stay. No children. The others have packed up and left, most after Moser's murder." Anna continued to listen as she slowly made her way among the men, reclaiming the cups as Adam followed behind her.

"Perhaps, you all should have left. I ain't much for givin' advice but, seems to me, ya all should be over the mountains. How many little ones ya got there?" He looked at the cabin door where Mary stood, holding the baby, while the two little boys watched the soldiers with awe.

"And you? Did you send your wife and daughter away?"

"Yep, sent them to my father's in the Shenandoah Valley over three weeks ago. Good thing, too. At least they're safe for now. The wife's used to my absence since I've been soldiering for four years now."

A scowl spread across Michael's face. "We are here to stay. Your job is to protect and warn us. I hope your men are up to it. They look like a difficult lot." Michael surveyed the waiting men, variously attired, most unshaven. Their mounts reflected the appearance of their owners, and Anna saw doubt on her husband's face.

"Well, each man must make his own choice, and you have made yours. I wish you well. I intend to do everything I can to protect these valleys. Do not be misled by the appearance of my men." Dunlap lowered his voice. "They are all fighters and hate Injuns. They may be a handful, but I have Woods over there. He is loyal to a fault. The two of us will instill order once we are established at the fort. If them savages cross the river to these valleys, we will know. You will be warned. These are bad times we live in, friend."

"I know. I know, but I will not lose this land. We have worked too hard, too damn hard these past years." Michael shrugged and dropped his gaze to the ground.

"Well, keep your doors and windows bolted and do not go out alone. Keep your rifle close, and you better arm your wife too."

"She can load and fire all right."

Anna thought of Killbuck. Walking straight to Dunlap, she could not refrain from asking, "Killbuck? Does he lead these raids against us?"

"We think so. He's been active for over two years now since he left this area four years ago. Some say he has dozens of notches on his spear, one for each white man he killed. Lives in a village on the Ohio River and is their war chief. The French supply him and his warriors, help him lead the raids sometimes too. But it could be another bad one, Shingas the Terrible they call him. Can't know for sure which one leads these war parties. Some even think the French lead them."

Anna's face turned pale, and she saw the image of Killbuck in her mind, an image of a half-naked man with an evil sneer, walking toward her.

Michael interrupted before she could ask another question. "Anna, go inside and mind the children."

Before she turned to leave, she sought Dunlap's eyes. "Thank you, Captain Dunlap. I wish you and your men well. God be with you."

"Thank ye, mam. You have a fine family there," and he looked at the children gathered in the doorway. "We'll do the best we can. Twill be a blessing if boredom is the only thing I have to confront with these men."

Anna noticed that Dunlap looked at her husband with sympathy. "He thinks we are doomed," she thought as she turned to the cabin and her waiting children. Her pleasure at seeing the soldiers gave way to fear as she herded her children safely into the cabin and shut the door behind her while the sounds of men and horses gradually disappeared.

April 15, 1758

It was noon when Michael entered the cabin, slamming the door behind him and leaning his rifle against the wall. He hung his leather coat on a peg by the door and proceeded to the fire to warm his cold hands from the chill of a cold, rainy day. Anna watched from her seat at the trestle table, continuing to coax her children to eat their hot stew.

"Be prepared to fort. You will have no choice. I must go with others soon to purchase supplies. You cannot stay here when I go."

"Go to Seybert's stockade? Cannot I stay here unless the soldiers warn us of an attack?"

"No. There is no guarantee that Dunlap can warn you in time. I will not allow you and our children to remain here."

He was often cross with her for no reason, and resentment welled up within her.

"So we can expect more savages to attack?"

"Yes. You know that. I am sorry it has come to this. We have no choice."

Anna's heart fluttered, and nausea threatened to take hold. She managed to control herself but dreaded the thought of living in a fort with five children and many, many others. She knew there would be no privacy. It was too much to bear, thinking about living in such conditions for more than a day or two.

"You will leave me and five babies in a flimsy stockade with few to defend us against those damnable savages? I do not know if I can stand it. Why do you have to be the one to get supplies?"

"It is my responsibility, along with a few others in the militia. Pray that the savages do not return before we do. I do not know what else to do. I did not want this, you know. I want no harm to come to my family." She noticed his moist eyes and suddenly realized how difficult his life had become.

But she could not stop herself. "Why, why didn't you get supplies last week or the week before? Why?"

"You know why. We thought we had enough lead to hold us over until the British sent reinforcements. But we don't. Several local men promised to aid us, but they lied. They packed up and disappeared, lead with them. Jacob says there is still enough time. Savages will be held up at the great council the French are holding at the full moon. Big ceremony. Big medicine for the Indians. Tomorrow is the full moon we reckon, and the French will keep them busy for days. Got to get them riled up for the raids. Then the trip here takes at least nine days from their villages. Earliest they could raid us is the first of May I think."

"Then leave tomorrow."

"Can't. Nicholas Heavener and I need to wait for Jacob's sons-in-law to ride with us. Jacob is staying since he is the commander of the fort, but his kin are good shots and reliable men. We need them."

She did not see any sense in his reasoning, but she could no longer protest. She felt as though the world were crushing her, and she would soon disappear into the ground with no trace. She saw only blackness in her future and could no longer concentrate on anything. Once in a while a thought did jump into her muddled mind: she was carrying another child.

Chapter 6

April 17, 1758

As the full moon loomed above on this chilly night, Chief Killbuck and his followers, both Shawnee and Delaware, some of who had just returned from a very successful raid, sat around a fire in front of Fort Duquesne, listening to several French officers outline a plan of attacks upon the English settlements in Pennsylvania, Maryland, and Virginia. The French promised guidance, supplies and manpower. But Killbuck's mind wandered as he listened to various officers drone on and on about the British, their forts, their land grabbing claims, and the numerous settlers who, despite danger, continued to move westward, paying no attention to Indian treaties. He had heard it all before, but he kept his promises and had assured the French of his attendance at this great council.

Although he spoke both English and some French, the war chief never paid any attention to the speakers unless they spoke his native language, so he waited for the interpreter.

The arrogant Frenchman explained, "My red brothers. The British must be stopped so that we can secure our trade routes and trade with our brothers, the Indians. The earth is sacred and belongs to all, not the English who take it by force."

Somehow, Killbuck doubted that this Frenchman was his brother. "The French know nothing of brotherhood, but they do not devour the land as do the English." The uncontrollable British settlers continued to increase, more moving westward every day, and showed no signs of letting up. In his heart, he feared no effort would be enough to stop the surge of whites, and he feared his people were doomed regardless of efforts he might make.

"Kill two settlers, and four more appear to take their places," he had warned. Now, over one hundred disgruntled warriors agreed to conduct raids, and Killbuck and sixty of them were to head to Augusta County, attack the two forts, kill and scalp the militia, and capture desirable settlers. Others would head to Pennsylvania for the same purpose.

"Bring us scalps of the English, and we will reward you. The English are your enemies, and you must rid yourselves of their presence on this side of the mountains. We, your French brothers, must keep our trade routes open. The English are like rabbits. They multiply and move west every day. They must be stopped, my red brothers."

"Yes," Killbuck thought. "We must stop the English, but their numbers are great, perhaps too great. There are not enough of us."

Looking directly at the Frenchman, Killbuck demanded silence and then shouted in French, "We will bring you scalps and captives. You have my word."

Only a month before this night, Killbuck's loyal follower, White Otter, and others had traveled to Virginia, successfully raided several remote areas, and returned with scalps, horses and young captives. Additionally, they had knowledge of the new forts.

White Otter had reported, "My chief, we can take these English forts easily. The garrison is small, and the eastern fort has no militia. The English cannot not withstand our attacks. The spirits will aid us."

"Ah, that is good news, brother. I, too, have seen signs of our success."

The great council dragged on, and the French continued their entreaties and promises. A bored Killbuck sat cross-legged on the ground and recalled his association with his white brothers during the years he had lived in Virginia, the peaceful years before the British and French declared war on each other. Having knowledge of English and the terrain, Killbuck knew he was well suited for the task.

At the conclusion of the French entreaties to their Indian brothers, Killbuck stood near the fire, watching the gathered warriors perform their war dance, illuminated by firelight under a fleeting moon. The night became a nightmare of human shapes with raised tomahawks, gesturing toward the East, the noise of chanting, the beating of drums, and the shrieks of war cries, while the French quietly distributed rum to the now-crazed Indians.

And, so the night came to a close as Killbuck, avoiding rum, pulled his hand-picked followers aside and removed them from the chaotic scene. "Prepare your weapons and be ready to leave at first light. The spirits are with us on this journey. You must not drink the French rum for it will destroy us."

He wanted none of the rum-drinking, war-crazed warriors on this trip. None of his chosen refused his commands, but a few left reluctantly, remembering the warm, burning taste of the liquor and the feeling it would produce.

Killbuck was encouraged, for now he could continue to exact revenge upon these arrogant white settlers whom he had known, but who had not given him the respect he deserved. Obviously, these settlers had no intention of allowing Indians to keep their land and desired only to secure more acreage.

"At least the French are not interested in carving out farms and putting up of fences. They are traders and respect the land and its inhabitants." Killbuck, a pragmatic man, had allied himself with the French and now scorned the British, but he knew alliances were never permanent.

Extremely confident, Killbuck planned to leave at the first light of dawn for the trip to the South Branch area. He returned to his resting men. "The Upper Tract Fort is now garrisoned and is a more difficult target than random cabins in the woods. I need strong, rested warriors. We must not fail, but I do not trust these French."

April 26, 1758

Anna

1 p.m.

The time has finally come, and Michael is taking us to Seybert's fort this hour. I have gathered all I can and prepared our five children. Mary is very afraid, but Adam looks upon it as an adventure. The three little ones do not really understand. We will go by horseback, Michael with the little boys, me with Sarah and Mary behind me, and Adam on the old mare. Then Michael will return to our cabin to hide our horses except for the one he will ride when he leaves this afternoon with the militia. They will cross the mountains for supplies and return in a few days, we all hope. In the meantime, we must fort to be safe from the rumored Indians in the area.

Of course, the Indians have been rumored to be in our backyards many times for the last few years. I have not seen one since that morning several years ago, but I sense that they watch us. So many times we have prepared to fort at Seybert's stockade, but we have yet to do so. But after poor Peter Moser's murder, I knew it was coming.

I hate to leave our cabin but cannot stay alone during this time. Sometimes during the day when Michael is gone, I am terrified. So now it has come to this, and everyone is fearful. I pray every night for our safety and the safety of our little ones. It feels like God has forsaken us in this wilderness. I wonder why? Is it because this land truly belongs to the Indians? Have we not made fair treaties with them? We are caught up in government disagreements, and it is not so different than the land we left behind, the old country where we never knew who was in charge and what they might take from us.

I worry about our cabin and livestock. What might become of our animals, our livelihood? Michael will hide the horses in the forest and let the cattle and hogs run free. Maybe the Indians will not find them. What if they burn our cabin? I cannot stand the thought of having to build another one, such labor. I guess we do not have much of value to lose, except our lives. That is what keeps me going.

I will look forward to seeing our neighbors at the fort, especially the Mauses, whom I rarely see. They have six children now, some the ages of ours, so the little ones will see adventure in our forting. I suppose I will have to see Roger Dyer, who, I fear, does not like me much. I have always suspected that he does not like Germans nor hearing us converse in our native tongue. Yet his sons-in-law are German.

3 p.m.

When she saw the wooden stockade ahead, Anna shivered even though the day was warm and pleasant. She held Sarah tightly while Mary wrapped her arms around her waist as the three sat astride the mare. Anna felt her daughter's body pressed tightly to her back. Michael rode beside them holding the reins of both animals as they plodded slowly up the rise to the gate. Adam followed on the old mare who was more interested in her scampering colt than the small boy who tried to urge her forward and keep his balance among the baggage tied to her broad back.

The family stopped short of the gate. "Seybert, it's Mallow. Open the gate for us."

Anna waited while Jacob swung open the heavy wooden gate and took the reins of her horse to lead them into the stockade yard. Relieved, she then handed her baby to Jacob, dismounted and caught Mary as she slid from the horse. After George and Michael were safely deposited on the ground, Michael began to unload the baggage and pile several bags against the fort wall while Jacob rescued Adam from the mare's broad back.

"Thank ye, Jacob. I guess the time has come. We have brought what we could spare." Michael swung a sack of corn meal to the ground.

"God help us," thought Anna as she watched her husband and Jacob. "This cannot be happening." She did not know what to do so she simply stood with her children waiting for instructions.

Michael returned to her side, put his hands on her shoulders and kissed a smiling Sarah on her pale forehead. Then he kissed Anna hard on the mouth. "I would give anything to stay with you and our babies. You know that, don't you?" He lifted her chin and sought her eyes.

Anna tried not to cry. "Yes, I do. Your sense of duty . . ."

"My duty is to protect my family and my community. That is why I go. It is the lead and supplies that will protect us. There is time. We will ride all night and should return in three days. Do not worry."

Anna put her fingers on his lips. "Hush. We are all worried. I will pray for your safe return."

Michael dropped his eyes and released his wife. He turned to Mary and Adam and kissed them both. "Protect your Mama. I will see you all soon." He hugged the two small boys and turned quickly to mount his impatient gelding. He grabbed the reins of the other two mounts and rode through the gate, the colt trotting behind. Anna watched her husband until Jacob pulled the heavy structure closed and bolted it. He then walked to her side.

"Anna, your husband will be all right. It will only be for a few days, and there are many here to help you. Maria and my girls will help care for your brood. Come now. We will find you a place to settle in the blockhouse when night comes."

She followed Jacob as her children kept close and held Sarah tightly. They entered the rectangular wooden building that sat in the middle of the stockade. Adjusting to the dark room Anna recognized two pallets along the far wall, each occupied. A small figure sat next to one of the pallets.

"Oh, Lord Jesus. How many of us will have to share this small space?" she thought.

Jacob saw her distress. "Anna, you know my mother, Hannah. She is having a difficult time since Henry was killed. George, George Moser lies over there with his wife Eve beside him."

"Mama, you know Anna and her children."

"Yes," Hannah rasped. "Dear Anna, I am so sorry that I cannot aid you and your children. Forgive my condition. Pray for George though. He is much worse off than I am. Oh, how I hate this land, you know. It took my Henry . . ."

"Frau Lorenz." Anna interrupted Hannah's rambling. "Do not despair. We are grateful for your son's help and will manage. I hope my children do not disturb you."

Anna was startled by the sitting figure who now stood in front of her. "Frau Mallow, I am Eve, Eve Moser. George is not well but he will be better. I know he will."

Uncomfortable, Jacob said, "Well now, I must leave you all for there are things to do."

Anna squinted her eyes in the dim room. "Yes, oh, yes. I know." She did not want to converse at all and simply wanted to leave her blankets and supplies and return to the fort yard. She did not want to stay in this oppressive room with two sick people, but she knew she would have no choice at dusk.

And so she ignored Eve and spread her blankets. Then she quickly took her leave and walked out into the sunny fort yard, her children close behind her. She heard Hannah say,

"Anna, dear Anna. Stay outside as long as you can. This is no place for you and your children."

Relieved once she and the children stood in the bright sunlight, she looked for Maria and her daughters. Shortly, she found them and was soundly embraced as the girls quickly took the baby and the two little boys on a tour of the fort. Putting her arm around Anna's shoulders, Maria said, "I will catch you up on our neighbors, the Regers," and she pointed to a solemn group of two adults and six children gathered in the corner of the stockade. "John and Dorothy came yesterday with their six. Frankly, I think Dorothy has lost all of her senses. She never has adjusted to frontier life. John has trouble controlling her outbursts, you know, when she tells whoever will listen that God has forsaken us. Or that God is punishing us. And that oldest son of hers is almost as bad. A sullen, sour faced youth if I ever saw one. But her girls, they will be fine and take care of the three little Regers."

"Poor Dorothy, I never really talked to her, you know, even though they have been here several years."

Maria waved at another family happily unloading supplies and going back and forth to the block house. "You remember the Mauses? They came this morning. George and Catherine have filled buckets with spring water for us. Their children are such help, and young Elizabeth is a charmer."

"What about the Woods? Martha and her girls? I know her husband is garrisoned at Fort Upper Tract. We saw him when the soldiers stopped at our cabin for water the first of April."

"Woods should have sent his women north to his family, but he sent them here instead. She, Magdalena and Katrina are here somewhere."

"My God. There are too many of us in here. Not enough men. Too many children. Poor Jacob. He must be overwhelmed with it all."

"I know, I know." Maria's voice was pained. "There are only six men here including old William Heavener, Elizabeth's father-in-law. Of course, my Nicholas and Henry can shoot, and we have flintlocks for them, but precious little lead. I cannot complain. Jacob is doing the best he can, you know."

"Oh, I am not criticizing Jacob. It is not his fault that Michael, Nicholas Heavener, and Dyer's sons-in-law simply dropped their families off here for Jacob to care for while they and the others left on a trip for supplies."

"I know. I do not understand the ways of our menfolk sometimes. But I know they do the best they can under these terrible circumstances. Now, I must see to supper for all of us. We are roasting some venison. Will Dyer brought in yesterday, should feed us all today and tomorrow. He will hunt for us while we are cooped up in here. There are plenty of biscuits, and Mauses brought cheese to share. We'll make do, for a while at least. There's a cow tied behind the blockhouse, and she should provide milk for your Sarah and the other little ones. Oh, and there's an area beyond the cow set aside for our personal needs. Hope the wind blows in the right direction." Maria laughed and turned to walk to the group gathered around the fire.

Anna remained where she was for several minutes, observing the chaotic scene around her. Seeing Adam and Mary playing with the Maus children, she moved to the stockade wall and sat down, her face toward the warm sun, and rested before her children returned with their endless demands.

April 26, 1758

Midnight

Killbuck was tired but relieved. He and his men were safely hidden a quarter of a mile west of the South Branch River upon which lay his first target, Fort Upper Tract. He was certain that no British scouts had observed his sixty men during their eight day journey from the fort that lay where the

Ohio River began its course. Motioning to a nearby warrior, barely discernable in the blackness, Killbuck whispered, "Come. I will show you something."

Leaving his tired comrades, he led the warrior stealthily through the dense forest to an opening where both could observe a dark ribbon of black winding its way below. The men stopped while Killbuck searched for his target. It took several minutes of silence before he noticed a glow emerging through the dark shapes lining the eastern river bank. "Firelight, the fort. There, you see. That is our target, the fort with soldiers. We will take the fort at first light."

"But they will see us crossing the river."

"We will cross before the sun rises. Up there." He pointed north to a place where the ribbon of black disappeared from view. "We will not be seen around that bend."

The warrior Shenango nodded in agreement, and the two men turned to make their way back to their resting comrades.

Before they reached their silent companions, Killbuck abruptly stopped. "Shenango, I have seen signs of our success. Moneto will protect us, but I have seen forty summers now, and must make a request."

"Anything you ask of me, great chief."

"Should I fall in battle, you must commend my spirit to the gods and bury me deep so that the wolves cannot desecrate my grave. Remove this talisman from my neck."

And he pointed to a small bag dangling from a leather cord around his neck. "Give this to my son when you return to our village. It is my Manitou, and he will need the power it holds."

"As you wish, but we will not fail."

Killbuck nodded and the two men returned to the silent war party.

Chapter 7

April 27, 1758

7 a.m.

Before the first rays of sunlight had broken through the dense foliage, Killbuck and his war party had secured themselves in the trees below the Upper Tract Fort. They had quietly crossed the river north and were satisfied they had not been seen. The war chief knew that the fort bastion always held a lookout who observed the river below, but he also knew that the view was limited. The soldier could not have seen sixty warriors cross the stream in twos causing few ripples and making no sounds.

The chief kneeled behind a large sycamore and watched the gate of the fort. He was certain that the gate would open sooner or later and was prepared to wait until it did. Then he would decide whether to hit the fort with a barrage of bullets and arrows or simply storm the structure. The gods would give him a sign. He felt the sun on his back as it began to rise above the tree line and hoped the glare would aid them when the time came.

Less than an hour had passed when the silence was broken by the creaking of the gate as it swung slowly open. A lone man emerged, a young man apparently unconcerned by the thought of Indians, for he made his way hurriedly to a grove of trees within twenty feet from Killbuck's hiding place, where he relieved himself with a loud sigh. He then sat down with his back against a large oak, facing the sun, and closed his eyes in obvious relief. Killbuck waited until the man's jaw dropped, his eyes closed and deep breaths emitted from his opened mouth. Then, Killbuck looked toward the gate. To his amazement, it remained open a crack, just a slight crack, but unlatched.

The chief listened to faint sounds from inside the fort and knew the soldiers were awakening and their senses might be dulled from sleep. Using a hand signal, he ordered a nearby warrior to kill the sleeping soldier. The deed was completed in seconds, and the warrior crept back into the trees, a bloody scalp in his hand. Seconds passed in silence, and then, at Killbuck's signal, four warriors made their way to the gate, stationing themselves on either side and motioning the others, hidden in the forest, to come forward. With a hard pull, the warriors yanked the gate open as far as it would go, and Killbuck yelled, "We will have revenge, brothers. Take their scalps and leave no man alive."

Screaming and shouting filled the air, and the soldiers, most sitting or kneeling next to the fire, watched with horror as the warriors entered the fort. The unprepared men, crying in pain as the life flowed out of them, made feeble attempts at surviving what would soon become a massacre. The fort enclosure became a tapestry of browns and reds, dust and smoke. The eighteen rangers were no match for Killbuck's sixty, highly-charged warriors wielding tomahawks, spears, and rifles, aiming at anything that moved.

Killbuck halted to observe the bloody scene unfolding before him. His eyes soon fixated on two couples cringing next to the blockhouse, the two young women screaming in terror while their men tried to shield them.

"I want their scalps." Killbuck pointed to the four. Within minutes, the two couples lay dead in a bloody heap while two angry warriors took their scalps, and soon a clump of thick auburn hair hung from one of their spears.

Not yet satisfied, Killbuck searched among the dying soldiers and pulled one up. "Where is your leader and I will spare you?"

The stricken man did not hesitate to point out a soldier and warrior in a life and death struggle by the fire. Without hesitation Killbuck took his knife and slit the surprised informant's throat before rushing to the struggle.

"He is mine." Killbuck shoved the warrior away.

"You will lead no more soldiers against my people. You will sire no sons to fight." He easily overpowered the wounded Dunlap and struck him with his tomahawk. Dunlap fell immediately and rolled over, his eyes with a vacant stare, and Killbuck took his scalp.

The sun was high when the fort's inhabitants finally lay dead or dying while the crazed warriors tore through everything, securing weapons, food, rum, and whatever useful items they could carry while others scalped and secured the grisly remnants on their waists or their spears. The two horses, loose within the fort, had been caught and were loaded with contraband and a bag of coins taken from the dead and dying. As they were led outside the gate, Killbuck ordered two warriors to ride them back to the villages as their share of the plunder.

"Fire this fort, this monument of white invaders. No more of our people will die by the hands of those who lie here."

Immediately, several warriors took hot embers from the fort's fire, placed them by the wooden stockade and blockhouse, and fed the fire until the flames began to climb the logs. A slight breeze encouraged the slow burning wood until the entire structure began to smoke and flame in earnest. The bodies had been piled next to the wooden blockhouse which also was ignited, and it was not long until the crackling and roar of the uncontrollable burning was heard. The massacre was complete.

It was with great satisfaction that Killbuck and his war party watched from the nearby trail as the fort's flames rose high above the trees and smoke billowed above, hindering the view of the clear, blue April sky. Some held their noses in an attempt to escape the odious smells of burning flesh now permeating the area. Their eyes became reddened and burned, and they stood watching their deed in silence.

"It is done." The war chief stood with his arms folded across his blood splattered chest. "These whites will take no more land or kill our warriors. The cleansing is good, and the whites will know our wrath. These men will not have sons to take up arms against us. We will not stop until all white men have fled over the mountains to the great waters, and we can return in peace to our ancestral lands. Now we have a journey ahead before we rest. We will not stop to destroy the log houses of our enemies. We will journey to another fort holding many women and children. We will have many scalps and captives to take back to our villages, and the French will pay us well."

After a brief rest, Killbuck led his warriors to the Indian trail to move on to their second target, Fort Seybert, nine miles southeast. His men were bloody and exhausted, yet the warriors would travel within two miles of the second fort. Much to their surprise, they encountered no one during their silent march, and Killbuck was pleased that there would be no more killing on this day.

For seven difficult miles the war party followed Killbuck as they moved quietly towards Fort Seybert. They saw several cabins, devoid of human life, for their owners had left weeks before. They did not stop to burn these reminders of encroachment but rather moved toward a more important objective. They had twenty-two scalps, a goodly number for payment from the French, and they would soon have more.

By late afternoon the Indians were comfortably established off the trail in a hollow near a small stream where they rested, cleaned their weapons, munched on jerky, and prepared themselves for tomorrow's task. Some scraped and cleaned the scalps while others repaired their war paint. Dunlap's scalp fluttered from Killbuck's spear.

Darkness filled the area by seven, and the Indians rested and talked quietly. Guards were posted in case some hapless settler might be out after dark, but the possibility was remote. It was cool and damp after the sun disappeared, and the Indians slept early to awake at first light of dawn. Killbuck watched his men with pride and tried to rest, but sleep did not come easily.

April 27, 1758

Noon

Anna had taken her restless children out of the oppressive blockhouse shortly after dawn and fed them cheeses and hard biscuits. Two-year-old Georgie was fussy and refused to chew on a tasteless piece of bread. Anna, nursing Sarah, looked at Mary. "Please. Try to get your brother to eat or at least drink more milk." She turned to her attention to back to her baby.

Suddenly, Anna was startled as Jacob opened the gate to admit two young black men. She knew Seyberts had slaves but had only seen them from a distance. Now, she watched the young men listen intently as Jacob outlined the situation. She noted the puzzled looks upon their dark faces as they accepted the packets Jacob gave to them. They looked at each other and turned to scurry through the slightly opened gate.

"Sweet Jesus," Anna thought. "These young men have no idea what is happening."

She called to Jacob. "Where will they go, those boys? Why didn't you make them stay here?"

"I gave them a choice, I fed them. But they could have stayed with us."

"No, they did not understand. They do not know the danger they are in."

"They will survive. The savages, if they find them, will keep them as slaves, not kill them."

"Is that better?"

"Yes, it is better to be alive."

"Do you mean we are doomed here?"

"No, I did not mean that. We have time. Time for your husband and Heavener to return with supplies. See to your children now." Jacob turned from her and walked briskly away.

Lowering her eyes, Anna did not protest and walked back to her children.

She could not find fault with Jacob for he had supplied the fort with necessities and entrusted his wife to organize the food situation. Maria gratefully accepted what each family brought to share with their neighbors. Some had gathered firewood from the surrounding area while others filled jugs with water and organized the sleeping arrangements, some in the blockhouse and some preferring to erect temporary shelters in the fort yard, using oil cloths and blankets.

Regardless of the valiant effort of the Seyberts, Anna thought her worst fears had come true. The fort was teeming with children, constant activity, and noise despite their parents' efforts to subdue them. Nausea rose in her throat as she noted the number of people with whom she would be forced to spend the next indeterminable number of days. She counted at least forty individuals and knew that Hannah Lorenz and George Moser rested in the blockhouse. She wondered what would happen if the weather turned bad. The blockhouse could hardly hold a dozen let alone forty.

Anna tried to keep her sons occupied while Mary held Sarah. She began to show her young sons how to draw pictures in the dust at her feet. Feeling the warm sun on her head and the gentle breeze across her face, she tried to forget where they were, but it was simply impossible.

Anna was jolted from her task by a shout from outside the gate. She jumped to her feet as she listened to the conversation, fearing bad news. Jacob ran to the gate and held his flintlock. "Who goes there?" A deep voice responded.

"Robertson, name Robertson. My mare, she went lame on the ford. Need to find a new mount."

Jacob slowly opened the gate, and Anna observed a rough, leathery-faced frontiersman enter the safety of the fort, leading a limping mare.

Anna's boys, alerted by the commotion, clutched their mother's skirts when they observed a stranger talking loudly with Jacob. Anna quickly decided she did not like this man as he glared at the scampering children who surrounded him.

She watched the stranger size up the fort and knew he recognized its weaknesses and lack of man power.

"Oh," she thought. "He will have to stay with us. Another mouth to feed."

She noted his tanned, wrinkled face and unkempt beard and doubted that he had bathed in weeks, perhaps months. She listened to his description of his hard ride across the mountains from Staunton, Virginia, in search of land. Watching the limping mare, taken away by Anthony Maus, who efficiently hobbled her in the far corner of the fort yard, Anna fleetingly though of their old mare and the long-legged foal she had produced, wondering if she would ever see them again.

Jacob motioned the newcomer to stack his bedroll along the wall and join the others milling around the fire. Remaining where she was, Anna could not help but hear Roger Dyer take Jacob aside. "My God, Seybert. We're supposed to protect this mob of children and women? And now this stranger?"

"No choice. Poor timing for the others to be going for supplies. God knows we need ammunition."

"How long can we hold out if them savages attack?"

"Not long, I'm afraid. Mebbe the men will get back here before it happens."

"Hope my girl Sary will come in today. Ain't been able to get her here yet." An unhappy Dyer continued to follow Robertson with his eyes.

Overhearing Jacob's warning, Anna felt a chill and nausea rising in her stomach, and her head began to throb. She turned away from the men and ordered her children to follow as they made their way across the fort yard. Before she had proceeded very far, Elizabeth Heavener grabbed her arm. "Anna, stop. We have not yet spoken."

Anna recognized her friend and tried to smile. "This is so hard, and now we have one more to feed."

"And one more gun to defend us too. Come, let us sit down and visit for a while."

The two women and Anna's boys walked to the wall where the women sat down, Sarah now held by Elizabeth as she cooed over the fretful child who soon stopped fussing and closed her eyes. A relieved Mary and Adam ran to a group of children to join in their game of kickball.

Anna stretched her tired arms. "I cannot stand this but don't know what to do. The noise gives me a headache, and the children are so restless and unhappy. You are fortunate to have set up your pallets in the open for the blockhouse is unbearable, hot and full of sour smells. And then, poor George and Hannah, their breathing, the rasping and coughing, the dying. George is dying I am sure, but his wife refuses to accept it. She is such a twit anyway. Why did our husbands leave us here in this dismal and oppressive place? I would rather take my chances in our cabin, but the children. It is the children I worry about and cannot handle alone."

"I know. My girls are older and do not require care. I, too, hate this place, but know it is for our safety. Keep praying for our husbands and our safe delivery from the savages."

"We left everything of value behind, at the cabin. Michael buried what coins we had and let the livestock run free, hoping the Indians would not catch and kill them. He took the horses deep into the woods and hobbled them. We will never see them again should the Indians locate them." Anna stopped and wiped her moist eyes.

"Have faith. The Indians may not be on their way here. No one knows for certain. Nicholas and Michael would not have left if they thought we were in imminent danger, you know."

"I know, but . . ."

"Remember, too, Dyer's daughter Sarah Hawes is still out there. I don't think Roger would have allowed her to do so if he thought the Indians were close by although her brother Will brought her daughter Hannah here yesterday. Sarah would not come in, he told me. She and that young indentured servant of hers."

"Indentured servant, how I hate that term."

"No, it is a good thing. Young Will has a chance to pursue his dreams in this country."

"Oh, stop. What dreams? Is this what you expected when you moved here? I hate this land and never expected to fear for my life and the lives of my children. It is not fair."

"No, I guess it isn't, but we are here now and must do our best for our children."

Anna sighed and closed her eyes. "Elizabeth," she thought, "is too much like Maria Seybert. I wish I had their optimism, their strength, but I have only fear."

The women ceased speaking, and Sarah fell soundly asleep, but there would not be much time to rest because supper would soon consume their time.

7 p.m.

The night was clear with no breeze to carry the smell of the still-smoldering remains of the Upper Tract Fort to the Fort Seybert area. A moon hung in the sky while the sounds of night creatures filled the forest. The group in Fort Seybert had no inclination that a massacre had taken place on the other side of South Fork Mountain and that sixty warriors were within striking distance this very evening. A small fire burned in the stockade while Anna mingled with other families around its warmth, conversing quietly as darkness began to encompass the area.

As women clasped their shawls around their shoulders and murmured to their restless children, Anna knew it was time to take her family into the center blockhouse to prepare for the night while some of the men walked the stockade yard and smoked their pipes, quietly discussing their precarious situation.

Dreading an encounter with Eve Moser, she had watched young Eve run back and forth from the blockhouse where her dying husband lay. Anna saw the young girl's eyes, wide and frightened, as she feared that she might be left a widow at sixteen. She sympathized with the young girl but did not know how to comfort her.

"I am too young to die," Eve said to anyone who would listen. "I should not be here."

Anna felt anger rising within her. "Eve, none of us should be here. But we are. Please be still. There are children here. You must not scare them."

Eve did not answer Anna's plea and continued her pacing.

Entering the blockhouse and settling her children, Anna tried to rest. Placing her children on the pallets in the corner, she closed her eyes, but sounds and sights frustrated her until she could stand it no longer. Admonishing Mary and Adam to watch their siblings for a minute, she quickly made her way to the door, afraid she might retch before she reached it. She stepped outside and stood against the wall, savoring the night air and the comforting smell of the remnants of the fire, breathing slowly and deeply.

Observing the quiet and those who were trying to sleep on the uncomfortable ground, she noticed two figures quietly talking. Although she felt guilty, she could not help but overhear their conversation and observed Robertson relaxing against the stockade logs, smoking his pipe, and Roger Dyer.

She heard Robertson muse, "Dyer, do ya ever wish ya hadn't moved here?"

"No, things ain't pleasant now, but in 1745 when we came, no Injun trouble at all. I've prospered y'know, lots of land, good sons-in-law, grandchildren, and a respectable daughter-in-law, a tad sober for my tastes, but a good wife to my son Will. Last few years have been hard though, no help from the government, damn government won't send help against these savages."

"Can't see the Injuns givin' up their land without a fight."

"True, but they sold it to the British. We have lawful claims, but it'll be years before we get title to these lands.

"Guess you'll ride it out."

"Damn right I will. We've all worked hard for these farms we made here in this place. But this spring trouble came, big trouble, Injun trouble. Ya picked a bad time to have a lame horse, friend. We could be here for weeks waiting for government soldiers. I hate it, but we must consider our families."

"Why didn't you send them east?" Robertson persisted with his questions.

"They wouldn't go, though I tried." Anna watched a scowl appear on Dyer's face.

"Well, ya can't go back now, and I guess we're all stuck here, but I thank you for allowing me to join you. Don't much like Injuns myself, and I reckon I don't want to be scalped by one of them neither. But there ain't very many men here to defend."

"'Tis true, but at least the Upper Tract's garrisoned. The government gave us that much. They're our first defense. If Injuns come into the valley, a ranger will warn us. We'll manage." Anna immediately thought of William Woods and the soldiers she had seen several weeks ago.

"Well, friend, think I'll curl up in my blanket and try to sleep. Better take advantage now before those noisy children decide to wake up."

When the conversation ceased, Anna waited until Dyer took his leave of Robertson who finally wrapped up in his blanket. She then watched Dyer peer through a slit in the stockade wall as he made his way slowly around the structure, smoking his pipe. Hoping neither man had seen her, she silently returned to her children and attempted to find the elusive sleep she desperately needed.

9 p.m.
Anna

I cannot sleep and I think too much. I am confined in a small stockade with five children and no one to aid me. My husband may not return for several days with our needed supplies, and, in the meantime, I am angry. I must not let the children know that I am distressed. I will not let the others know either, since they have their own problems. Poor Dorothy Reger is not holding up very well, but then she never has since they arrived here several years ago. She is not of frontier stock, I fear. Eve Moser is another one; she is young, of course, and simply cannot decide whether to cry or laugh or help her poor, dying husband. Hannah Lorenz, Jacob's mother, may not live long either but at least has old William Heavener to comfort her. Ah, what a mess we are in.

I have never been so afraid in my life nor felt so alone but with too many people around me. If God wills my death, then let it be, but I pray that my children will live. Michael should not have left us. I am thankful my dear friend Elizabeth Heavener is here. But I fear God has forsaken us in this wilderness. Was it a mistake to come to this country? I cannot yet say, but things are not good, and I am fearful, very fearful.

Within the blockhouse, the crowded families tried to ignore the stale air, the smells of cooking, and the restless movement. As night settled upon them, Anna, holding her baby Sarah, soothed her young sons, George, who was distraught over not seeing their mare's colt, Michael who missed his father, and Adam with Mary, stoic as usual. She quietly hummed a German lullaby and rubbed her sons' backs. She felt her eyes closing, baby Sarah on her chest, and Mary clutching Adam while George and Michael finally slept peacefully.

Midnight

Before midnight, the inhabitants of Fort Seybert finally slept with only one male awake, on guard. Roger Dyer, having overseen his wife and their family settled in a makeshift shelter rather than the crowded blockhouse, walked the stockade yard, periodically peering through holes in the stockade wall to look for movement in the area beyond. But he could not see much, the night becoming overcast and very dark with the moon finally disappearing beneath the clouds.

And so the night progressed with only one soul awake but seeing nothing.

Chapter 8

April 28, 1758

Early Morning

Even though the first rays of dawn hovered above, heavy fog lay over the valley like a shroud. There was little movement in the thick blackness of the forest despite sixty Shawnee and Delaware warriors moving single file, silently, toward Fort Seybert. It was early, some light filtering through the mist, when the war party stopped at a signal from Killbuck about one mile from their destination which stood three hundred yards beyond the bank of the South Fork Branch of the Potomac River.

Blending in with the trees, the warriors, vividly painted in red and black, silently observed a lone man, kneeling on a rise, flintlock pointed toward a doe feeding in a small glen in the distance. The hunter was William Dyer sent out to procure meat for the more than fifty settlers who, for several days, had been contained within the stockade for protection from the very group headed toward them. Dyer had located a deer within a short time. An excellent marksman and hunter, thirty-year-old Dyer, intent on his prey, did not sense nor hear the Indians.

Killbuck silently halted his war party to observe the lone man. Satisfied that Dyer was alone, the chief said in a hushed whisper, "Bring me his scalp."

Two warriors crept closer and closer until they were within twenty yards of their prey, still concealed by the heavy woods. Before the doomed Dyer could turn around, they fell upon him, grabbed his flintlock as the weapon went off in the air, and threw him to the ground. Within seconds one brutally tomahawked the struggling man while his comrade began the process of scalping. It was over in minutes, and now the dying Dyer lay slumped in a heap, blood flowing freely over his face, life draining from his eyes. Killbuck did not move a muscle until he was presented with the grisly reminder of the dead man.

Nodding to his men in approval, Killbuck thought, "And so it begins again. This man will not warn his people, and he will not supply them with meat."

Silence again prevailed, and soon, Killbuck ordered the war party to continue on their way, the bloody scalp hanging from the waist of one of the warriors. Shortly, the anxious war party passed a clearing with a small cabin, and, thinking it was empty, the owners having sought the protection of the fort, were surprised when a female voice was heard in the distance above the tinkling of a bell.

Abruptly Killbuck ordered a stop and complete silence. Again, the warriors halted while two of them, with stealthy, silent steps, quickly moved toward the sound.

"Will," a female voice shouted. "Catch her so I can sheer her."

"Yes, mam," called a lanky, blonde boy ahead of her. He sprinted toward the fleeing ewe and fell upon the animal in obvious glee. "I got her."

A few minutes later screams were heard, and soon the two warriors returned with a female and a young blond boy in tow. Both were terrified, the boy limp and speechless, but the woman still struggling. The female, not more than eighteen years old, exhibited defiance, her green eyes blazing, and continued to pull at her bonds.

"Let me go. Please let me go. For God's sake, Will. Help me." But she saw young Will could not aid her, and he was quickly taken away from her sight. As soon as she was gagged, an insolent warrior roughly pulled off her cap revealing long red hair, greatly admired by the Indians.

"Ah," said Killbuck who had returned to the warriors who had captured her. "A red head. We must not kill this one. She will be a valuable addition to our clan. A fighter too."

The young woman finally ceased her useless struggling, caught her breath, and allowed her captor to pull her into the line of admiring warriors, most of whom envied the young warrior, White Owl, who had captured this lovely female.

After a brief pause, the war party and their captives continued on the trail that began to skirt the river on the way to the fort. Fog continued to hang over the area, and the air was close and still on this spring morning. Soon the trail edged closer to the rocks scattered next to the river. In a rash moment, Sarah threw her body at White Owl, shoving him into and then over the rocks.

Losing his balance, the disgruntled man released her and fell sideways into the shallow water. However, there would be no escape; no sooner had the splash been heard, when another warrior roughly grabbed and held Sarah securely while the water-soaked man hastily climbed back to the trail, cursing the white woman who caused him embarrassment.

As he lifted his hand to strike her, another warrior stopped him, laughing. "Squaw man. You let this young squaw get the best of you."

The anger on White Owl's face dissipated quickly as he saw Killbuck awaiting his reaction. "It is so, but it will not happen again."

The amused Delaware leader pulled at Sarah's red hair. "Brave woman." As he watched White Owl rebind and gag the captive woman, he heartily approved of her actions. Although she was older, she would make an excellent addition to his tribe.

Directing his comrades forward, the war chief led the way ever closer to the confined, unsuspecting settlers. Sarah, pushed forward by her captor, moved along with the war party. Killbuck knew there was no chance of escape, and she was unaware that Wallace's blond scalp now adorned the spear of a warrior who trudged along the trail ahead.

At a bend of the trail, the wooden fort, framed in mist and fog, loomed ahead on a rise several hundred yards west of the river. Since the fog had begun to lift and expose the cleared, flat area, the Indians would be seen if they tried a frontal attack. Behind the fort a ravine provided natural protection. Following Killbuck's instructions, the war party stopped to secret themselves in the boulders and the brush by the river. A spring lay exposed about twenty yards from the fort's gate. Surveying the situation the warriors waited for a command from Killbuck, who had brazenly crept close to the spring where he could not be seen due to a depression in the cleared ground.

"The great spirit is with us." Killbuck lay on his stomach observing the silent fort. He heard the scream of an eagle and watched the bird circle above the tree line. He knew that the eagle was a sign that their mission would succeed, and he smiled in satisfaction.

Shortly, a woman carrying two buckets quickly emerged from a slight opening of the gate and hurriedly headed toward the spring. Killbuck made no sound but rather allowed the unobservant woman to dip her buckets into the pool of water and then make her way back to the fort. She did not notice him nor see the hidden Indians or Sarah, who was held with a warrior's hand clapped tightly over her mouth.

Allowing the woman to return unharmed was not Killbuck's choice, but he did not wish to alarm the fort nor risk being shot by an observer within its stockade. His scouts determined that very few men remained to defend this fort; and so, satisfied, he waited for a few minutes and silently, the way he had come, made his way back to the river and his waiting war party.

He spoke softly to his warriors and all listened intently. "We will surprise them. They fear our arrival, but no one has warned them. We will stay here, concealed in these rocks and trees. When the time is right, I will order an attack. I have seen a sign that we will succeed. They will bargain for their survival and will believe what I promise for they will have no choice. We will kill all of the men and take the women and children captive. Do not kill randomly for the captives will replace those who have been lost to white men's guns or disease. But we will take the scalps of the men when the time is right."

Anna

It is early, but I do not know what time it is. It is not long after dawn, but I have been awake much of the night. We are extremely uncomfortable and crowded; the baby has been fretful all night, and my two little boys have been restless. For two days we have forted with fifty or more other settlers because of the grave Indian threat. I am very tired and scared as are most of us by now. Michael is gone with Nicholas Heavener and others, but insisted we come to the fort for safety. I did not object; five children are too much to manage alone, especially under these conditions.

My Mary has been such a help for a mere nine-year-old, and Adam would defy me if it were not for her influence. It is easier to care for my eight month old baby Sarah and little Michael and George with her motherly aid because I am so tired and so drained, and I fear I am carrying another child.

How awful this year has been. I am constantly afraid and angry, and I want to go back to the old country, across the ocean. At least I knew what I was up against there, but I am not prepared for this danger here. There is nothing I can do, and Michael does not like my complaining. I think he fears as much as I do, fears for our five babies.

Ignoring nausea, I force myself to rise from our uncomfortable pallet surrounded by restless people of all ages. The smells of so many unwashed bodies does not help. I smooth my wrinkled shift and gently pick up my Sarah. She is awake and yearns for milk. I will have to locate some and hope that someone has thought to milk the cow this morning. Sadly, I could not nurse her for more than six months. I have not told Michael. I am not ready for a sixth child. I am only thirty-two and have been pregnant most of my married life of ten years.

Others begin to move, and quiet conversation among the families begins. I walk out of the blockhouse into the fort yard where Captain Seybert and his son Nicholas are standing, looking concerned. I want to speak to them, but they turn from me as we hear a shot in the distance. We are all alarmed but listen for a repeat, but none is heard. It is very quiet, too quiet. They are talking about William Dyer who left an hour ago to hunt for us. We will need meat I know. We may be here a long time, a very long time.

Many of the settlers have now joined us in small groups, all very alarmed. Practical as always, Elizabeth is worried about water. We need to fill the water barrel, but the spring lies twenty yards outside the stockade. It is necessary for someone to venture outside the gate with buckets and go to the spring. Captain Seybert and others peer from all sides of the stockade in an effort to see movement, any movement at all that might suggest Indian presence. It is difficult to see, however, because the fog still hangs over the area by the river. The air is moist, and we are warm even though the temperature is moderate.

Time passes, but no movement is seen, and all seems quiet, too quiet if you ask me; but no one does. I am not consulted and still do not speak English very well. I think that some of the women resent my presence in the fort because I do not speak English as well as the other Germans. Only Dorothy Reger has less knowledge of the

English language than I do, but she rarely speaks at all, for she is too busy crying and complaining, as if that were helpful. The Dyers do not understand German, and Roger Dyer has never liked the Germans much, even though two of his daughters have married them.

Elizabeth volunteers to go to the spring for water. She gathers two pails, and the gate is opened slowly while her two daughters, Katrina and Maria, plea with her to stay. Paying them no heed, she is cautioned by her brother Jacob and proceeds gingerly through the gate and down the slope toward the spring. All of us watch her progress and observe the surrounding area. We see nothing, and she returns with two pails of spring water for which we are all grateful. The gate closes quickly behind her, and we go on with our business of morning chores such as they are within this stockade.

Nicholas, the oldest Seybert boy, watches the river intently while holding his flintlock through the slit in the stockade. He seems to be certain the savages are out there. The shot alarmed us. I become even more afraid as are the others still standing in family groups. There are only six men to protect us; besides Captain Seybert, they include the Irishman Roger Dyer, whose son is probably dead, George Maus, John Reger, old William Heavener, and the whining Robertson. With a shout, Nicholas fires his gun and exclaims with glee that he has shot one of the savages. Jacob peers through the slits to confirm his son's kill. They see feathers floating in the distant river and assume he has achieved his purpose. There seems to be some confusion, and we glimpse movement along the shore and behind the rocks. Nicholas reloads and waits to shoot again.

I huddle with my children, trying to calm and quiet them as do the others. That annoying Robertson does not help but rather argues with anyone who will listen. He thinks we are doomed. He would run if he could, but wouldn't we all if we could? We wait for what seems like hours, but the sun is not high so it is not yet noon. Then it begins, a barrage of bullets and arrows, then silence. We do not move but are paralyzed with fear, our children clinging to us. Out of the silence we hear a booming voice from near the river, calling to the captain. As they peer through the slits in the stockade, Seybert and Dyer observe a painted savage, a savage who speaks English and wishes to bargain with our leader. Walking slowly toward the fort, he summons one of his men to his side. A warrior appears in the distance with a captive woman in front of him. It is Dyer's daughter, wife of William Dyer who has not yet returned and who, we fear, was the victim of the shot we heard earlier. Sarah, despite the hand covering her mouth, seems to be indicating for us not to surrender. She scuffles with her captor, who roughly drags her back into the shelter of the rocks. Jacob, against the advice of many of us, decides to leave the fort and talk to the Indian leader. We fear he will be shot before any conversation takes place. I become speechless.

10 a.m.

It was Killbuck's plan to take the fort as swiftly as he could because he feared that the militia might return and did not want to lose another warrior. Anger filled his heart when Nicholas' shot had hit its mark, and he watched his warrior drift down the slowly moving river, feathers floating with him. The shot had passed through the dead man into another warrior who was severely wounded but could be taken by litter back to the Ohio River villages.

Deciding to show his superior strength and void of any fear, Killbuck directed his warriors to initiate rapid firing at the fort. For more than fifteen minutes, a barrage of bullets and arrows hit the walls of the log fort in rapid succession. The settlers, having taken defensive positions, returned the fire to no avail. No one was hit on either side. The firing ceased as suddenly as it had begun.

"Brothers, our moment has come. We will take this fort. These whites will surrender, and we will have our revenge."

Before Killbuck ordered the firing, White Owl, who had secured Sarah Hawes, pleaded, "This woman. She will make a fine squaw. Spare her." He looked longingly at his beautiful, red-headed captive and put his hand on her shinning tresses as she glared at him with hate.

"Remain here until I call you." Killbuck ignored the request. White Owl did not protest and stood still, waiting for the signal to storm the fort and the war cries of his comrades.

An excited Killbuck made his way slowly across the flat area toward the fort, beckoning White Owl and Sarah to follow, and White Owl reluctantly complied. The trio stopped fifty yards from the gate. Holding his rifle in a ready position, the imposing Killbuck stood his ground and waited for Seybert to open the gate and take a few steps toward him. Knowing that time was of the essence, Killbuck intended to promise anything the settlers wanted but would keep none of them.

"Hear me. Listen to my words. We will not harm you if you surrender. What say you?"

Seybert and the others not only heard the words but also observed movement through the stockade wall. With shock, Seybert recognized the young widow and became angry that Roger Dyer had not forced her to fort. Anna and the others now stood frozen with fear, and Seybert knew what he would do. Warning the waiting Nicholas not to shoot and stepping cautiously outside the slightly opened gate, Seybert observed the area, having no idea how many warriors lay hidden behind the rocks and how many remained within the cover of the forest.

Standing face to face now, a dignified Seybert and the dark and confident Killbuck began to negotiate, their voices loud and harsh.

"We are at war with the English and will give you no quarter unless you surrender. I have come with sixty of my warriors to warn all settlers that they must return to the East or face the wrath of my people. We will take this fort as we have taken others. And we will show no mercy if you do not surrender." Changing his tone to a conciliatory one, Killbuck added, "But do not fear, for we will take you to the trail that leads across the mountains to safety."

"How can we trust your words? You did not spare our neighbors when you raided this area a month ago. You murdered our friends in cold blood with no mercy. You have taken our women and children. Why should I expect your words to be truthful?"

Killbuck contained his fury. "Have my people not been the victims of the white man's treachery? Have you not made promises and violated treaty after treaty? Have you not encroached upon our hunting grounds and depleted our food supply? Have we not lost young men to your soldiers? Do not question my words. You will have to believe me as we have had to believe your people." Killbuck's steely eyes were unflinching. "You have our terms. Do not be foolish. We are strong and will succeed. Now give me your answer. My warriors are restless, and you have already killed one of them. I will not lose more."

"I must take your words to my people, and then I will give you our answer." Seybert turned quickly to enter the stockade, knowing they were hopelessly outnumbered, and the impatient Indians could not be trusted.

Eyes downcast, Seybert entered the fort, and, as the gate slammed behind him, the fort's waiting inhabitants began to all speak at once in varying degrees of fear and rage.

Sixty-year-old, graying Roger Dyer, silenced his defiant son. "We cannot trust these savages. But, my God, they have my foolish Sarah and will kill her. How many of us will also die at their hands?"

He was interrupted by Robertson who demanded they surrender. "We must surrender. We can't outlast them savages. We have but six men to defend. I ain't about to die for women and children. Some of us can make a run for it."

"Stop, you coward" spat Dyer. "I say we fight and hope our men or the Redcoats rescue us. We can hold out awhile. They won't kill my Sarah but will take her captive and she will live."

"Not enough lead, Dyer. Not enough." interrupted John Reger. "I am not a coward, but I have six children to consider."

George Maus, his crying wife hanging on his arm, argued, "So do I, so do I, but we cannot trust them. They will kill us anyway. I'd rather die fighting."

Courageous and dignified, Seybert silenced them all. "It is not just lack of men. We have scant ammunition, and I fear we cannot hold them for more than a few hours. They will overwhelm us and fire the fort."

"Maybe we can hold until the militia comes," suggested Seybert's sister Elizabeth, vaguely hopeful that her husband and sons might return in time.

Jacob's voice became raspy. "It is Killbuck who leads this raid. He and his clan lived here until several years ago. I thought he accepted us. We traded, and he brought me meat. I never thought. . ." He looked at Anna. "Anna, you met him several years ago."

Anna did not respond until she recognized that all were silent and looking at her. She waited for the earth to swallow her, but it did not, and she was compelled to speak.

In halting English, she heard herself respond in an unfamiliar voice. "Yes, he came to our cabin for food several years ago. He did not harm me but could have." She looked at the sea of faces in front of her. "I think we should not surrender. I prefer death for me and my children rather than living as slaves or dying in Indian villages."

"Do not listen to that woman," yelled Robertson. "She can't help defend us. Can you shoot, woman? Can you load a flintlock? Probably don't have one anyway." He glared at Anna, who became pale and thought she would faint. Mary began to cry. "Mama, stop that man; he is mean to you."

"Hush, Mary. It will be all right." Anna stood as tall and straight as she could and looked at the sneering Robertson. Before she could respond, Dyer said, "Jacob, we know you will decide. It is not my life I fear for. See there," and he pointed at a group of three women and five little ones. "Those are my kin, my family. I don't want to lose any of them. But I agree with Anna. Surrendering is a death sentence. My boy here, James, he can shoot, and old man Heavener over there," and he pointed to an elderly man holding Elizabeth Heavener and her daughters. "He can defend. We can hold out for days."

"Dyer, you know your son Will lies dead out there. You all heard the shot. We have a chance to save lives. Killbuck assures me he will escort us to the Shenandoah trail. He wants our supplies, our valuables."

"He's a savage liar. Can't trust none of them savages," shouted Robertson. "Surrender and get it over with, Seybert. Some of us will run."

Anna could no longer look at the rough frontiersman, and she knew that he would be the first to run if he had the chance.

George Maus shouted, "Jacob, what kind of valuables do we have anyway? Did you all bring hoards of gold coins? Silver jewelry? I think not. Do you think the savages will be satisfied with a bag or two of flour? Our old kettle over there? How about your bay horse? Our valuables will hardly satisfy Killbuck."

"Shut up, George," cried Reger who had clapped his hand over his wife's mouth for fear she would scream incoherent obscenities to God himself. "I stand with Jacob.

Surrender, Jacob, and hope the savages will let us, or at least some of us, live. But I think all of us know that the men who stand here today are doomed, regardless. Perhaps our children will live."

Hearing the angry debate, Jacob's son Nicholas and several others adamantly objected to surrender, but Jacob ignored the dissenters before he opened the gate for the last time. "It is my decision to make as captain of this fort. I do not know if it is the correct one, but it is my responsibility, and I take it. We will surrender and pray that God will instill this savage chief with some sense of pity to take on us. Otherwise, I fear that some of you will be right. We will be doomed."

Before Jacob turned toward the gate, Maria clutched his arm and stared into his pained, dark eyes, eyes and said so that all could hear, "God be with you, my husband," as he gently pulled away from her and sought the gate.

It was as if the world had stopped, and only silence prevailed. The sun had refused to come out of the low clouds that remained over the valley, and low areas still suffered remnants of the earlier fog. It was as if nature itself was aware of the catastrophe about to take place.

Chapter 9

April 28, 1758

11 a.m.

Knowing their fate was sealed, one way or another, the fort's inhabitants froze as all realized surrender was imminent, and Captain Seybert would soon swing the heavy gate open to the painted horde awaiting the spoils. His son Nicholas was a portrait of defiance, standing, gun ready to fire upon the vicious chief who had talked his father into surrendering. Time stood still, and the forest was ominously silent, waiting. Even the small children stopped their crying as if they, too, knew their fates were in the hands of the Indians.

Anna looked to the sky, praying fervently that her family might be spared, while Dorothy Reger screamed, "The devil is at the gate. He is here and we are doomed." She then prayed for her soul and those of her family. Anna watched Dorothy with pity as the gate swung open in slow motion, inch by inch, allowing her to see movement beyond, her fingers clawing into the arms of her children. The sounds of muffled prayer began to fill the area.

As the heavy gate creaked and angled open, dozens of painted, yelling warriors materialized in the rocks and trees. Seybert now stood in front of the waiting chief. "We will accept your terms. We surrender, and you can have anything that is here. We expect you to take us to the trail. Do we have your word?"

Looking satisfied, Killbuck replied, "Did I not say it was so?"

"Then it will be." Jacob turned toward the gate, eyes filling with moisture.

Before he could enter the fort, Killbuck strode toward him, tomahawk in his uplifted hand and struck him with the blunt end of the weapon causing the surprised man to stagger back and cover his mouth, now bleeding profusely.

"Do you think you will see the light of another day, white man?"

Nicholas had run to his stricken father and aimed his rifle at Killbuck's chest, but his father knocked the weapon out of his hands. The warriors hesitated in shock expecting to see their chief fall, but that did not happen. The shot hit the ground in the dust at Killbuck's feet.

A second passed before Killbuck looked at Nicholas. "You have given us a sign, a good sign," and he grinned at the shocked boy who was shortly grabbed by two angry warriors. The war party, now enraged, prepared to mount their final assault and storm the fort.

"You lied," screamed Nicholas as he was thrown to the ground by an angry warrior. "You had no intention of helping us. You have no honor. I will never give in to you. Never." He glared at his father but was stunned when he saw the blood begin flowing from his father's mouth. Having rushed to her husband's side, his mother quickly tore off a piece of her skirt and placed it firmly on her husband's mouth in an effort to stop the profuse bleeding.

Looking sadly at his son, Seybert said, "Nicholas, stop. It is too late."

Anna watched the events unfold in slow motion, She heard the words of surrender; she saw Killbuck strike Jacob and heard the crack of a shot as Nicholas tried to kill the war chief. To her amazement, Killbuck still stood. It was then she was overwhelmed with the failure of it all. It was over, she knew.

Blinking back her tears, she had not moved for an hour while her children remained clustered around her, and she held Sarah crushed against her chest. Her breath came in short gasps as the gate opened, and she tried to fix the images of those within the fort into her mind. If she lived, she would remember the scene before her.

Colors became enhanced, and she saw the brown earth at her feet, the graying logs of the stockade, the green trees peering over the walls, and a few yellow-red coals remaining in the fire pit. She smelled the dying embers and the horses as a soft breeze moved across her face.

She tried to memorize the faces surrounding her. She noted John Reger's pinched face as he tried to contain his hysterical white-faced wife, eyes hugely round and unsettling. She saw the furrowed forehead and gray heavy eyebrows of the bearded William Heavener, more hair on his face than on his head. She saw George and Catherine Maus, their pained faces merging into one as they looked at each other and their children, terrified looks upon their pale faces.

She recognized Martha Woods and her daughters blending into the wall as one marbleized statue. She noted the grief-stricken Seybert girls glide to their parents while William Dyer and his son James stood at the wall, eyes fixed on the Dyer women and children at the gate.

Her image was broken when Robertson, next to the gate, rushed through the determined Indians who paid him no heed, so intent were they to search the fort. Seconds later, the Dyer women, carrying and dragging five little ones, ran through the maddened warriors toward the rocks by the river. Anna soon lost sight of the women as they pushed their way through clouds of dust, smoke, and figures of screaming Indians. Following close behind were Elizabeth Heavener and her two daughters.

Anna watched, stunned, until the dust, smoke, and angry warriors began to obscure her view. But through the haze

Anna could see poor Maria Heavener, lagging behind her mother and sister, caught by a lone warrior who tripped her as she passed. Maria was unable to elude his grasp as she screamed for her mother and sister, but her voice was absorbed by the war cries of the warriors and the cries of the victims still within the fort.

Suddenly, time began to move very quickly. New images began to form, and Anna saw rapid movement. She was aware that young Anthony Maus and Johnny Reger zigzagged through the rampaging warriors, hysterical women and children until they were caught. She heard the harsh bellow of the old cow quickly silenced, but still she could not move.

Killbuck had one goal, the destruction and annihilation of both the fort and its inhabitants and did not order the pursuit of those who managed to flee. He had no interest in young children who were liabilities anyway. It was the men he hated and feared and desired to kill.

Confusion escalated, and noise increased. Shouting with rage, the Indians rampaged through the stockade and into the blockhouse, gathering anything of value they might use later. On Killbuck's orders, they confiscated pots and a large kettle; they took blankets and any available clothing; they grabbed guns, knives, and ammunition. The settlers were thrown to the ground, searched for valuables, and mistreated profusely.

While the warriors searched and destroyed everything in their paths, the terrified prisoners cried and pled for the lives of their children. Anna watched Roger Dyer stoically braced against the stockade wall, lips moving in silent prayer that his wife and family were now safely hidden among the rocks. She had no idea if the warriors had pursued the women and children, and she too prayed that they had escaped the grasp of the seemingly-inhuman beings destroying all of their dreams. Seeing that Dyer's weathered face was racked with pain, tears in his eyes, she feared that this day might be his last. Awaiting his fate, he held his son James securely.

Anna watched as several warriors stormed the blockhouse, and she knew that Hannah Lorenz could not rise from the pallet upon which she lay. Sounds from the blockhouse were hard to distinguish, but Anna listened for Hannah's screams. She failed to recognize voices but knew that Hannah and George would die. She heard the yells of triumphant warriors and watched several leave the structure, a bloody scalp held high in triumph. She did not see Hannah's long, gray hair, however. It was George's scalp she saw.

Another screaming warrior emerged from the blockhouse, a figure of a woman in his arms. Through the dust and chaos Anna recognized Eve Moser, taken to the gate where she and the man disappeared from view.

Standing near Anna and her whimpering children, Martha Woods made every effort to shield her two daughters. She looked at Anna, and their eyes met briefly, both women terrified and afraid for their children. Hearing the carnage within the blockhouse, Martha pushed her daughters against its wall and defiantly stood in front of them. Anna saw that her efforts were in vain for Martha and the girls were separated, each held and bound by Indians who took them outside the gate where the captives were forced to gather. Anna waited for the inevitable to happen.

Two mangy brown dogs ran aimlessly through the area, ripping at anything moving, while barking continually. With shock, Anna watched as, one by one, they were silenced by one of the warriors. She sought the horses but did not remember where they were and could see little in the mounting dust. But she knew that, including Robertson's lame mare, three had been hobbled behind the blockhouse with the cow. Surely, the Indians would not kill the animals, she thought.

Paying no attention to Anna or her children and shouting with delight, other warriors ran back and forth with their plunder while one secured a large pot for the purpose of holding jewelry, coins, and useful cooking utensils that would be carried back to the Indian villages. Still others brandished the weapons they had secured from the settlers.

Anna's view was obscured by the lame mare who trotted aimlessly within the stockade, whinnying and kicking, but ignored by the warriors. The two sound horses were quickly subdued and mounted by warriors who managed to gallop them through the confusion of people and head toward the river bank. Anna knew that Jacob, for the last time, witnessed his favorite gelding bolting down the slope to the river and disappearing among the trees.

Now, watching all of the carnage and destruction, Killbuck stood in front of the group of captives who had been dragged outside the protective walls of the fort. Forced to watch, Sarah Dyer Hawes was held securely by White Owl while the settlers were rounded up and marched out.

A trembling Anna clutched her daughter Sarah and prayed that she would not cry. Her younger two sons choked on dust and fear while Mary held her brother Adam as firmly as she could. Anna's mind wandered again, and she saw her husband Michael, she saw her cabin, and she saw images of her past passing before her eyes. She tried not to see the Indians or their painted faces or listen to the horrible sounds surrounding her.

As the dust in front of her began to settle, she watched a figure emerge. Then she saw him, Killbuck, just as he had appeared in her dreams, a savage grin upon his painted face. In English he said "Ah, we meet again."

She tried to scream, but no sound emerged from her opened mouth. Three warriors suddenly appeared behind the chief. "This woman. Do not bind her but allow her to carry her child. The older two." Killbuck pointed at Mary and Adam. "They can stay with her, but these two young boys, these two young boys will be taken to our villages. Take them to the river where the horsemen wait. And you." He reached his hand toward Anna. "You will follow me." Although he now spoke in his Delaware tongue, Anna knew exactly what he meant.

He turned abruptly as the warriors grabbed the young boys. Anna felt the scream finally emerging from her opened mouth, and she pressed Sarah even closer with one arm and futilely reached for her sons with the other. Mary refused to let go of young George but was pushed to the ground while Adam's grip on Michael was quickly severed.

The boys screamed in fright while they were roughly thrown over the shoulders of the dark, bare-chested men who took them. Roused into action, Anna did not hesitate to run after the chief and his men with Mary and Adam following.

Paying no attention to the settlers gathered outside of the gate, Anna attempted to follow her abducted sons as they were taken toward the river, but was roughly halted by a warrior who shoved her into a line of settlers. There was a hushed silence while Anna pleaded for her sons. She heard Georgie's cries turn to whimpers and Michael's scream cut short by his captor. She watched them taken farther away towards the river where she recognized the horses, now controlled by Indian warriors who grabbed the boys and wheeled the animals into the trees along the river.

Anna's cries echoed across the valley, and she felt sick and helpless and thought of death. She grabbed Mary's thin shoulder and pinched her hard enough that Mary cried out in pain.

"Mama, stop. Stop. They are gone."

Anna no longer saw the horsemen and knew Mary's words were true. Her sons had been taken from her, probably forever. She glared at Killbuck, standing nearby, and screamed at him. "You took my sons. Where, where did you send them? May the devil strike you dead." And she sobbed uncontrollably.

Killbuck walked to her and said quietly in English, "Be still woman. Your sons are better off. I chose them to live, to live as warriors in our villages. Young children will not survive our journey, but yours will live."

Anna's sobs ceased, but her shaking did not, and she tried to turn his words over in her mind where a glimmer of hope hovered in one corner. Then, she saw the horrified looks on Catherine Maus' face as she looked at her baby in her arms and John Reger's pained expression as he held his child tighter to his chest.

When the miserable band of humanity had been forcibly assembled outside, three warriors remained within the fort, and the sounds of wood chopping and breaking could be heard. When the men had gathered the wood needed, they carried their plunder to the river bank and proceeded to make a litter, using the broken wood and vines from the river bank. Killbuck planned to use the litter to transport the wounded warrior now lying with a comrade by the river, barely surviving in his pain. If he did not live, one of the captives would replace him.

Before the final act of the burning of the fort, Killbuck ordered each captive attached to a warrior, some bound by their wrists and some with ropes around their necks. Terrified mothers attempted to carry their youngest children in hopes of protecting them from obvious harm to come. An hysterical Dorothy Reger carried her youngest while her husband John carried two more. Killbuck stood some distance away, observing his captives in silence.

No one heard old Hannah's screams through the din, and most had temporarily forgotten her and George Moser, so intent were they to survive themselves. Killbuck watched Anna as she stood silently among her neighbors, her face reddened and tear stained. The Seybert children had been separated and moved away from their stricken parents who remained silent, pain and horror evident on their faces.

Some distance away, Nicholas, however, still furious at his father's surrender, continued fighting and cursing at the amused warrior who held him. Seybert himself, mouth still bleeding and teeth loosened, stood, now bound, and looked at the ground while Maria tried to comfort him.

Mary tried to gain her mother's attention. The child verged on hysteria and clutched Adam with one arm and her mother with the other. Anna was busy cradling her baby and did not hear her daughter above the noise and confusion. She did not want to think at all.

Briefly awakening from her grief, Anna heard Killbuck. "Fire the fort. I want nothing left when the English get here." The warriors obeyed, and several re-entered the structure with large branches that had been stripped of their leaves. Soon she heard the crackling and popping of a fire and saw orange flames rising above the fort walls. She again thought briefly of Hannah and George, and then she recalled old William Heavener, who had fled to the blockhouse when the gate opened. She did not see him.

Noon

Over an hour had passed since the fort had been fired, and now the sun reluctantly peeked out of light cloud cover as smoke began to obscure the area. The devastation was observed by the victorious Killbuck and his warriors. With hand signals and a glare, Killbuck brought his war party to a kind of order while smoke thickened as the fort began to burn in earnest. Most settlers, watching their last sight of their home for several days, slowed their outrage and cries to whimpers, waiting for the next disaster.

It was not long in coming. Killbuck ordered the three smallest Maus children, all under six, brought forward while their distraught father fought unsuccessfully with his captor. Their hysterical mother fell to the ground, arms outstretched in a useless plea for mercy.

"No crying," he warned. "Indian children do not cry. Silence your children, and they may live."

Knowing that the Maus children would not cease their cries, he intended to make an examples of them. Signaling their captors, he ordered their slaughter. With no hesitation, the three warriors holding the three small children grabbed their hair and, pulling upward, used their knives to scalp the helpless, crying children, who died quickly, covered with blood, mourned by all settlers as terror mounted.

Killbuck paid no attention to Anna who had resumed her uncontrollable sobbing. He ignored Catherine Maus' pleas for mercy and looked with disgust at Dorothy Reger, vulnerable as a frightened child, as she lay upon the ground while her husband attempted to gain her attention. His warriors maintained tight grips on the older boys for fear some might try to escape. The Maus children were not mourned by the warriors who left their broken bodies in front of the fort and its captives.

Killbuck then ordered the preparation for the long march ahead, but determined James Dyer had had enough. With a quick movement, the slight and agile boy jerked free of his captor and ran as fast as he could toward the river. His father Roger pleaded with him to stop, but the fourteen-year-old-boy made the run of his life and almost succeeded had it not been for the river itself. He had distanced himself from his captor when he reached the water, but his hesitance at that point allowed the Indian to gain ground. He was captured at the bank and thrown to the ground. The warrior smiled as he secured the boy for his trip back to the group of captives, all of whom had silently prayed for James' success. His sister Sarah watched as he was pushed past her, tears cascading down her dirty face, and she froze in fear.

Killbuck, observing the boy's efforts, mentally put him on his list of captives to take to the Indian villages. Nicholas Seybert, too, was on this list, another brave boy. Killbuck considered all children over six as worthwhile and valuable for trade or inclusion into Indian families. The adults were another story, however. There was no doubt the men were expendable and dangerous and could not live to fight the Indians again. He had not decided the fate of the women, but he had observed some bravery in a few: Anna, Sarah Hawes, and the dark haired, attractive Martha Woods.

Although the distraught Eve Moser had shown no indication of bravery, Killbuck considered her youth an asset, and she was unencumbered with children. The Mallow baby and the Reger young ones would be eliminated, for their crying irritated him. The war chief knew very well that crying, small children were liabilities on the nine day march back to the Ohio River. The distance was great, and only the strongest would survive.

As a still defiant James was roughly placed back in the line of captives, Killbuck observed all of this destruction in silence. He did not relish killing, but he feared for his people. He did not trust the French much more than the English, but the French respected the land, the earth that was sacred to all and could not be bought and sold.

Having lost both friends and family in this struggle, Killbuck recognized his duty and the responsibility thrust upon him. For over two years he had fought the white man and killed many. Having seen his warriors killed and members of his clan slaughtered, he felt no remorse at his violent deeds.

As chief it was Killbuck's duty to perform these vicious acts in every effort to stop the westward movement of the English. Killing meant fewer men to kill his own people. He knew he participated in a death march of sorts but was unsure of the outcome.

Anna
2 p.m.
I have lost all track of time, but it does not matter. Smoke burns my eyes, and tears have dried on my cheeks only to be replaced by new ones. Sarah's damp body lies against my chest, my arms encircling her small body as she whimpers and coughs. I could not bear to look at the mangled bodies that lay before me nor can I look at the Mauses and their hysterical children. Three babies lie in the dirt. I close my eyes because there is nothing I can look at. I am only slightly aware that my children still live, not for long, I fear.

I do not know where my Georgie and Michael are. I wonder where the militia is and will they arrive soon enough to save us. I think not.

All of us are now controlled by a painted savage. Besides smoke, I smell unfamiliar and unpleasant scents. My God, can it be burning flesh? This cannot be happening. The three in the flaming blockhouse, I cannot bear to think of them . . . in the flames. My God, help us, help them. Mary holds my arm while clutching Adam's hand. We are together now except for the presence of a horrible fiend behind each of us, constantly watching our every move.

I cannot control my thoughts, and they wander. I watched that daring James Dyer try to escape and prayed he would. I imagined him crossing the river to freedom and help. But that was not the way it happened. I see Robertson locating our returning men in time. But it is not to be.

We are getting ready to leave this place. I cannot understand the words of these savages as they talk back and forth, but I can sense our imminent departure.

I am numb and do not know how to keep things together for my children. George and Michael are gone; that I know. I pray they will live, but George is frail and might not survive a long ride to the Indian villages, and Michael is young. Hopefully, he will survive, and some squaw will hold him as her son.

Oh, God, how I hate this land, the land of our dreams, shattered now that God has forsaken us, the God who gave us this new land only to take it away. Is this what hell is like?

Chapter 10

April 28, 1758

The war party, tired from their bold successes, were anxious to leave; and, with much pushing and pulling, forced the hapless captives to move. Each captive was the responsibility of a warrior, most of whom treated their charges roughly. The captives, disheveled and dust-covered, and the warriors, still painted, some blood-spattered and sweating, began a single file march up the old Indian trail towards the Upper Tract area and South Fork Mountain, which divided the two valleys. Black smoke drifted along the tree line, obscuring the cloudless blue sky. In the deadly silence, Anna took no notice and did what she was told.

It was now early afternoon as the group of warriors and captives moved farther from the fort. The smell of smoke lessened, and the scent of spring began to emerge. The trees and undergrowth were green and thick, and wild flowers appeared in patches, promising a lovely spring. Silence prevailed among the captives who realized that crying was not helpful and perhaps a death sentence.

Anna trudged quietly through water, overgrowth, and new vines that covered parts of the trail. Her feet became damp and her clothes dirty, and all tried in vain to keep the remaining small children quiet in fear that they would receive the same fate as the hapless Maus children. But, most of all, she avoided looking at the grisly reminders of death hanging on belts or spears.

Struggling had ceased, and the forlorn captives contemplated the fate that might lay ahead. Except for the

Dyer offspring and Nicholas, no thought of escape entered their minds. Grief numbing their thoughts, the captives followed the person walking ahead of them. Anna and the other women, mothers all, suspected death was imminent for them as well as their still-whimpering children. No one could comfort the pathetic Mauses, who were inconsolable, and even the presence of their three older children could not distract them from their grief.

Dorothy Reger by now had retreated into her own world and was beyond the help of anyone. Briefly, Anna thought it was a blessing because Dorothy alone would die with no memories of the massacre unlike Anna who would never forget the horror of seeing her young sons taken from her.

Silently weeping, Anna could not bear to look at the tragic figures of the four men left, Jacob Seybert, George Maus, John Reger, and Roger Dyer. She had no doubt that they would be killed, when or where she did not know. She knew that Jacob, feeling tremendous guilt, was not condemned by the others, for they knew he thought the decision was the best one for them all.

"God forgive me," she heard him mutter over and over. Her dislike of Roger Dyer had faded into admiration, and she knew he prayed for his valiant family who had managed to escape. She had seen no evidence of their recapture, and no new scalps adorned spears that she could see.

Following behind the group struggled four warriors carrying a litter, hastily constructed from logs from the fort, which held the wounded warrior who, they hoped, could be taken to a village to heal. Lastly, walked two disgruntled men carrying a log which held a kettle containing the valuable items taken from the fort. It was obviously heavy, and the two had difficulty in keeping up with those ahead of them.

Less than an hour had passed since the trip up the mountain began, when suddenly, Killbuck ordered a stop. "Move those logs." He pointed to where he wanted them placed.

No longer moving, the captives were jolted into awareness, fearful of what this might mean. Motioning to his warriors, Killbuck said, "Children on that one," and he pointed to his left, "and adults there." Then he pointed at the three young Reger children and motioned for them to be secured with the adults.

The action took several minutes, and when it was done, the older children sat on one log while the adults and small children had been yanked and pulled to the other.

"We will rest." Arms folded across his painted chest, he then pointed at Anna, Eve Moser, and Martha Woods, seated with the adults. They were roughly pulled from the log and pushed to the other side. The captives, now divided, knew that those on one log would survive and those on the other would live but a few more minutes. Most warriors wanted the bloody business completed so they could return home with their contraband.

Anna did not struggle for she knew that it would be in vain. Instead she once again fixed the faces of her two small sons in her mind. She still clutched Sarah but no longer knew of her presence. It was Mary who tried to keep the child quiet, knowing all too well that the child might not survive much longer than the Maus children. Adam simply watched in fear and clutched his sister's arm.

Eleven-year-old Maria Heavener caught Anna's attention, and she turned to watch the child who had not stopped crying since she had been dragged back to the fort as her mother and sister disappeared from her view. Pushed and shoved to the log with Anna and the others, Maria refused to sit. Anna realized, too late, that Maria intended to flee. She wanted to grab the child but did not have a free hand to do so.

Anna had no time to cry out and saw Maria bite her captor on his bare forearm. The young girl managed to loosen his grip and, without a backward glance, fled into the forest behind the log. Her captor, holding his bleeding arm, hesitated just long enough for Maria to disappear among the thick trees. The warrior then pursued her but, after a few minutes, failed in his effort and returned to the clearing minus his captive. Shrugging his shoulders at a glare from Killbuck, he settled into the line still holding his bleeding forearm. No effort was made to pursue the girl, who, Killbuck thought, would not survive a night alone in the forest nor have any idea how to reach a friendly fort. It was not worth their efforts. She would die.

Experiencing new shock and horror, Anna had finally realized the purpose of the two logs. Death awaited those who sat across from her while she and the others would live as slaves or Indians. Stomach in knots, she pulled Mary and Adam as close as she could and waited for the events to unfold. She saw the warriors remove their tomahawks from their belts and closed her eyes for she feared she would faint it she watched the brutal murders.

Killbuck could wait no longer. He knew it was time to rid himself of the white men before a search party located them. He looked at his waiting warriors. "On my command, those seated there," and he pointed to the group on one log. "Those will die. Their women too."

At his command, the victims were brutally tomahawked and scalped at the same time. Eyes closed and baby clutched close to her breast, Anna did not see Dorothy and John and their three young children die, nor did she watch the Seybert adults' last moments. She did not see the relief in the eyes of George Maus before he died quickly nor hear Maria Seybert's short, then silenced, screams. She did not see the tomahawks fall upon the heads of any of them, but she knew it had happened and would not remember much of the next few days. The bodies of the slain lay where they fell, Dorothy Reger's arms stretched in vain over two of her slaughtered children. The war party now had additional scalps to take back to the French who would pay a bounty for each.

Killbuck had watched young James Dyer react with fury when he heard the sound of a tomahawk on his father's skull. "You bastards. I will never forget this evil slaughter," and he choked on his rage.

Suddenly, James screamed again. "Sarah. Sarah, get up." He saw his sister Sarah, who had been seated with the doomed, lying in a heap on the ground, her scalp still intact. A hushed silence overcame the warriors as they gathered in front of her body.

Quickly, White Owl breathed a sigh of relief. "Brothers, we cannot kill this woman. Her spirit is powerful and can leave her body to do us harm. We must not take her life." The warriors murmured, "Ahs," and stood in reverence above her inert form.

Without a word from Killbuck, White Owl jerked her up and shook her to consciousness. Sarah's eyes opened in horror, and she started to scream, but a fierce look from White Owl silenced her. He moved her firmly toward the other log and glared at his comrades and Killbuck.

"She must be saved. Her soul can do us harm if I do not control her. She is mine and I will keep her spirit from leaving her body."

Killbuck frowned but considered the power of witches and did not want to disturb the spirits who had aided their journey so far. At a nod from Killbuck, White Owl pulled Sarah to the log with the remaining women and children.

The massacre had taken less than an hour, and now the survivors were to continue their march. The only adults who still lived included thirty-year-old Anna, Sarah Hawes, Eve Moser, and Martha Woods, the oldest of the four, in her late thirties. Beset with another tragedy, Anna briefly wished she had died with her neighbors. She had seen more evil on this day than she could have imagined and could not comprehend God's plan, if indeed there was one. For the first time in her life, she questioned her faith and could not imagine a God who would sanction such horrific murders.

Thinking ahead, Killbuck knew that Anna would be an asset in controlling her daughter Mary and her young son Adam, both of whom were desirable captives. Of children under five, only Anna's baby remained alive, and Killbuck would offer a chance for its survival if Anna could silence her. "Do not allow your child to cry, and she can live."

Anna and the captives, abruptly forced to move again before the horror of the moment would cause hysteria, reluctantly drew themselves up and allowed their captors to move them into line. The group continued walking along the trail away from the bodies of their family members and neighbors who lay in bloody heaps next to the trail. Anna could not look back at the hideous sight, but the images remained etched in her muddled mind.

The group walked for several hours until the sun began to fall below the horizon of the forest. Numbness overcame Anna as she trudged along the path and looked neither right nor left but rather fixed her eyes on the feet in front of her. She noted occasional hoof prints indicating the recent passage of the two Indian horsemen carrying her boys at a fast pace back to the Ohio lands.

"Please, God, please allow my boys to survive," she prayed over and over, more from habit than from faith.

Cap discarded and black hair falling in clumps on her shoulders, Martha concentrated on her daughters and prayed constantly that they would survive. Twisting and turning, eyes seeking relief from pain, young Eve Moser could not be silent nor could she grasp the situation as she was pushed and pulled forward, but Anna, looking only at the babe in her arms, dully trudged along in quiet contemplation and grief. The sun had disappeared, and the forest sounds became overwhelming, finally silencing all muffled cries and sobs. Even Eve ceased her excessive movements and walked, head down, in perfect silence.

Several hours passed and, at Killbuck's signal, everyone was ordered to stop to make some semblance of a camp, near a spring. The captives were allowed to take care of personal needs under the supervision of their captors, but there was no food except for some jerky hastily eaten by the Indians. Anna's tired, hungry child was not hard to silence. Anna settled on the hard ground, Sarah tucked protectively within her arms. Adam and Mary cuddled next to her as darkness and chill settled over them.

It was with complete mental and physical exhaustion that most were asleep, entwined in each other's arms, within a short time. Several warriors remained alert in case a search party would appear, highly unlikely they thought.

Chapter 11

April 29, 1758

Predictably, the weather mirrored the tragedy of the day before, and fog again filled the primal forest as the captives and their still-painted captors began to stir at the first sign of daylight. Sounds of sighing, crying, and hushed conversation broke the eerie silence in the clearing and competed with the steady gurgle of the nearby spring. Deep shadows surrounded the group of about fifty individuals of varying ages, many of the warriors having slipped away during the night in haste to return to the Ohio villages where they would receive handsome rewards for the bloody scalps they carried. Although the threat of being followed now seemed remote, Killbuck intended to move quickly, taking no chances of being surprised by a group of raging settlers or relentless pursuit by the militia.

While Anna was experiencing the first pangs of hunger, she and the other captives were roughly aroused and forced to stand. Cool air tingled on her face as she dragged her aching body to a standing position and picked up her whimpering child. After being allowed to relieve herself and cup water with her hands to quench her thirst, she was quickly put in line, moved to the trail, and signaled to move with the others.

"Please," she pleaded to the warrior who followed her. "Please find my children."

The warrior complied and motioned Mary and Adam to Anna's side and uttered "move" in the Delaware tongue.

Killbuck led the way, conversing softly in his guttural Indian tongue with two comrades, seemingly his lieutenants.

Eyes focused only on her baby, Anna followed behind the Seyberts, Nicholas being bound and watched carefully by a scowling warrior. Last came the Dyers, purposely stationing themselves behind the group as far as they were able, but not far enough to pursue any plan to escape. Watching James carefully, White Owl kept Sarah as close as he could because he had no intention of losing his prized captive.

Although the Indians dispersed themselves among the captives to prevent an escape and bound the hands of the older boys, the massacre had swallowed all hope.

Killbuck knew that all were hungry, but there would be no stopping this day for food. The war party was accustomed to going for long periods without nourishment on raids such as this. They would not stop to hunt before evening, putting as much distance as possible between them and the charred remains of the two forts.

As the ghost-like figures moved westward, a slight breeze materialized bringing the acrid smell of smoke and burning embers. Anna smelled the bitter odor and briefly thought of Fort Seybert. She was vaguely aware of Martha Woods and her daughters who followed behind her. Suddenly, Martha, too, thought of her husband and the Upper Tract Fort, but the Indians showed no wariness.

With a muffled scream, Martha abruptly stopped. "The fort. I smell the fire. William is there. My God, you killed them, killed them all, didn't you?" She looked at the inscrutable Killbuck who moved quickly toward her.

Her screams had caused those behind her to halt before she was harshly grabbed and pulled along to catch up with those ahead. Anna had turned at the scream and realization engulfed her as she remembered the Upper Tract Fort and the men who were garrisoned there.

Killbuck yanked Martha out of the line. "Silence woman. The white men in that fort live no longer. They will not come to your aid. It is your daughters you need to concern yourself with." He shoved her back onto the trail and trotted forward to the front of the line.

Although most of the children were unaware of the nearness of the fort, Anna thought of James Dunlap and his visit to her cabin. "Those poor men," she thought. "They are dead at the hands of this fiend who leads us, Killbuck."

Now, thinking she could handle no more grief, Anna and the pathetic group of captives trudged further along the narrow trail while Killbuck and his warriors spoke little and maintained a determined pace, ignoring any questions about the Upper Tract Fort.

"How much more tragedy can we stand?" she thought. "All of us have suffered greatly, and I see no end in sight." Trying not to think anymore, Anna obsessively watched the regular movement of the calf muscles of the Indian in front of her as she moved in step with him.

New growth covered the forest floor, and the path was partially obscured by vines and wildflowers and tall grass showing little evidence of the passing of the Indians five days before. Portions of the path were unobstructed, however, and rock solid from use over several centuries by these natives and those for generations before. The Indians never hesitated and followed the trail instinctively even when it became covered by dense growth.

Although the fog had lifted before noon, the sun rarely emerged for long, keeping the April air chilly. The trail wound its way around mountains, across ridges, and along creek beds, most running quickly from spring rains. The forest was thick and green even though growth was not yet dark and mature. The sound of birds filled the air while numerous flying insects suggested what was to come when the weather warmed. At times, Anna could not see the sky as the path, shadowed by ancient trees, became dim and forlorn; occasionally, bright sunlight would appear and disappear too quickly, taking its warmth with it.

The trek became monotonous and grueling, and Anna was barely aware of Adam and Mary who walked behind her, their feet nipping at her heels. All kept heads lowered, tear stains evident on their faces. There was no thought of escape because the captives had no idea where they were or where to go if they managed to elude their captors. Some thought of home and families, now destroyed, while other thought of nothing but the immediate task of moving. Anna thought only of her lost sons and the baby she crushed against her chest. She tried not to think of the future, which would come soon enough. She was hungry, damp, miserable, and devoid of any thought of rescue.

"It is death that stalks us now. It is all around us, and God has shown us no mercy." Anna clung to her pain in silence.

There was no doubt Killbuck admired young Nicholas Seybert. He thought him resourceful and loyal, loyal to his five siblings who looked to him for comfort and protection, even his older brother Henry. The Seybert sisters, Margaret and Catherine, were excellent captives, slim, tall and physically fit from years of frontier life. All six Seyberts were prized by Killbuck, and he recognized their value.

He considered their anger and hate toward him as assets on the journey. Sustaining their anger was helpful because this emotion would help them survive, and Killbuck meant to feed their anger.

Killbuck saw the hate in their eyes and understood their losses. With the exception of Nicholas, Killbuck knew that the Seyberts would not attempt to escape. They were too intent on the survival of the entire family. Although the girls spoke German believing that the war chief could not understand the language, he did, in fact, comprehend a little from years of living among the South Branch settlers. He heard Margaret say, "That chief is an ugly, horrible being who has sucked the life out of our family. He is the devil, and I will spit at him first chance."

"Do not let him hear you say that. He will kill us on the spot," Catherine whispered.

Killbuck was not the least bothered by their comments and knew they would never forgive him or his warriors; he only wanted them to survive. He knew, too, that their mother Maria's dark hair, streaked with gray, hung from a warrior's belt and continued to be a constant reminder of the massacre of their parents.

Besides Nicholas, only James Dyer of the older boys held Killbuck's interest. He marveled at James' curiosity under these conditions. He knew James hated him, but that did not stop James from being, by far, the most observant of the smallest details. Killbuck suspected James memorized landmarks with the thought of escape foremost in his active mind. He was also aware that James watched his warriors, especially the two carrying the heavy kettle. He chuckled at James' interest in the confiscated items because he knew the pot held no valuables but rather standard household utensils and tools which the Indians greatly desired. These settlers did not hold hoards of gold coins, and, if they had, they smartly buried them before coming to the fort for safety. Killbuck knew that tools and the kettle were far more valuable to the Indians than coins.

The procession followed the ancient Indian trail leading over the mountains toward the Tygart River Valley, not yet tainted by white settlers. Now, the forest became cool and humid, and clothes embraced the dampness and clung to their bodies. For four hours, the group walked along a rough trail, over rocks and vines, through thickets and swampy land. Their shoes became threaded, and some were discarded, and their clothes became ripped and shredded. The hair of the females now hung in clumps over their shoulders and down their backs as most had discarded their caps.

These disheveled, unhappy captives were in no mood to observe the rugged, but beautiful, scenery through which they passed. None had been further west than the Upper Tract area and did not have the desire or the energy to appreciate the spring landscape, rich with the promise of summer and warmth. Most were still numb and processing the events of the previous day. Little thought was given to the future, if, indeed, any existed.

Anna rarely thought of the other captives, but tried to concentrate on her three children. Most of her attention was spent caring for the needs of her weakening baby while Mary watched over Adam who was becoming more and more interested in the warriors who controlled them. Martha Woods, too, was concerned about the Mallow child.

"Anna," Martha offered. "Let me carry the child for you so you can rest from the burden."

"No, no. I cannot let her cry. I cannot, and it is so hard. She is so frail and so hungry. I cannot even keep her clean. Her dress is soaked with urine. I cannot lose this one, too." Anna felt panic rising in her body.

Carried on the litter behind the group, the wounded warrior made mournful sounds, and a death rattle emitted from his throat, and it was obvious that his wounds were fatal. It was only a matter of time. He would not live to see his home in his Ohio village. Anna heard the sounds and tried to ignore them. She recognized the sounds of death but did not care because she thought only of her weakening baby.

"I hope he dies." She felt no guilt at the thought of wishing for a man's death.

As she tried to subdue her panic, she became aware of James Dyer whom she had always liked and knew he was keenly aware of their surroundings. She saw him hesitate and occasionally stop until the warrior who controlled him forced him to continue walking. The two Indians carrying the heavy kettle had mysteriously disappeared with no one paying much attention. James noticed. "The kettle, our parents' valuables. They will hide it, but I will remember this place."

Anna made no attempt to remember landmarks nor did she care about the kettle. Michael had buried what few gold coins they had. Her only concern was her baby. In her heart, Anna knew frail, young Sarah would not survive. Her pale young daughter had had little nourishment and continually cried softly. Anna tried to give her water by soaking a piece of her skirt in a stream and squeezing it into the baby's mouth. It was temporary at best, and Anna knew it. She cradled the baby in her arms covering her with her apron, but she could not rid herself of the chill which engulfed her entire body, the only warmth being her chest where the baby was pressed.

Mary, dark and hollow-eyed, silently cried for her baby sister but was overwhelmed by fear and helplessness.

As the monotonous march continued, Anna's captor became more agitated at the child's muffled cries. Try as she might, Anna could not stop the noise, soft as it was. Killbuck wanted no noise, none, and it was an impossible task. Abruptly and with no warning, Sarah was grabbed from Anna's arms and roughly handled by the glaring warrior who held the fretful baby with both hands. Then holding the child by her feet, he bashed her little head upon the rocks next to the trail.

"Enough," he snarled as he swung the baby toward the rock. Arms outstretched in a pleading motion, Anna screamed at his action and fell to her knees with a wave of pain.

"No, my God no." She covered her eyes with her hands. "Tis a dream. I will wake up soon, please let me wake up soon . . ."

She was roughly pulled up by the murderer of her helpless child and forced to walk away from the bloody remains. It was over in seconds. As they passed, one by one, the captives tried not to look at the small, bleeding body lying on the side of the trail.

Covering their mouths in shock, Sarah and Martha watched as the child was killed, and Sarah stumbled, retching in horror. Both James and Nicholas stopped abruptly and glared in hate at the murderous warrior who paid them no attention, nor did the rest of the war party who barely hesitated at the action. Many of the captives ignored the disruption because they could endure no more tragedy.

Forced to keep moving, blinded by tears, Anna no longer thought or saw images of her boys or her deceased Sarah. She paid no attention to Mary or Adam, try as they might to rouse her out of her stupor. The world did not exist, and she slipped into a black hole where sound and light could not penetrate. She saw the face of insanity and could not see, could not think, could not care. Life, as she knew it, was over, and it would be days before reality emerged again. Even then, her life would never be the same.

Monotonous hours of marching continued on narrow paths, up and over steep hills, and deep into the lush, green mountains. It was close to sunset, even though the sun had hidden itself the better part of the long day. At least no rain had hindered them during the forced journey. Killbuck was proud of his choice in captives, for they all marched well, seemed physically fit, and did not exhibit the hysteria that he had sometimes seen in captives. He was always amazed at the desire for survival exhibited by these white settlers.

Although Killbuck knew he was a ruthless man, hardened by years of witnessing the losses of his people and the land, he was not devoid of compassion and was well aware of the terror within the minds of the captives. He had no hate for those whom he had slaughtered. It was simply a matter of necessity. These captives, as many before them had, would adjust to Indian life, much preferable to their harsh lives as settlers.

Intrigued, Killbuck watched James as two more warriors disappeared during the last hour. None of the captives seemed to notice their absence or care for that matter except James, who had watched the men fade away with bows and arrows, swallowed up by the forest. Killbuck wondered if James knew that many warriors had already departed and taken some of the bloody scalps with them for bounty payments by the French.

"A smart young man. Watch him at all times," he warned his warriors. "He will always attempt to escape and will never adjust to our ways."

When the light began to wane and sight became difficult, Killbuck ordered a stop to prepare for the night in a narrow ravine. A rippling brook nearby offered refreshment and the opportunity to splash water on dirty faces. Anna simply stood silently, a vacant look in her moist, dark eyes. Mary held her hand and tried to interest her in the clear water, but Anna did not respond.

"Please, Mama, drink. Sarah is gone. You must save yourself and us. You cannot change things."

Although he had tried, Adam had finally given up trying to rouse his mother from her stupor and simply followed the warriors' instructions.

Soon, a small fire was prepared by the Indians, dark skins aglow in the sunset. The captives were then placed in a half circle around the burning logs while most of the remaining war party observed them from the other side. Two warriors were posted as sentries and guards to divert any captive from running, but no one had the energy to try after such a long, exhausting walk.

Anna simply sat, legs sprawled in front of her, hands in her lap, noting nothing, not even Mary, who might have become hysterical had not Martha come to her side. In a futile effort to comfort the distraught child, Martha held her to her breast as tightly as she could while Adam simply watched in wonder, thinking now mainly of food.

"Mary, dear Mary. Your mother is grieving and needs time. She will never forget, but you and Adam must stay by her side and comfort her."

"She won't answer me." Mary sobbed and turned away from Martha.

After the fire burned sufficiently, two grinning warriors appeared carrying the carcass of a small doe, which they hurriedly skinned, gutted and placed the remaining carcass on a spit over the now-blazing fire. The meat crackled and cooked while the captives watched in fascination and severe hunger, their bellies growling in anticipation of food.

When the Indians decided the meat had been cooked enough, one warrior, disregarding the heat, pulled a hunk of meat from the slab on the spit and placed it on a rock while waving his hand from the heat. As soon as the meat cooled, he broke off pieces and handed them to several of his comrades who immediately devoured them.

After the Indians had eaten over half of the cooked meat by grabbing hunks directly from the spit with their tomahawks or knives, the captives were invited to partake in what remained. The Indians removed the spit, placed the meat on a large flat rock, and tore it apart. The captives, having been released from their bonds, were each given hunks that they eagerly chewed in seconds.

Eat," Nicholas ordered to everyone around him. "We must keep up our strength even if we have very little to sustain us."

Finally, the bones were passed from warrior to warrior and chewed for whatever meat remained. Murmurs and grunts of appreciation followed from the now-satisfied warriors who gathered up the bones and reverently covered them with earth and rocks.

"Why do you not just throw them in the forest," questioned James.

"The spirit of the deer would not be pleased if we did not take care of the remains," Killbuck explained.

Far from satisfied, the captives, at least, received some nourishment that would help sustain and perhaps allow them to sleep easier. A pale Anna had been forced to eat a piece of venison, but did so without emotion or knowledge. She paid no attention to her two children who were becoming more and more distraught at her strange behavior. Pulling on Anna's dress and hitting her arm, Mary unsuccessfully tried to elicit a response from her mother.

"Mama, please, Mama, look at me."

Again, leaving her daughters, Martha moved to Mary's side and looked at Anna. "Anna, dear Anna. Your daughter needs you." Anna made no reply nor did she look at Martha.

"Frau Woods," Mary cried. "What can I do? I do not know what to do."

"Perhaps time will take care of this. We must wait until she is ready to join us. Pray God for patience."

Leaving the grieving Mallow children with their non-responsive mother, Martha crept back to her daughters.

Finally, exhausted, the captives settled on the ground, some trying to cover themselves with leaves to ward off the chill of the April night. Others lay as close as possible next to each other to conserve whatever warmth their bodies emitted. Most had been unbound, as the Indians had little fear that anyone would attempt an escape. They were now deep in the mountains, farther west than any of these whites had been, and Killbuck knew escape would mean death.

Having watched the murder of the vulnerable Mallow baby, Eve Moser, now a widow at sixteen, was extremely distraught and inconsolable. Hate was etched on her dirty face, and her arms flailed at her sides. As the evening became quiet and, without warning, she suddenly focused her bleary eyes and screamed at Killbuck, who stood silently among his warriors watching her display of anger pierce the silence. "I can't stand this. God, I hate you. You are savages, ugly, blood-thirsty savages. Kill me and get it over with." She lunged at Killbuck, while her captor grabbed her arm roughly.

With characteristic scorn, Killbuck allowed no more than seconds of her rant before indicating that her captor should silence her. The scowling warrior followed the command immediately by striking her across the mouth and slamming her to the ground only to jerk her up by her long hair. Eve immediately stopped her cries and glared at the angry chief, blood seeping from her cut mouth. Shaken and bloody, she ignored Sarah Hawes who came to her side offering comfort.

"Eve, be still. Do not put the rest of us in danger. Do you want to die? Look at me and listen."

But Eve ignored Sarah who quickly silenced the angry girl and pulled her to the hard ground where they would remain for the night. Sarah had no intention of allowing Eve to cause additional unrest among the Indians.

As the settlers finished preparing for the night's rest, the warriors formed a circle and began a slow monotonous chanting that continued for at least an hour. Their comrade, carried for two days on a litter behind the group, had died and was unceremoniously covered with rocks and buried in a nearby cave in the side of the mountain. Watching the captives as a hawk watches his prey, Killbuck silently mourned the loss of his warrior but would replace him with one of the captives.

Except for Anna, the night passed slowly for the captives,

most of who slept very little. Anna slipped quickly into a dark sleep, but the others could not shut out the echoes of the Indian chanting and smelled the remnants of pipe smoke and burning wood. Shuddering in fear, they heard the cries of the mountain cats and the howls of the distant wolves. They were chilled by the damp night air, and the noise of the forest stayed alive and chilled them even more.

April 30, 1758

The third day of this forced march emerged cold and wet. A steady rain began at dawn and continued throughout the long day, and the entire party was miserable. It was as if the forest were weeping in sympathy, and storm clouds, in turn, waited to let loose their fury. Clothes were wet although the bare-chested Indians scarcely noticed. The captives, however, were cold and uncomfortable with their clothing clinging to their bodies, their feet wet and sore, and their stringy hair plastered to their necks and shoulders.

Most of the captives, on this day in particular, would have preferred death had they been given a choice over this long march, up and down, over rocks, stumps, vines, waterways and endless mud. There were trails so narrow one person could barely pass and deep crevasses waiting to catch a careless walker. With no noticeable discomfort, the warriors walked with little effort, hacking vines with their tomahawks when necessary and maneuvering captives along treacherous paths. Only once were the captives hurriedly dragged off the trail into the forest and ordered to remain silent while the warriors listened. However, no humans appeared, and the warriors proceeded without further alarm.

Despite her children's pleas, Anna could not focus nor did she acknowledge their touches. Her thick, dark hair hung in greasy clumps to her waist, and her face was splotched with dirt. Her dress, no longer covered by her apron, hung damply on her body. As rain slapped her in the face, she simply allowed herself to be led or pushed along with the others, Mary having given up arousing her unresponsive mother.

The group wound its way down a steep path and through a dark wood that abruptly opened at the edge of a fast flowing stream. The captives stopped while the warriors gestured and spoke among themselves. Deciding the stream was too deep and fast to cross at this point, Killbuck ordered the group to move upstream, searching for a more suitable crossing. Walking a half mile or so along the rocky bank, the Indians noted a shallow area where a sandbar formed in the middle of the stream, a more suitable crossing.

The warriors had no fear of water and most had been swimmers since their first summer. Most of the captives, however, did not know how to swim and were terrified of the swiftly moving stream.

"Watch," Killbuck told his warriors. "These whites are afraid of the water. If we had time, we would cleanse them of their white blood. The water spirits would rid us of the smell of these whites who do not use the gift of water."

Observing their apprehension, Killbuck briefly felt disgust at those who expressed such fear and the whites who failed to teach such a basic skill to their children. It would amuse him, however, to watch their efforts in crossing.

Having given up on his mother's help and watching the others, young, shivering Adam stood on the bank, unsure of what he was expected to do.

"Mama, someone, help me. I cannot swim and the water is fast."

A smiling warrior lifted him up and perched him on his shoulders. Clinging for dear life, his arms around the warrior's neck, Adam watched in fear as the water came up closer and closer to his thighs. Laughing, the warrior whooped and jumped up and down in the fast, cold water.

"I will cleanse the little warrior of his white blood."

Closing his eyes, Adam waited for the ordeal to end and to feel hard ground again. Soon, the warrior gently placed him on the shore and ruffled his hair with a touch of kindness. Mary watched with apprehension, but Anna paid no heed to her son.

Killbuck laughed as, one by one, the captives were led into the water and across the cold stream, their discomfort increasing with every step. Rocks cut their feet, and garments became drenched. The youngest were hoisted on the shoulders of the warriors and carried across while the women were roughly supported and held by other Indians until they fell, exhausted, on the far bank. The older boys were left on their own with no fear that they might run.

Watching the Seybert children, Killbuck was intrigued that they showed no fear, but remained close together, thanks to the encouragement of Nicholas, who watched over young George, while keeping up the spirits of his younger sisters. Nicholas was not about to discourage any of them. Margaret hesitated at the water's edge, looking at the cold, swiftly moving stream. Catherine clutched her arm in fear, but Nicholas moved behind them. "Move, both of you. Do not show fear. The water is not deep, and you will come to no harm."

Holding hands, the girls slowly made their way across the rocky stream bed, much to the admiration of Killbuck, knowing they hid their terror. The warriors laughed and watched Nicholas and Henry lead their young brother across. With a sense of humor, several warriors mimicked the children and held hands while crossing the cold stream, running back and forth, laughing heartily.

Anna did not laugh nor did she watch any of the antics. Instead, she walked straight into the moving stream, looking neither right nor left. Killbuck watched her with growing concern. Although he understood her grief, he thought she would gain her focus and look to her two remaining children for comfort. But she showed no signs of doing so and did not seem to care that her son Adam was slowly moving into the Indian world.

The river crossing completed successfully, Killbuck, a slight smile on his dark face, observed his charges with pleasure and felt pride in his choices. As the thunder faded into the distance, he stood on the bank as, one by one, the captives joined him.

"You will soon adjust to our ways. We will make good Indians out of all of you. Your life will be much better than the life you now lead."

Killbuck was very careful in allowing the captives to relieve themselves. He noted the direction of the flowing water and always demanded relief be a good distance downstream or away from the water used for drinking and cooking. He knew instinctively that water used for human consumption must not be tainted by human waste or grime from bodies. Indian villages had enforced such rules for centuries, and the clans had remained free from diseases. But then the whites came, and diseases for which the Indians had no immunity surfaced and killed thousands. Killbuck did not understand why this was so, but he continued to follow age old traditions.

"Never, never relieve yourselves near water that you will drink. It will cause you great suffering. Drink only water that has not been tainted by your bodies." He directed those who wanted water to walk a short distance upstream and waited until their needs were satisfied.

Suffering a great deal, especially after the river crossing, many of the captives no longer had anything upon their feet which were sore and cut. Some had wrapped pieces of cloth around them and now watched the remnants float quickly down the stream. Others began to discard their shoes, and soon most would be barefooted.

"Your feet, the soles of your feet will soon become hardened, and you will no longer feel pain."

As the day wore on, the captives were continually chilled and miserable, and their only solace came during the rare times when they were allowed to rest by a spring or creek and make useless attempts to get clean and massage their sore feet. Killbuck deliberately walked close to James admiring his demeanor; it also was pleasurable to be close to his redheaded sister, a very attractive female who would certainly end up in his village. The two Dyers kept him entertained, unintentionally, on this third day of walking over the dangerous terrain.

More than once the chief caught Sarah's arm in an attempt to keep her on the narrow path. Although she cringed at his touch, Sarah maintained her dignity and refused to acknowledge his presence. Killbuck simply laughed and knew she recognized that he desired her and would not kill her. He also knew that James watched for an opportunity to shove him into an abyss or push him over a cliff. He never got the opportunity. Clearly, James was learning, and the warriors watched him closely, fearing that he might attempt an escape.

The captives now knew the routine and methodically relieved themselves and drank stream water at the rare stops. The weather had slightly improved, and the drizzle had abated. Occasional rays of the sun seeped through the dampness and fell upon the weary captives. All thought of being followed had evaporated, and moods were improving remarkably.

The Indians had enjoyed the river crossings and the discomfort of their captives and took pride in showing their knowledge and their lack of fear. By evening, two warriors, who had left the group earlier, reappeared, this time with an elk, a large beast that many captives had not seen up close before. The party was excited at the kill and anticipation of plenty of meat for this evening's meal.

While the meat cooked over a large fire, a second fire was built over which the Indians placed a small kettle, stolen from the fort. Parts of the elk's intestines were placed in the water along with greens gathered from the forest, making a nourishing broth which was distributed in two tin cups passed among all.

"You." Killbuck pointed to the two Seybert girls. "You will distribute this broth to the prisoners." Although they looked at the broth with much distaste, the girls readily obeyed the chief's command.

Their clothes still damp and plastered to their bodies, the captives felt the warmth of the fire and began to lose some of their discomfort. The tasteless broth warmed their stomachs, and they ate hungrily without distaste. Their exhaustion helped fade memories of this awful day into thoughts of rest and sleep.

Having been forced to eat for the second night, Anna remained incommunicative and unconcerned, still with a blank, vague stare. Unresponsive, tangled black hair in clumps along her shoulders, eyes unsettling, she sat on the ground, staring at an unknown object in the distance, eyes devoid of recognition, an occasional tear running down her face.

Clearly, Mary's concern for her mother had only intensified, and she began to feel anger towards this unresponsive woman. Adam, on the other hand, was puzzled, but he was beginning to watch the warriors and learn from them. Most of the younger captives began to have periods of time when they no longer thought of the tragedy, and the horrible images retreated into the recesses of their minds.

April 31, 1758

Late on the morning of the fourth day, having crossed rivers and covered more than forty miles of rough terrain and mountainous paths, Anna showed no awareness. If she were hungry, she did not know it, if someone talked to her, she did not respond, if her children tugged at her, she did not care. She stayed locked in a world of her own, having no will to join reality.

Soon, the group came to a lush, green valley that spread out in sun washed beauty. The distant river became a ribbon of glittering silver, winding its way toward the horizon where it disappeared from view. The weather was warm, and the sun shone through the trees, drying off clothes and improving the moods of the captives. Frowning, Killbuck observed the Mallow woman. Because he had seen captives descend into madness, he did not want to see this fine, dark-haired woman join their ranks. He suspected she was with child and had observed her retching on occasion at relief stops. He would speak to her. He knew the value of a captive. French traders would pay well for her services if she were sane.

The valley was alive with movement, but the intruders interfered with routines. A red-tailed hawk flapped his wings and screamed out as he perched on the limb of an ancient sycamore and watched the captives pass far below. Cavorting in the tall grass, a fox and her five kits scampered to safety when they heard sounds of the trespassers. The warriors watched intently as a doe and her fawn floated effortlessly over the tall grasses in the distance.

Thinking more about Anna's value to the French than her unborn child, Killbuck did not want to bring a deranged woman into the trading village. In the past his choices of captives had not only been excellent replacements for the

Shawnee and Delaware, but also had brought good sums as slaves. Anna's age would place her into the latter group, and the French traders would pay well as long as she was sane. No one had any use for a mindless creature, no matter what she looked like, and the pragmatic chief did not particularly want to see her killed.

Maneuvering through the line of silent warriors and wretched settlers, Killbuck secured himself beside the blank, staring woman. He spoke slowly and quietly in English. Listen to me. I know you carry life. Hear me woman." He pinched her shoulders and turned her abruptly towards him, pulling her off of the trail while the others continued on in silence.

No response came from the woman. "You have life in your belly. Do not despair. You have new life to replace one lost." He put his large, scarred hand over hers and placed both on her belly. "Do you hear me? You carry life, a new warrior."

Anna paused and slowly glanced down at the strange hand over hers, eyes beginning to focus for the first time in two days. She looked up at the dark, unpleasant-looking man beside her and recognition came swiftly with shock and horror. Her eyes slowly focused. "I am dead. It does not matter. I do not care. You are a savage murderer. You have killed my baby and taken my sons to their deaths."

"Ah, I have seen some of my own family killed, and I still live and do what I must. We cannot carry small children over the mountains to our villages. They would not survive and would suffer greatly if we had not killed them. We will make good warriors out of your living sons, the dark ones taken by horseback to our villages. Your daughter will make good Indian squaw."

Struggling with English, Anna whispered, "I cannot understand all of your words. I am German born and wish I had never come to this land. My husband brought me to this place and these harsh times, worse than those we had in Germany. He is at fault. I wanted to go back to Pennsylvania, but he would not hear of it. Do what you wish with me. I no longer care."

Puzzled, Killbuck thought of the Pennsylvania raids and suspected Anna did not know that she would have been no safer there than Virginia. There was no place to hide for these settlers, but he did not speak of this. "Do you not care for your son and your daughter, for the flesh born of your body? Be strong, woman. Think of the seed you carry and live for him."

Anna looked down again at her belly, realizing that life existed within her, Michael's child. Seeking her eyes, Killbuck smiled, satisfied, and knew he had reached her and planted a seed of survival, if not for her, for her unborn. He somehow knew she would bear a son to replace her lost daughter, and he quickly returned to the front of the line while Anna resumed her position with a slightly more determined step. Her eyes began to focus, and her mind formed images for the first time since her baby had been brutally murdered.

"A child. I carry Michael's child. I must live for this child, but it is a terrible time for a babe to come into this world. How will I manage?" and she began to sob.

As the group continued to travel through the valley, the sun warmed their sore bodies and aching muscles as well as their spirits. The path spread out, and the new grass blew softy in the gentle breeze. The valley was alive with the sounds of birds, insects, and the rustle of grass. Instinctively, the warriors sought the movement of game while the captives simply embraced the first real warmth they had felt for days. A spark of survival and love of life emerged slowly among some of the young captives, but it would take much longer for others.

Chapter 12

April 30, 1758

Anna

Ah, suddenly I feel warm. I hear the voices of my children and am thankful that two have survived. I know that Sarah is dead, but I cannot, no, will not, remember the details. I do not know if George and Michael will survive. I cannot endure that pain and must imagine them together in heaven above, no longer to suffer the trials of life. I must think of other things because we are still in danger although I suspect we are worth more as captives then dead settlers. I must pray for strength.

I must remain vigilant. I must help Mary and Adam and not think of the massacre, the deaths of those I knew and some I loved. God help us all. Give us strength.

I cannot think of Michael. He may be gone from my life forever. He may think we are dead. My God, how awful it would be to return to the fort and find one's entire family gone, perhaps dead. I must not think of this now. I must not, cannot. I must live for the moment. God forgive me, but I must not think of my loss . . . or of Michael.

Perhaps anger and hate will sustain me and keep me alive. How I hate that chief. He repulses me. Why did he spare me? It matters not why; rather it is how I will survive and help my children. God help us all.

Pulling on her mother's arm, Mary smiled for the first time since the massacre. "Mama, mama, are you all right?"

Anna smiled at her daughter. "Mary, my dearest daughter, I am as all right as I can be under these conditions. Stay with me, child. I need your presence."

The two briefly managed to cling to each other before being forced to continue forward. Mary was relieved, as were the others, that Anna had not succumbed to madness, and the concerned Martha watched in relief.

Anna had finally become aware of Martha who continued to try to help her family in any way she could. Anna suddenly remembered that William Woods had been garrisoned at the Upper Tract Fort.

"Oh, William, your William. The fort was destroyed was it not? And Captain Dunlap? All of them gone?"

"They are all dead at the hands of these savages. Why do they let us live?" Martha began to cry.

"I am not sure. I think because we are women with children, and they want our children for their villages. You and I are old by their standards. I think we will be sold as slaves to the French and our children taken from us."

The question would haunt her, and she would never understand the reasons for her survival, if indeed there were any.

Anna never complained, but she did have one annoying problem, however. Her shoes were gone. She had thrown what remained of them away the day before, and now her feet were brown with mud and red with small sores and cuts. Martha, too, had lost what was left of her shoes.

Anna had noticed that, for days, the young warrior, Shemaneto, had followed Martha and studied her. On this day the warrior produced a pair of moccasins from his pouch. He pulled the surprised Martha from the line and sat her down on a nearby log where he softly wiped her feet with a damp piece of cloth and gently slipped the moccasins on her sore feet. Martha looked at him in gratitude and smiled for the first time in three days. The warrior returned her smile, pointed to his chest saying, "Shemaneto," his name in Shawnee. Anna suspected that Shemaneto would see to it that Martha and her daughters would arrive safely at his village.

Not without concern Anna watched his gaze toward Martha's daughter Magdalene, and it occurred to her that Magdalene was his real objective. The dark-eyed Magdalene at fourteen was a beauty with every promise of being a handsome and capable woman. However, Anna sensed that Indians did not indulge their carnal desires while on raids, so she dismissed her fears for the moment and watched Martha enjoy the comfort the soft new moccasins provided.

Now that Anna had emerged from her stupor, Killbuck spent much of his time learning as much as he could about the other captives. He soon dismissed the Regers who remained aloof from the others and made no attempt to communicate. Try as the talkative Seyberts did, none were able to get more than one word out of Regers' mouths. John, the eldest at twelve, had no patience with his sisters or any of the captives for that matter. Killbuck watched the sullen Johnny continually warn his sisters, ages ten and eight, to be quiet. The girls obeyed and remained still and terrified.

Killbuck suspected young Johnny was a coward at heart. He was puzzled by this boy. He thought that Johnny's father, who had died well, would not be pleased with this son of his. Killbuck measured men by their courage and loyalty, and he believed that this lanky young man lacked them both unlike the Dyer and Seybert boys. The chief recognized the anger and disdain in Reger's face. It was not like the defiance exhibited by James and Nicholas. Rather, it seemed to be a pathetic attempt to distance himself from the situation and responsibility. Reger would run if he had the nerve, but Killbuck thought he did not, unlike the other two boys. Killbuck thought that the scowling young man would never survive a gauntlet and would just roll up into a ball, cowering from the blows, and be killed. However, it was of little concern to Killbuck.

It was young Elizabeth Maus who caused the most trouble and amused her captors. She was a feisty seven-year -old and despite warnings, continually attempted to escape to no avail. All the warriors and Killbuck liked the bright-eyed Elizabeth, and all thought she would be an excellent addition to their clans. They discussed among themselves when she might try to break away from the group, and her captor was envied for his position as her guardian, and his status was enlarged among his comrades

On the second day, Elizabeth had broken from her captor and actually ran one hundred yards or so through the thick forest, only to be caught by the ankle by her captor who rolled on the ground, Elizabeth in tow, laughing. Later that day, despite being bound, she managed to trip her captor and run to the stream bed before he, again, tackled her in the water. Spitting at him, Elizabeth was jerked up while the warrior simply laughed and patted her behind, sending her back to the others.

Just last night she managed to stay awake, hoping to outwit her captor. She fought exhaustion and watched him beginning to doze. She waited for her opportunity and, thinking he was asleep, very slowly moved her body, only to have him grasp her leg with a laugh and pull her back to him. Her older brother was no help, nor was her younger sister. Clearly, she intended to take care of herself despite the apathy of her siblings. "I will get away from these savages. You will see; I will succeed."

Anna heard James and Nicholas questioning where they were and where they were going, and she knew that most of the captives could not read or write. She had tried to teach Mary to recognize German words, but was soon left with no time for such tasks, and had said to Michael years ago, "When we left Pennsylvania, you assured me that our children would receive an education and they have not. Neither of us has had the time to teach them, and there is no church to help us. I fear that our children will remain illiterate."

"I cannot change the situation we are in," Michael had told her. "We will have a church one of these days, and our children will learn. None of us foresaw that fear of savages would consume our days."

Despite several attempts at questioning Killbuck, the boys received no answers, and the chief relished their apprehension. He would not tell them their fate or where they were headed, and he suspected that they could not read white men's maps or words. Although Killbuck did not need a map because the land was etched in his mind, he had seen French maps and knew of the great river valleys, one of which was their destination.

May 1, 1758

Greeted by the sun and awakening with the feeling of warmth, the captives rose to a moist spring day with the promise of heat, unlike previous mornings when the chill permeated every part of their bodies. The fresh smell of the forest became tainted with the odor of sweating bodies. Sunlight streamed through the trees, lighting patches of the forest floor and its covering of dried leaves. For the first time, many of the captives relished its warmth, the soothing of sore muscles and the drying of their garments.

Although she felt nausea upon awakening, Anna sought her daughter and allowed herself to be led to the spring where the two splashed water on their dirty faces and attempted to clean their bare feet and hands.

"Why are you sick, Mama?"

"I think I am carrying another child. It is too soon to be certain. I beg you not to tell anyone."

"Oh, Mama, where will it be born?"

"I do not know yet. It is months away, late fall I believe."

Anna's nausea increased as she began to realize that Adam, at six, was impressionable and would eventually look upon the warrior as his father. She had observed Adam's admiring look when the warrior instructed him how to find signs of game. Young Adam ignored her but sought out his captor with whom he had begun to establish a trust. Anna feared memories of his father were beginning to retreat to the back of his mind, and he was beginning the slow transition into the lives of the Indians.

Anna was torn but pragmatic enough to know that Adam's chances of survival were better under the tutelage of this warrior. Perhaps it was good, but it broke her heart. Michael was his father, not this savage.

By noon, the blazing sun high in the sky, the captives became warm, very warm, and their clothes remained damp with perspiration and odor. The glorious sun had turned into a brutal orb of heat, distressing the captives as much as the cold and dampness had. The females lifted their skirts as much as modesty would allow while the boys removed vests and unbuttoned their shirts which clung to their bodies.

Offended by the smell of unwashed bodies and the lack of clean clothes, Anna, with her new found strength, ignored the unpleasantness, and tried to think of Mary and Adam. But Eve Moser was beside herself more than usual. Her greasy, damp hair was plastered to her skull that itched and caused her much discomfort. Torn and dirty, her dress smelled of moisture and body odor.

As the afternoon waned, and the sun began to sink behind the trees, Eve could no longer abide the clinging, sticky clothes, the smells, and her sweaty hair sticking to her neck and shoulders. Late in the afternoon, the group reached a small stream and hesitated at its bank, looking at the shallow water and rocky bottom, covered with large flat boulders. Forgetting that she was a captive, Eve could no longer stand her condition.

"I cannot stand the filth, the smells." She broke from her captor and ran into the rocky stream where she sat in the fast moving water, arms outstretched, legs spread. She suddenly lay backward, allowing her hair to be covered with water running over her face. Her body was submerged in cold water, grime and dirt loosened by the fast flowing stream. Her dress floated and billowed while she ran her hands through her greasy hair and loosened her collar. The warriors watched, spellbound, and then grinned at the spectacle while the other captives observed her and took immediate action.

Within minutes, Anna dragged Mary by the hand. "Come, we will get some relief and try to get clean."

Anna and Mary followed Eve into the cold water, splashing it on their bodies and eventually sitting down as Eve had done and allowing their hair to be covered with water. Soon, all the female captives sat or lay in the cold stream, attempting to wash away days of dirt and grime. One of the warriors stepped into the stream, grabbed a handful of sand and rubbed it on his legs, allowing the water to remove the sand. Anna followed his example as did the other captives who grabbed what sand they could find and rubbed their arms, legs and heads, allowing the current to carry the dirt down the stream.

Soon the stream was full of captives finally relieved of dirt after so many days. The warriors watched and laughed at the captives' antics and allowed the cleansing to finish. The sun still shone on the rocks, so the Indians offered the women their blankets. Anna and Mary removed their dresses and covered themselves with blankets while the Indians made camp next to the stream. As the clothing dried and the captives relaxed, the warriors prepared and cooked meat brought in by a small party.

And so they all settled in camp for the evening.

Anna

In the warmth of the late afternoon sun, I washed the grime away and watched the water flow across my body. What a wonderful feeling, and I forget...for a moment, but the images continue to return. I cannot block them out. But I no longer feel death hovering over me. I can think, despite the awful images. I saw the others enjoy the cleansing. It is the little things, food, water, sleep, things of the moment that will sustain us. That must be how people survive.

My hair feels clean, and my scalp no longer itches. I cannot remember the last time I washed my hair, perhaps months ago. I have forgotten how a clean scalp feels. I have forgotten what clean skin feels like. I suspect the Indians bathe regularly, and we do not. It was so difficult to clean five children, to boil water, to dry wet bodies. I never had enough time.

May 2, 1758

Anna

It has been a week since I lost my three babies. I awake, amazed that I am still alive, that life lives within me. My Mary is with me, but Adam is gone I know. He has taken to his captor who seems to care for him. That is a good thing, but I despair that he is lost from me forever only to be engulfed into Indian life. At least he will live, but our lives are changed forever.

And where is my God in all of this? He has forsaken us I fear. It has become very difficult to believe in a God who ignores his people during this tragedy. I can no longer pray. God is indifferent to my pleas.

Martha, dear Martha, has supported me on this journey. It is a strange relationship since we did not know each other before we forted. She has been very kind and concerned, perhaps because she feels fortunate that she and her daughters still live. She does not speak German, but patiently listens to my halting English. She has lost her husband, we believe, because Fort Upper Tract was destroyed. Yet, she looks ahead and comforts not only her daughters but also the rest of us.

Sarah Hawes is a survivor and is also ready to escape, she and her daring brother James. However, they are careful not to put any of us in danger, knowing we have children to protect and cannot escape without them. She torments Killbuck with her questions, her demands, and her refusals to cooperate, but she never goes too far.

For instance, Killbuck asked her why whites do not eat horsemeat but will partake of hogs, dirty animals, he said. She firmly stated that horses are noble beasts, not created by God for food but rather for labor and pleasure. Surely the Indians do not want to displease their God by eating such beautiful animals. Killbuck has not come up with an answer for that so far.

May 3, 1758

On the seventh day, the party reached the Monongahela River, a fast moving, wide stream that flowed northward to Fort Duquesne where it merged with the Allegheny to form the Beautiful River most whites had never seen. Standing on the shore, Anna, holding Mary's hand, observed the river in front of her. Much to her distress, Adam was enlisted to aid the warriors in securing the canoes necessary for the crossing, and the warriors quickly located several which had been purposely sunk over two weeks before. They whooped with joy and set about draining and floating the crafts for the trip across the river.

The process had only begun when a thunderous roar caused everyone to gaze at the western sky. All watched in awe as the sun disappeared, and a huge black cloud passed above them, millions of crying birds, passenger pigeons darkening the sky in their passage. The captives had never seen such a sight, but the warriors had and looked in reverence at nature's bounty, taking the passage of the birds as a good sign.

After the canoes were readied, Nicholas, eyes still on the sky, pointed at a small flock of birds in the distance.

"There. Wild turkeys frightened by the pigeons."

Killbuck grinned. "You have sharp eyes. It was you who killed my warrior."

"Yes, and I would have killed you if my father had not prevented my aim."

"Ah, I thought so. It is good you did not kill me because my warriors would have stopped the attack and headed home. It would have been a bad sign."

Nicholas did not return his smile.

Anna watched Nicholas as he was forcibly seated in the first canoe with Killbuck, two warriors, and his two older sisters. Henry Seybert was placed in the second canoe with the Dyers while Anna was led to another with Mary. After the crafts were loaded, they slid forward in the fast moving water while the other captives waited on shore for the canoes to return for them.

Anna waited in silence until all stood on the northern shore. Her heart sank when she saw Adam smiling at his captor as he was lifted to the river bank.

I have lost my son, she thought as she turned to Mary who watched her brother with tears in her eyes.

She put her arm around Mary's shoulders. "Do not cry. There is nothing we can do. Perhaps his life will be spared."

"But, Mama, he likes them. He is becoming one of them."

"We cannot know what will happen."

After the successful trip across the river, the captives were hurriedly positioned to keep moving while the canoes were sunk for future travel. Killbuck sighed in relief, knowing they were close to their destination and that the captives were healthy and the crossing successful.

The group proceeded north with no more excitement. The captives were tired and subdued, and it was not long until the chief ordered them to stop for food and the night.

Seated near the fire as the embers died a slow death, Killbuck watched his captives' faces and saw relief and exhaustion. He noted that much of their anger had disappeared from their pale faces, and they had begun to accept their fates by concentrating on day to day survival.

"It is good these captives are strong and will survive. Some will forget their lives as settlers." But he said to White Otter, "Dyer and Seybert. They will not give up. They will try to escape and will never forget. We must watch them. The others, ah, the others will adjust to our ways. Some already have." He looked at young Adam and George and smiled.

May 4, 1758

As the pink streaks of dawn emerged, a haggard group of eighteen children and four weary women proceeded as ghosts of their former selves as they prepared to follow the Indian Trail leading to villages on the Ohio River northwest of Fort Duquesne. There was little conversation, the women going through the motions of herding the younger children into their appointed places in the line, interspersed with determined warriors who anxiously wanted to return to their villages with their spoils.

Mary was forlorn and despondent, having no idea of what might lie ahead for her.

"Where are they taking us," she asked her mother daily.

"I do not know. A village I suspect. I fear we will be separated at that time. There is nothing we can do but hope that your father and the others have found our trail and are following us."

"Oh, Mama," Mary said hopefully. "Do you really think they might find us?"

"We must pray that they do," but in reality Anna had lost all hope of a rescue. Her greatest fear was that Adam was lost to her, and she had no hope of changing that. She rationalized that he was better off accepting his captivity, and she often pictured him dressed as a warrior, head plucked and feather attached to a remaining tuft of hair. She could not think about Sarah, Georgie or Michael. It was too painful.

Both Anna and Mary were now barefooted with feet covered in caked mud, blood encrusted from numerous cuts and bruises from the trail. Their skirts were ragged, partly from being torn for various purposes. Greasy and dull from lack of care, their hair hung down to their waists. Scratches and scabs from errant branches and thorns shown on their dirty arms and hands. Their faces were dark, partly from the sun and partly from dirt.

Anna refrained from looking at her reflection in the water, but she tried to keep her feet clean so that the sores would not become infected. A warrior aided in this regard. "Clean your feet. Put mud on the sores. The mud will help the healing."

Although stops always included water from springs or creeks, grooming had ceased to be important, and few cared about their appearances nor noticed that of others.

Anna tried, unsuccessfully, to remove the tangles from Mary's hair and clean the dirt away from her legs and arms, but she no longer cared how she appeared.

Anna

How many days has it been since I lost my precious Sarah and my boys? I do not know. Time runs together. But I am alive, and my babe lives within me. I try to pray for survival and strength, but no words come any more. I will bring this babe into the world for he deserves that. Mary will survive, I know. Adam will too, but I fear he will survive as an Indian. So be it then. He will live, at any rate. And what of Michael and my two boys? I cannot think of them any more than I can say a prayer.

Having traveled together for a week, all of us have become closer and look out for one another as much as we can. Martha, she has been such a help. We will soon be separated I suspect. But I will never forget her assistance. I should pray for her and her daughters. How I wish I could pray.

Chapter 13

May 5, 1758

Unaffected by the warm, pleasant sun-filled dawn, Anna was awakened by noticeably-excited warriors who were unusually anxious to get everyone moving. Feeling a spasm of nausea, she and the others were hurriedly taken to the nearby creek to relieve themselves and quench their thirst. The water mirrored the pathetic appearance of Anna's gaunt face, but she no longer noticed. Her aching and growling stomach and the weakness of her malnourished body took on more importance.

The group wound their way northward along the trail, fording tributaries and rivers, none as great as the Monongahela two days before. Five hours passed of almost continual walking with few stops. Anna's entire body ached, and her head pounded. She noticed several of the warriors move ahead of the group at a faster pace and eventually disappear into the forest. She briefly wondered why, but she could not concentrate on anything but forcing herself to move.

"Look," Martha whispered. "Some of the savages have left us and gone on ahead. I think we must be nearing our destination."

"Yes, I think you're right. You know that this means we will all be separated. Your daughters may be taken from you as my children will." Anna's voice broke.

"That is my greatest fear. I will hope to die if that happens. First William, then Magdalena and Sarah. I cannot lose my girls." Martha held back her sobs and covered her red-rimmed eyes. Anna noticed the concern on Shemanto's face as the warrior strode to her side, looking warily at Anna.

"It is too much to bear, too much for all of us. Perhaps death would be welcome." Anna trudged ahead without looking at Martha.

Twice, the captives were taken off the trail and hidden in the heavy woods in silence, and Anna relished the brief stops when she could rest even for a minute. Unlike days before, the group became aware of Indians passing, heading south on the same trail.

"We should call out to them," Eve said to those around her.

"Do you think they would be different than our savage captors? They could very well be worse, you know. I prefer to take my chances with Killbuck. At least he has not killed any of us yet," Sarah added, and then looked at Anna, who thought, "Do you not remember my Sarah, my baby, cruelly murdered in front of your eyes?" But Anna did not refute Sarah, but rather looked away and tried to suppress the image of her baby.

The soft noises of the intruders quickly evaporated, and the captives were motioned back to the trail. A short time passed before sounds of rushing water were heard. Before seeing water, Anna heard its presence, and soon found herself on the bank of a beautiful, fast-flowing river, swollen and black from spring rains.

"What is this water called," she asked.

Standing nearby, Nicholas answered. "My father has spoken of a great river, northwest of our valley and called the Great River, the Ohio River. Perhaps we have reached that river. We are close to their villages. Father spoke of the many villages on this river."

"Then they know," Sarah said. "The soldiers, they must know where we have been taken. They must be following us."

"No, they aren't. The savages have shown no wariness on this whole trip. They know the soldiers are not close. The militia is not coming, and we must take care of ourselves."

"Nicholas is right. Ain't no rescue party on our heels," added James who had moved towards his sister.

"Then there's no hope? I will become some savage's squaw? My God, I can't do that," cried Sarah as the words sunk in, and James pulled her to him.

Anna interrupted. "Stop. There will be no rescue. You can do what you have to do, Sarah. God has abandoned us, but Nicholas is right. Each of us must do the best we can under these horrid circumstances. We are alive, but that is all I can say."

As the group approached the bank, Anna looked at the far shore that had become alive with people, more people in one place than she had ever seen. Indians of all sizes and shapes, white men in Indian garb, and a few French soldiers in uniform mingled on the far shore. Whoops and yells floated back and forth over the water, words unintelligible to the captives who heard no English or German, just French and Indian words.

Anna's stomach began to churn, and she knew they were at a turning point in their journey. She suspected that it would not be long until she and Mary and Adam were separated, perhaps forever. Her future lay before her as a blank slate. She grabbed Mary's arm and looked for her son.

It was not long until the warriors had located five canoes left upside down on the shore, and they began the process of turning them over and sliding them into the fast moving water.

Mary pulled at Anna. "Mama, Adam is with them," and she pointed to a canoe that had been loaded with four children and four warriors. Adam and young George clung to the necks of the warriors who held them securely while two paddlers fought with the current. The canoe eventually moved at an angle across the river toward the mob of people waiting on the far bank.

"I cannot stop him now," Anna answered.

The remaining canoes were quickly loaded and shoved into the water while a handful of captives remained on the bank under Killbuck's control.

After the canoes dropped off their passengers, two returned, and Anna and Mary were motioned to the shore and helped into the craft. They were soon joined by young Elizabeth Maus, crying for her brother and dragging her feet, expressing the panic they all were feeling.

Reaching the far shore uneventfully, the captives were roughly pulled out of the canoes and dragged up a short slope only to be confronted by a hundred people, curious to see and touch these new arrivals. Anna felt she had been taken to a strange, new world, an unreal place from which she could not escape.

She held onto her daughter and tried to avoid contact with those who enjoyed the tormenting of the captives.

"Stop them, Mama. They are pulling my hair." Anna swung her arm toward a grinning squaw who had grabbed her daughter's long tresses.

"There is no controlling these savages. Try to ignore them, and we will soon pass through this crowd."

Anna

It is late afternoon, and the Indians, excited and agitated, march us to the center of the village. I have never seen anything like this village, filled with all manner of structures lining a wide expanse, now filled with people. The structures include everything, shacks, wigwams, and log cabins with no apparent order or design, a most unpleasant place, dirty and unattractive. The noise is overwhelming and also unpleasant to my ears, noise of shouting, chanting, laughing, all in languages I do not recognize. There are smells, very bad ones: smells of body odor, of campfires, of pipe smoke, of food I do not recognize. The smell of dead fish is the worst of all.

Indians and French flow out of the cabins to surround us. These people laugh, yell, whoop and generally accost all of us. I have been pinched; my hair has been pulled; and I have been hit with switches, not hard, but hit. Killbuck tries to stop this harassment, but it continues anyway. After we stop in the center of the village, Killbuck struts ahead to meet a Frenchman, a trader I think, because of his rough appearance and clothes.

In the meantime we are tied to poles where other pathetic creatures are already confined. The young men, Nicholas and the others, are separated from us and taken back towards the river while the inhabitants of this ugly village line up, making a line several hundred feet long. After the confusion, I see that these people line up facing each other and are carrying all sorts of weapons, rocks, sticks, switches, knives and so forth.

In all of this noise and confusion, I do not know what to expect but concentrate on Mary and seek Adam, who has been placed on the shoulders of his captor to watch whatever festivities are in store for us. Choking from the dust and trying to ignore our fears, Mary and I cling to each other despite the ropes on our wrists, binding us to a large pole in the center of the village. Several poles support roped captives including those we do not know. The older boys remain at the far end of the line that stretches toward us.

The strangers among us, captives also, must have been here for days or longer. They are pathetic creatures, starving, bruised from beatings, and hollow-eyed, looking at us with pity, knowing we may be in the same condition in a matter of days. Trying to overcome my terror, I try to see what is happening.

While Anna, the other women and younger children remained tied in the center of the village near the council house, the older boys, five in all, had been dragged back toward the river at Killbuck's command while the crowd yelled and screamed in anticipation of a spectacle, the infamous gauntlet run. The excited village had been waiting weeks for the return of their warriors with those who would entertain them. Anna watched the boys in agony. She knew they would soon be the victims of some unknown sport, a sport the crowd expected. She noticed that James and Nicholas remained as calm as possible, but Johnny Reger was truly terrified and fought with his captor who eventually picked the boy up and carried him to the river.

At Killbuck's signal, James was pushed into the line and told to run to the council house that stood at the end of the long line of people brandishing weapons, anxious for the run to begin. James took a deep breath and ran for his life, suffering hits all over his body from switches, sticks, and an occasional rock. He did not fall, and his speed aided in his effort; but he collapsed, finally, at the end of the line where a Frenchman pulled him up with cheers and a pat on the back. Killbuck laughed as the crowd roared its approval when they watched the slim figure of the sandy haired James, who had avoided many of their blows. He was loudly applauded and would live.

Several minutes later, Nicholas joined him, bleeding from beatings, but generally in good shape. He had fallen only once but managed to regain his feet and, in agony, made it to the end of the line. Henry, too, succeeded, but had been severely beaten. Killbuck was patted roughly on his back, and his warriors were cheered before the Maus boy managed, just barely, to survive the run.

Then came Johnny Reger, whom Killbuck had left for last, thinking that the sullen boy would provide great sport for the village. Johnny screamed and cried out and pleaded with his captors for mercy, but there would be none. The crowd screamed in delight as Reger was forced into the line and turned toward his destination. Sobs shook his lanky body, and tears streamed down his thin face, his dark hair falling in tangles on his forehead.

"I can't. I can't," he cried and received a hard smack across his mouth resulting in a bleeding lip. It was clear that Killbuck's men would beat him where he stood or the squaws would torment him as he ran. Johnny decided to run and take his chances. In the end, he was pushed violently into the line and shoved by those who beat him unmercifully. He fell after twenty feet, regained his balance, and fell again. But then something happened to the terrified boy. He struggled to his feet and ran and ran, ignoring the pain of the switches. Falling three times but regaining his footing, he eyed Nicholas and James at the end of the line and concentrated on them. Managing to crawl the last few yards, his back bleeding profusely, he successfully made the end of the run, and the crowd was ecstatic. He would live, and a sick, bloody grin spread across his bleeding mouth, revealing red teeth. Collapsing in a heap, Johnny was quickly dragged and taken away by two squaws, followed by James and Nicholas. Killbuck watched the scene and was pleasantly surprised that Johnny survived.

The noise and excitement waned, and the crowd dispersed into their various lodgings. Soon there was little evidence of a celebration. It would be twilight when they emerged again for the feast that evening. Only Anna and the rest of the captives remained, secured to the poles, finally watching the pathetic prisoners whom they had joined and wondering who they were and afraid they were seeing themselves.

Anna

We are divided after the gauntlet runs. I knew it was coming. Adam is forcibly taken from me but does not seem to object. With a bearded Frenchman following, Killbuck returns and unties me, giving the rope to the stranger. It is there that I am relegated to a piece of contraband, no doubt sold to this unkempt, ugly old man. My mind wants to descend into blackness again. I am taken to a nearby building by this stranger, and Killbuck enters the cabin after us and speaks with the trader. They negotiate a price, and it is done. Eventually, Mary is brought to me, and I rejoice. A sympathetic Killbuck looks at me, and I see concern. Perhaps he has done me a favor.

May 6, 1758

Early this morning, having slept very little, Anna sat in a corner in the lean-to, Mary crouched beside her, softly crying, when Killbuck entered the structure. The Frenchman, called Louis LeBoeuf, as Anna had learned the night before, greeted the scowling chief.

Yesterday, LeBoeuf had told her, "Madam, my name is Henri, Henri LeBoeuf. I trade and have bought you to sew for us. You can sew, can you not?"

Anna did not understand French so she remained silent. Realizing she had no idea what he said, LeBoeuf explained in English, "Madam, you," and he pointed to her. "You sew?" He made a sewing motion with his hands.

"Ya, yes," she answered in English and realized what he wanted.

Now, he was cheerfully humming and packing furs for a trip south where they would be sold for a high price, he hoped.

Killbuck stood in front of the pleased Frenchman, looking at Anna and motioning her to him. "I can still offer you a choice. I can take you to my village as a squaw."

She shook her head because she knew that she could not bear to look at him day after day. The Frenchman was not connected to the loss of her children and would not be a constant reminder of her losses.

"Then it is done. You belong to LeBoeuf. You will be his slave. Do you understand?"

"Yes, and so it will be. And what of my Mary and my Adam?"

"They will become Shawnee. They will live. Your daughter will go with you and LeBoeuf to the Scioto villages on the Ohio where she will remain. What LeBoeuf does with you, I cannot say."

"Why did you spare me?"

"You carry child."

"And what of my two little boys? Do they live?"

Killbuck hesitated and then placed one hand on her shoulder and looked at her moist eyes. "Woman, some things we cannot control. I will tell you the truth. Your sons are dead. The little one died on the trail, and his brother died in this village two days ago. Your little one slipped from the grasp of my warrior while crossing the Monongahela River. Your other son arrived here with sickness. He was not cured by the cold water or the chants or the French trader's squaw who sat by his side for two days. The spirits were invoked but did not intervene, and the child died peacefully in her arms."

Anna felt the pain and nearly passed out from the shock of this new tragedy, not that it was unexpected. But some strength emerged from the tragic news, and she maintained her balance before this chief, this man who was responsible for her great loss. She could not forgive him nor could she understand why this had happened to her. But this new strength sustained her for this moment. "I will survive for this child I carry, but I will hate you for all eternity. I would kill you if I could, and I hope God, if there is one, strikes you down. You are the devil, the devil himself."

"I do not understand your devil," answered Killbuck harshly. "I do what is expected of me. The whites are taking our land, our food supply, our warriors, the life we have had for centuries. Why does your God favor white men over the red man? Why should we not fight for our lands, our way of life? We have not seen your God. Your God did not visit the red man. Is it a fight between Gods? I think not. It is simple. We fight for our survival, and it is unfortunate your children were in the way. We do what we must to save our lands, our people. What rights do the whites have to take from us? What would whites do if the red men took their lands, their food, their warriors? The earth is no man's to sell. It belongs to all, to men and to the animals who inhabit it, to our ancestors who lie buried within her arms."

"I do not know." Anna wiped her eyes, trying hard to silence her sobs. "I only know I have lost my family. That is all I know."

"I, too, have lost family to your soldiers. I have been forced to move several times to escape from your white men. I have lost a child. My son lives, but I fear he has been tainted by the whites and will not make a great chief someday, and my heart breaks."

Feeling numb and knowing she could not possibly think about her young sons' deaths, she took a deep breath, turned her face from the chief, and walked to the back of the cabin to curl up in a blanket. Her life held no hope and was drowning in memories. She knelt at her crying daughter's side, placing her arms around Mary's slight frame. Burying her face in the child's neck, she whispered, "Mary, my precious daughter. I loved your brothers so much."

Killbuck stared at her and felt her sorrow, but he was hardened and would not relent from his position.

"My heart tells me that the whites will prevail and I cry in sorrow. There are many of your people, too many, and our clans are small. We must unite as one, but there is no Indian who has the power to achieve this. Now, I do what I can to save my people. There is no room for the whites and the red men to live in peace. You fence and ruin the land, the land that belongs to all, the gift of the Great Spirit. I believe this is true and I will continue to destroy as many whites as I can. I fear my efforts will not be enough."

Without a backward glance, Killbuck left the Frenchman's cabin. He secretly hoped the woman Anna would survive. He admired her now that her spirit had returned, and he felt her pain. Tomorrow he would return to his village taking several captives, including the feisty redhead, but not this fine-looking dark-haired woman.

Neither Anna nor Killbuck had answers to the war or the clash of cultures. From a personal standpoint both knew sorrow, loss, and anger, but both realized there would be no conciliation. The whites and the red men had no common ground in this fight. Anna resolved to save herself and her unborn child whatever it took. Killbuck resolved to save his people, and he knew killing was part of the answer. For some reason, Killbuck hoped Anna understood his position, but he would no longer pursue it. Anna, in reflection, knew she was caught up in this clash, but the sorrow would be eternal. She would never forget her losses nor would she understand this war that had destroyed her family.

Chapter 14

May 9, 1758

Rain had fallen for several nights, and the road through Logstown was full of ruts and rivulets of water, effectively eliminating any remnants of recent events within the village. Facing the main path, the French trader's cabin was not much more than four plank walls, a flat roof covered with mud and moss, and a skin-covered door opening just large enough for one person. The chief resident of this lodging, boasting a full gray beard with a few dark strands appearing randomly on his blunt, square face, was Henry LeBoeuf, a short, but powerfully built, Frenchman who had roamed the French trading routes for two decades. His Seneca wife, Sepi, shared the hut with him and had, so far, ignored the two white women with whom she now shared the dilapidated structure.

For four nights, Anna had slept on the dirt floor in a corner in the French trader's cabin, Mary with her. Exhausted, she had done nothing for three days but eat and sleep while occasionally observing the activity in front of the hut. Her fellow captives had been taken away by warriors from both the Shawnee and Delaware tribes. Now, all but suffering Johnny Reger, Anna, and Mary remained of the Fort Seybert group taken three weeks before. Huddled together were, however, a few unfortunate souls from earlier raids, still tied to the poles day and night, beaten, unfed, and dying slow, agonizing deaths for what crimes Anna did not know.

She had witnessed the death of one young man who refused to comply in any way with the Indians' demands. The night before last he continued to be defiant and was beaten severely until he could no longer stand. His imploring cries unanswered, he fell by the pole which held his tied wrists. He was immediately surrounded by shouting men, women and children who gave him no peace until it was obvious the blows had taken his last breath. He was untied and allowed to remain in place until the numerous dogs, freely roaming the town, had torn him to pieces. Anna could not look at the spot without remembering his bloody, mangled body lying in the dirt, and she wondered who he was.

"Why, why was he killed," she questioned Henri.

"I do not ask these Indians such questions. I do not question their ways. It is not good to ask such things if one wishes to be agreeable. I am agreeable, always. I do not wish to lose my scalp."

"Where will you take me?"

"We will go on long voyage, to the greatest river of all, the Mississippi. Your girl will go with us. She will leave us at the Shawnee village on the Scioto. I am to present her as gift to the great chief who lives there. She is fine young squaw, and the chief will be pleased. Sell me many fine furs too." He grinned revealing tobacco-stained teeth.

"Where are the others? What will happen to the others who were brought here with me?"

"I do not ask. They most likely will be taken to Indian villages and live as Indians."

"They will not forget their white lives or their homes."

"You are wrong. Why you think Indian life so bad? Warriors live to hunt and fight, not work. Good life I think. The squaws, they work, but I do not see them complain. Work no more than whites on your farms. Your people will forget."

Henri had given her a small, wooden box containing needles, a pair of scissors, and various threads and warned that the box was her means of survival. She had not yet been forced to participate in preparing for the river trip but knew it was expected.

Standing at the cabin's door and observing the sun as it began its slow climb in the east, Anna remembered Adam's departure, and a spasm of nausea seized her. She had stood behind the Frenchman and watched her young son hoisted on the shoulders of his grinning Shawnee captor. She saw affection between them, Adam laughing as he was secured. She noted, too, the look in the Shawnee's eyes. He liked her son and would be a protector, probably a family member. Adam was not yet seven years old, and time would soon dim memories of his earlier life, his white father, and his mother. Watching them as long as she could see their images, which soon merged with the foliage, Anna realized that she might not see her son again. He would be lost to her just as her younger children were taken in death.

A red-eyed Mary stood at her mother's side. "Adam did not say goodbye to us," and she began to cry softly, while grabbing her mother's hand.

"Hush. He will be fine, and the warrior will take good care of him, like one of his own. We, you and I, will be separated soon, my daughter. Our lives have taken terrible turns. Please know that your father and I love you, loved you all. We never meant for such horrible things to happen to our family. All of you will be in my thoughts the rest of my life. And your father's too, I know. There was nothing to save us, nothing, even if your father had been with us. He also would have been killed. At least he is safe, and perhaps one day, one or more of us will be freed to go home. Now, dry your eyes and know we shall have a few more days together."

Turning around to enter the trader's hut, Mary and Anna hesitated as the shadow of LeBoeuf fell upon them ominously. Mary quickly darted past her mother and the trader, to hide herself in a fur in the corner of the dark, musty cabin where she could cry silently as long as she liked.

"Madam, your son, he be fine with warriors. Do not worry," LeBoeuf said in his heavy French accent, paying no heed to the crying child. "Name? How shall I call you?" He folded his arms squarely across his barrel chest and waited for her answer.

"I am Anna Margaretha Mallow. That is who I am."

"*Oui.* Then I call you Marie, a good French name," he chuckled. "Now, Madam Marie, I show you shirts to mend. It is time for you to adjust and accept. Is that not what we do to survive? Sepi help, good woman." He sought English words. "Killbuck, he good Indian. Help me. Sold me you, Madam. Not to take you to village as squaw. Bad thing for you."

Anna was barely able to contain her anger. "Killbuck is evil. He caused the death of three of mine. How dare you praise him to me?"

"Hush, Madam Marie. It is good you live. We cannot change things. Be careful, Madam. Adjust and accept, did I not say? Now then, we will have pleasant journey down river, non?"

"I have no choice now, do I?"

"Non. You do not." LeBoeuf moved to secure the pile of mending from a bench along the wall. "You now must help, help Sepi. We leave at first light tomorrow." He handed her a bundle of shirts.

May 11, 1758

Anna

It is our second day on this river, and reality has set in for me. We left yesterday morning, Mary, me, the Frenchman Henri, and his Seneca wife, Sepi as she is called. There are others, too, who accompany us: traders, a few Indians, two other female slaves, four canoes in all. We, the slaves, are kept apart, not that it matters as both of the women do not speak German or French, but are English. The canoes are packed tightly with bundles of furs taken last winter and to be sold somewhere in the south. That is what Henri does, I have come to understand. He hopes to sell them for enough money and supplies to last the winter, and then he will come north again to Logstown to purchase what he can, and the process will begin again.

Besides the various trials I now endure, I must confront my language problem. It is unfortunate I am not more proficient in English. There are no German speakers here. I will, no doubt, be forced to learn French since my owner speaks it. Sepi barely speaks French at all nor does she converse in her Indian tongue, but she seems to understand what is expected of her and is kind to me.

I must sew for my keep. There are worse jobs, I think, so I will comply. I will be a seamstress, a slave seamstress. Henri knows I am carrying a child, and that he does me a favor by buying a woman who will soon have a child to care for. Sepi has no children that I know of, and I think she envies me. Perhaps that is why Louis bought me...for his woman who has not had a child but desires one.

I am seated in the rear of a packed canoe while dark, sullen Indians and a rugged French trader paddle, and the current takes us swiftly down this wide river, Belle Rievere, Beautiful River, the Ohio, as the Indians say. Although it is a pleasantly cool day, I am comfortable, surrounded by furs. My Mary sits at my feet, her back resting on my knees, staring ahead. I wonder what she is thinking. Surely she knows we will soon be separated at the Scioto village, but we do not talk about it. She is nine, but a very old nine-year-old now. Her eyes ask for help, but she knows I cannot help either of us. We converse in German, but the Frenchmen do not like it and make fun of our native tongue.

The Beautiful River deserves its name and is a magnificent sight, so wide, so full of life. Densely lined with huge trees, naked roots protruding from the bank, the southern shore has occasional breaks where watering holes appear. It is *these places where we see many animals, and today we saw huge brown ones with large heads and shaggy fur. I was told they are called buffalo, provide excellent meat, and are hunted in the land on the south side of this river, the land called Kan-tuc-kee by the Indians. We pass several Indian villages where the occupants beckon us to come ashore, but the traders make no effort to stop. There are no villages on the south shore, and Henri tells me, in his mixture of French and English, that Kan-tuc-kee land is sacred for all Indians and holds game and salt licks shared by all.*

We often see herds of deer and elk at the river's edge and occasionally a bear or two. Although I have not seen a big cat, we certainly hear their cries at night along with the howling of wolves and the hooting of night owls among other strange sounds. I have never paid much attention to such noises since I have always had a roof over my head, but now things are different. Last night we slept on blankets on the shore since the night was clear and not too cold.

I try to keep clean as we travel. I wish no infection to accost me on this miserable trip. Henri does not bathe, and his smell is often overwhelming. Sepi does not seem to notice but she, too, rarely bathes. On the nights when we settle on shore, I walk to the river and wade into the murky water where I clean myself as much as possible. I use sand to remove the grime and sweat, just as the Indians showed us on the trip. It does not replace the lye soap I made in Virginia, but it cleanses. If the evening is warm and there is no breeze, I wash the grease out of my hair and let the night air dry it.

May 13, 1758

Heavily laden, the four large canoes slid effortlessly around a bend in the great river amid much excitement shown by the paddling Indians. Two stood up carefully, aimed their rifles at an angle toward the sky, and shot several times, whooping and shouting. As the canoes rounded the bend, great noises emitted from the northern shore where a hundred individuals stood on the shoreline, several of whom returned the fire with much yelling, heralding their arrival.

"Have we reached the Scioto village?" Anna felt nausea rising in her belly at the thought of more Indians.

"*Oui,* we have. See how glad they are to see us. We will have a fine time here. Trade for many fine furs to take to New Orleans." Henri laughed and waved wildly at the colorful assembly on shore.

"New Orleans? Is that where we are going?" Henri was too occupied to answer since the canoes had finally arrived at the mouth of the Scioto River where several Indian villages clustered on the hillsides.

Shouting orders, Henri skillfully helped beach his canoe safely in a muddy, sandy cove just beyond the confluence of the two rivers where the current could not catch it. He quickly jumped out, boots sinking in the mud, and pulled the canoe to safety, helped in his effort by the two Indians. Soon all four canoes had been safely anchored on the muddy shore, and the traders began to unload passengers and supplies. Two kegs of rum were among the last items to be unloaded, much to the joy of the watching natives who looked forward to this event with much anticipation and thirst.

Removing her new moccasins, Anna, gleaming black hair tied by a strip of buckskin and falling down her back, was helped by Henri into the shallow water that reached her knees but not her new deerskin dress. Sepi had proudly given her this gift after a much-needed scrubbing in the creek at Logstown. Mary, too, had been scrubbed and dressed in Indian fashion. The two captive females very much resembled Indian squaws and were now tanned and reddened by the sun. Both were ushered up the bank by the grinning Henri who could hardly contain himself with an excitement matching that of the hundreds of Indians, traders, and a few French who whooped and shouted at their arrival.

Anna looked sadly at her wide-eyed, frightened daughter. "This village seems like a pleasant place. It may not be so bad, you know." She noted rows of organized huts and wigwams, the charming copper-colored faces of laughing children, and splashes of color that adorned clothing.

"And see there?" She pointed to a bright green patch of young corn, beans, and squash that lay next to the village, plants protruding in neat mounds, poles jutting upward to catch the new bean stalks as they moved upward towards the sun. "There will be plenty to eat, I think."

Mary did not respond but rather wiped the tears flowing from her dark eyes. Anna could say no more because pain and grief washed over her entire body, and she could barely move or think.

As the travelers moved toward the center of the village, the throngs of people, who delighted in addressing the newcomers, were pushed aside by a tall, elegantly attired Indian as he made his way to greet LeBoeuf and the other traders. It was obvious that the Indian was of great importance as he strode forward, clad only in breech clouts, leggings, and decorated moccasins. Silver bracelets adorned both arms, and the blanket thrown across one shoulder did not conceal the tattoos that covered his naked arms and chest. He held a spear from which a scalp lock dangled in the breeze, and memories like ghosts surrounded Anna.

The chief embraced Henri heartily and conversed in a mixture of English and French that the trader seemed to understand. The men gestured and laughed loudly with delight at seeing each other again.

"LeBoeuf, welcome, *mon ami*."

"*Merci, merci.*" Henri laughed as he firmly grabbed the chief's shoulders and planted wet kisses on the chief's cheeks. "I bring many presents, *mon ami*. We will celebrate, eh? I bring you a sister to complete your family. A gift from the great chief Killbuck. She is nice, eh?"

Henri turned from the chief and motioned Anna and the forlorn Mary to come forward. Pushing Mary to the chief, Henri made the sign of a gift as the horrified girl sought to grab her mother.

"Mama," was the only word Mary uttered as a tearful Anna stood stiff and calm while gently putting her hands on each side of Mary's small face.

"Do not cry. I will always be with you. Remember that your father and I love you so very much. Do not forget us. Someday," she choked on her tears, "Someday, we will meet again."

Anna's moist eyes spoke for her, and Mary knew that she now belonged to this fine looking chief who held her arm while he looked upon her with approval. Within minutes an older squaw, long, silver hair hanging down her back, appeared at the chief's side and took Mary's hands in hers, gesturing that the terrified girl should follow her. A tearful Mary obeyed but kept her head turned towards her mother as long as possible. Anna's eyes never left her daughter until the girl disappeared into a lodge that lay a hundred yards down the center path of the village.

May 17, 1758

Anna

Mary, my Mary is gone. I cannot endure this pain. God, why have you forsaken me and mine? I wish I were dead but cannot forget the life growing inside me...or Michael. I try not to think of him, for I may never see him again. What is he doing, thinking? My God, I do not know.

When we arrived at this large village overlooking the Scioto River, I was aware that Mary would remain here. Killbuck told me so, but I could not think of my loss until it happened, and now it has. I take small comfort in the fact that the older squaw who took my girl looked at her with tenderness and will no doubt take good care of Mary. Henri told me that the squaw was the chief's mother and that Mary would replace her daughter who died last year of small pox.

Sepi has remained by my side and constantly places her hand on my belly and smiles her wide, infusive grin, showing stained, straight teeth. The mosquitoes and bugs are plentiful along the river so she has shown me how to cover my exposed skin with bear grease that she carries in her pouch. This horribly smelling paste greatly relieves the terrible itching that I experience. I fear that I am no longer recognizable as a German wife with my reddened, tan face, and tan arms and legs. There is no doubt that my Indian garb is more practical than the shift, dress, and stockings I wore in Virginia. My deerskin dress is very soft and beautifully decorated with beads, thanks to Sepi's skill. I have become very attached to it.

I will see no more of my daughter. My heart breaks for her, for both of us.

After four days of feasting and trading, the French traders, their women and slaves, and three, restless Shawnee warriors took their leave of the village, loaded the canoes with more bundles of furs, and left gifts of not only rum, but also ammunition, cooking utensils, and a large kettle. As Henri herded Anna and Sepi through the crowd gathered on the shore, Anna tried to shut out the unfamiliar sounds that pierced her ears. She understood very little conversation but observed many rapid hand movements.

Henri observed her puzzled look. "Madam, they are making signs. It is universal language. We all understand the meanings." He laughed as he shoved Anna and Sepi into the canoe.

Anna had lost all hope of seeing her daughter who had not appeared since she entered the chief's lodge. Her eyes filled with tears as Sepi seated her among the bundles that filled the craft that would take them hundreds of miles away from anything Anna knew.

"They have taken my girl. What will become of us?" Sepi's homely, but kind, round face, was the only ray of hope that Anna had, but Sepi did not answer because she did not understand German.

Henri became impatient and glared at the women. "Madam Marie, stop your tears. Your girl will be fine."

Although Anna had shown no interest in the other travelers since leaving Logstown, she finally became aware of two English women, also enslaved, situated in the other canoes.

"Who are those women, and are all of us headed to the same place?"

"Slaves, like you, but not as good as you I think. Pay them no attention. I do not know what their owners will do with them, Madam. You are my only concern."

Anna knew that they were going west, farther and farther away from her remaining family, and she might not see anyone she had known again. She fought to adjust and accept, as Henri had said. She no longer prayed, for God was not with her anymore. She did not understand what life held for her, and she hardly cared at all.

The canoes, packed with both people and bundles of furs of various kinds, soon glided with the river current around a bend and out of sight of the village and those who waved and yelled from the shore. As before, the two Indians and the Frenchman paddled, while Henri squatted in front and issued orders when necessary.

He looked with pleasure at the clear blue sky. "Madam, this wonderful, warm day. Are your spirits not improved?"

"How can you ask such a thing? I have just lost my daughter, my only daughter. What kind of a life can I envision as your slave?" She turned away from his smiling face and wiped her eyes on her sleeve.

Anna refused to speak for the remainder of the day as the group traveled many miles with the fast moving current. She tried to concentrate on the gentle feel of the water as it lapped on the sides of the heavily laden canoe sitting low in the water. Henri made certain that the canoes made regular stops where all could stretch their legs and eat the food the Indians had provided for this first day on the river.

That night, after the canoes were secured to the shore and the passengers had disembarked, Anna slowly trudged along the rocky, muddy shore, trying to make sense of her life, but she could not. Aching loneliness spread over her, and she saw nothing but blackness.

May 23, 1758

Six days passed in relative tranquility as the oarsmen leisurely paddled down the peaceful Ohio River. Rain had come only once, and Anna was miserable as she crouched underneath an oil cloth, covering both her and the precious bundles of fur. Five canoes now completed the flotilla, the addition being a small canoe piloted by three Shawnees from the Scioto village. Anna watched them with wariness as her fear of warriors had not abated. "Why did those savages come with us?"

"They want to see the greatest river of all and the villages on its shore. They hunt for us too. They are good paddlers and will help us when we reach the great falls."

"What are the great falls?"

"You will see Madam. But you will see from the shore."

Before reaching the stretch of water known as the Falls of the Ohio, the traders ordered the canoes to be beached while the passengers waded to the shore. Anna looked warily at the rapids before her and heard the monotonous roar of the frothing white water that stretched into the horizon. She and the other females were told to walk along the river while the experienced oarsmen rode the rapids and beached the canoes safely down river. An hour passed before Anna was again settled in her accustomed place in Henri's canoe, the traders pleased with a successful rapid run.

Despite being grief-stricken, Anna had a few moments of satisfaction. She realized that no one spoke German so she took some pleasure in commenting in her native language.

"How can you tolerate that sour smelling old man?" she asked Sepi.

"I would tear your heart out if I could," she said to Henri. "I will kill you if I can secure a weapon on this trip."

"Speak English or French. No more German," Henri ordered every time she spoke in her native tongue.

The night temperature would permit comfortable sleeping on the river bank where clearings and fresh water miraculously appeared. Anna welcomed this evening ashore where she could stretch her protesting limbs, especially her aching back from long hours in the canoe. She watched the brash and confident warriors disappear into the dense forest even though the traders worried about hostile Indians waiting in ambush to steal furs and kill them.

When the evening meal had been consumed, Anna could no longer contain her curiosity while Henri sprawled on a blanket, watching her. "Why are you so cautious about putting out the fire?"

"We must be on the lookout for the Cherokee war parties who would kill us and take our furs."

"Why? You French are their allies."

"No, Madam. Not the cruel Cherokee. They are the friends of the British. They roam our trading routes and could attack us at any time."

"One more thing to fear, but it no longer matters to me," she muttered in German.

Despite the threat of danger, it was a relief after darkness covered the river when she could lie on her back, breathe fresh air, and stare at the sky, marveling at the millions of stars. For a few moments, she could push the past from her mind.

May 26, 1758

It was late afternoon when the canoes glided toward the north shore below a seventy-foot bluff shadowing the river and its travelers. The oarsmen located a suitable inlet and paddled with difficulty up the narrow, but deep, stream until they found a suitable beaching area large enough for the five canoes. Quickly and efficiently, they secured the crafts with ropes to trees along the banks. Sepi helped Anna disembark and said in halting French, "There," and she pointed to a narrow trail that wound up the side of the bluff. "We go up there."

"What is this?"

"French fort. We stay day or two, here."

"I will stay in the canoe. I do not want to see any French." She turned from Sepi to walk back to the canoe.

"*Non*, Madam," Henri commanded as he grabbed her arm. "You will come with us. Now make haste."

It was a steep journey up a muddy, slippery path that eventually reached a wide expanse of land where a huge fort suddenly materialized, much to Anna's surprise. Two disgruntled guards had been left below to protect the canoes and valuable cargo. On a broad, flat plain sat a new French fort called Fort de l'Ascension, which afforded a magnificent view of the river below. Boasting four bastions, the structure was built of wood and surrounded by a ditch with deadly spikes.

Henri explained, "This fort is a fine fort, you see. The river," and he spread his arms in both directions. "No one surprise this fort. Soldiers can see for miles, both directions. No British can surprise the men here. No Cherokees either."

He laughed heartily. "There are one hundred French marines to secure our trade routes. We are near the great muddy river and are protected from the British."

"It is French, and I will not like it." However, Anna thought it was an impressive structure when she saw the fort loom ahead. She liked the feel of the hard ground and the thought of sleeping under roof.

Reaching the fort's gate, the traders, Indians and women were met by several young French marines who ushered them into the fort yard where other occupants greeted them, wanting news of the British and the Indians to the east.

"What do you hear of our enemies?" asked a French officer of Henri.

"Fort Duquesne is still in French control. I hear nothing of the British making plans to attack it, but they will one of these days." Henri shook his head in disgust as he followed the Frenchman who soon stopped his ceaseless questioning.

Shortly, the visitors were led into a long log building where a fire burned brightly in a huge fireplace at one end. Tables, covered with oil cloth, and wooden benches on each side held platters of salted pork, venison, wild turkey, sweet potatoes, green beans and corn bread. Arriving conveniently at supper time, the visitors were able to join the French marine officers for a meal, much to their delight.

During the plentiful meal, Anna spoke little but understood some of the French. She was recognized as Henri's slave and treated as such, mainly ignored unless someone wanted to know about Virginia.

"Madam," a young marine questioned in broken English. "Tell me about the Germans in the Virginia colony. How did you become the slave of the trader? Why did you come to this new land?"

She refused to comment on her situation or the means by which she arrived at this French fort. The officer could not get her to talk, much to his disgust, and he soon turned from her in silence.

During the extended meal, the extremely jovial Henri and the other traders stuffed themselves, joked, smoked pipes, and consumed great amounts of rum and brandy. Anna tried to concentrate on the conversation, but could not absorb all of the French. Deep melancholy surrounded her, and tears remained ready to surface at the slightest affront. The men's enjoyment could be heard far into the night, long after Anna and the women had been settled in the barracks. Ignoring questioning by the English women, Anna was given a cot and had no difficulty in rolling up in a blanket and falling asleep.

Chapter 15

May 28, 1758

The day dragged on in mostly silence under dull, gray skies and threatening rain, matching the moods of most of the men. Having left the fort early the day before, the voyagers were still recuperating from a late night. Suddenly, the Indians began to exhibit a flurry of excitement, recognizing that the river was moving ever closer to the Mississippi. They could not contain themselves, having never been this far west, and shouted and pointed while motioning to the traders.

"We are close," Henri warned.

"Close to what?" Anna asked.

"The greatest river, madam. You will see soon. It is a magnificent sight. No more talking. We must take care."

He immediately shouted orders to the oarsmen and began to watch the river and landmarks closely, noting their positions and maneuvering the canoe close to the south shore, cautiously slowing down. Soon the Ohio began to widen, and currents swirled, fought, and twisted as the river began its emergence into the dark, muddy river called the Mississippi. The paddlers worked the canoes close to the shore, back paddling, as the canoes entered the fast moving currents.

It was difficult to keep the canoes steady and hugging the now-eastern shore of the mighty river, full of debris from spring rains. Anna clutched the side of the canoe and shut her eyes while praying the canoe would maintain its balance. Sepi responded to Henri while he shouted orders and kept the canoe remarkably stable. An hour passed quickly before the canoes safely floated south along the eastern shore.

Eventually, all breathed sighs of relief when movement stabilized, and the paddlers began to relax. The fifth canoe, however, had headed north, and the excited Shawnee were furiously fighting the current so that they could get to a northern village, their destination. Anna soon lost sight of them as the river rounded a bend. Although the sky had darkened considerably, the rain held off until the canoes floated safely. Then it came with a vengeance.

Anna, having just relaxed, felt the drops, heard the thunder roar, and saw the lightning dance across the dark sky. The river began to churn in the frantic wind, and all held on while the paddlers frantically tried to maintain course. After a tumultuous half hour, the storm disappeared as quickly as it had appeared. Again, all relaxed. They were safe, but the furs would have to be dried, a small price to pay for safety. Anna marveled that she had not embraced death but rather feared it.

"We are alive" and she smiled at Sepi. She did not understand why she suddenly wished to survive. She no longer prayed and did not credit God with her will to live.

Soon curiosity awakened her senses, and she turned her head toward the western shore of this wide river where she saw a rolling prairie dotted with clumps of trees, huddling together, as far as she could see. For a minute she marveled at the vast emptiness of it all, and felt she was seeing land that was unclaimed, wild and beautiful. Knowing nothing of the continent beyond Virginia, she had been continually amazed at its variety. Although she could not put it into words, she knew that history was being made in this new land but could not imagine what it would be. Occasionally, she realized that she could be one of the few white women to observe this dark river, this rugged land, and the thought overwhelmed her.

June 10, 1758

After endless days on the river, the monotony of the river's movement, the soft whisper of the breeze, and the silence of the men abruptly changed around noon as a loud yell pierced the air. The trader in the lead canoe pointed to smoke rising above the forest in the distance. Shortly, a clearing appeared upon which lay an Indian village, wisps of smoke emitting from neatly arranged huts and rising above the trees.

Curled up in the rear of the canoe, Anna was aroused from her rest by Sepi, who shook her and pointed to the eastern shore. "Tunica. Tunica."

"What is it? Who are those people?" Anna squinted in the sunlight as she tried to see details.

Looking to her left, Anna realized they were paddling towards a flat area, devoid of trees and planted with various crops. Lodges were visible within the village, home of the Tunica Indians, long the friends of the French nation. Observing the canoes gliding toward shore, the village inhabitants were aroused from their monotony, and a hundreds of souls gathered at the river's edge. The traders returned the welcoming gunfire and flag-waving as they made their way toward the shore.

"Tunica, a friendly village. We stay there, Madam. The French, they protect this village from the Cherokee who would scalp them all if not for the French soldiers. You will soon feel the ground beneath your feet, and your belly will soon be full."

The four canoes were pulled safely to shore by strong,

naked men and anchored securely in a small inlet. Shortly, the traders and their women were welcomed profusely and led to the center of the village by excited women and children. Anna and the two English women were eyed with curiosity, but not accosted, for the Indians were familiar with these traders and unconcerned about their women.

Tunica provided welcome diversion for the tired travelers. Henri was jubilant, and even Anna felt a smile cross her face. The small lodges were neatly arranged and surrounded by patches of emerging corn, squash, pumpkins and beans tended by bare-chested women. Shaggy ponies grazed nearby while a few chickens and hogs ran loose within the village. Strips of buffalo meat hung from tree branches, drying in the sun next to piles of buffalo waste from the recent buffalo hunt.

An imposing chief, covered with tattoos and a buffalo robe thrown over his shoulders, escorted the travelers into a council house where they were seated on the floor to enjoy a feast of venison, bread made from corn, and vegetables of sorts simmered in broth. The women relentlessly presented a variety of dishes, frowning if anyone refused their offerings.

Despite the presence of Indians, Anna greatly enjoyed the feeling of the hard ground beneath her feet and Indian bread lying heavily in her belly. When the meal was completed, the men remained to smoke pipes and share tales while the women were led outside where Anna rested against a tree. Soon, the men joined the women, and the evening's festivities began. Anna watched the copper-colored Indians, illuminated by firelight, perform their dances and chant their unfamiliar melodies. As darkness fell, she dozed only to be awakened by Sepi and Henri.

"It is time. Come. You will sleep in that lodge," and he pointed to a rude structure nearby.

Minutes after the three entered the lodge, Anna curled up in a bearskin and was asleep momentarily. No bad dreams disturbed her welcome sleep on solid ground.

June 24, 1758

It had been two weeks since the traders had left Tunica and continued down the mighty Mississippi, which twisted and turned as it plowed its way south. Short nights had been spent on shore, and the abundance of day light allowed for long hours on the river. The weather became warmer, the water swampier, the bugs more numerous, and the humidity rising daily.

Anna could not bear the mosquitoes and the red spots appearing on her limbs and face. "These bites, they are unbearable, and the heat is making me ill."

Sepi frowned and soon produced some foul-smelling salve and helped Anna spread the ointment on her bare arms and legs. She soaked a cloth in the murky water and gave it to Anna, allowing her to wipe her face and hands. She refused to allow Anna to drink river water and instead collected water from springs or clear streams she managed to locate during the evenings on shore. She kept a supply of fresh water in leather bags and refused to share with anyone other than Anna and Henri.

Making only necessary stops, the traders glided past many Indian villages but stopped at none for they were in a hurry to get to the port of New Orleans in order to sell their furs and purchase needed supplies for the trip upriver, a much more difficult undertaking.

Henri had told her, "I hire paddlers for trip back up river. You see return trip much more difficult. Canoes are very heavy with gunpowder, lead, tools, cloth, sugar, coffee, and tea. Trip take months."

"Who will buy these furs?"

"French ladies, of course." He chuckled. "The French ladies, they love their beaver coats and hats and pay dearly. Good for traders. Good while it lasts."

Anna could not comprehend the fact that women would pay high prices for furs that she had enjoyed in abundance. But she gave it little thought. The new continent was so vast that she could not imagine the traders running out of furs to sell.

Eventually, the river began to widen and mingle with many small tributaries entering the murky water. The land became swampy and bug-infested, the water almost black, with moss-covered trees extending their arms out from the shoreline. The four canoes slowed as they encountered more traffic moving to and from the busy New Orleans port in the distance. Now, Anna saw canoes and barges, traveling in both directions.

Finally, she observed large ships, some with sails furled in the wind and some anchored at wooden piers along the west side of the wide river. She recalled the port of Philadelphia from the distant recesses of her mind and briefly thought of Michael. The harbor was busy, much noise drifting up the river, people moving along both banks, some on horseback, some driving carriages, many afoot. The activity on the docks included the loading and unloading of all types of cargo and the stacking of goods high on the piers. Young black men worked strenuously, lifting and carting goods back and forth from wagons to ships. Captains yelled commands, merchants bartered, and ships of all sizes plowed their way to and from the many piers available. The dusky smells of dead fish lay heavily in the air.

Arriving in the midst of the activity, the canoes of Henri and the other trappers slid easily to one of the smaller piers where men awaited to help unload the bundles of very desirable skins to be sold and taken to France. The weary travelers disembarked from the crafts and stretched their legs on the narrow wooden dock.

Henri motioned to Sepi and pointed in the distance. "Take the women to the trader's hut, up there," and he pointed beyond the pier to a dusty road that would lead them to a dilapidated cabin run by a friend with whom he regularly stayed when he came to New Orleans. Sepi was familiar with the place and hurried the women along towards the partially obscured cabin in the trees off the dirt road. Two other Indian women and the English slaves from the other canoes trudged after them.

Anna obediently followed Sepi along the dusty path while she swatted the numerous flies and mosquitoes away from her damp face. Her dark hair was plastered to her skull, and strands hung in clumps despite being tied at her neck. She liked the feel of hard earth beneath her feet, but it was small comfort compared to the discomfort she felt over her unclean, sweating body. She thought only of water and hoped she could wash her face or, better yet, submerge her body in a pool of fresh water. However, she knew better than to expect such a treat.

Arriving at the cabin door, a tired Anna looked at Sepi. "How long will we have to stay here? It hardly looks large enough for all of us."

"Big enough. Stay here until business done. Two or three days, maybe longer."

June 27, 1758

Anna
Seven women living in one room in this small, dirty, smoky cabin in this horrible heat is extremely unpleasant. I have no choice, and Sepi defers to me in hope that she can keep me content knowing I am carrying a child. She has insisted on

giving me the most comfortable spot near the window while angrily keeping anyone from taking my place. There is hardly any breeze inside or out, and the bugs are horrible. I use bear grease often, and we all smell badly. There is fresh water available in a small spring behind the cabin. I spend much time there sprawling on a wooden bench and splashing water all over my body, clothes and all. It helps for a minute, and then the pleasure disappears. My two items of clothing, a deerskin dress and a skirt, are barely adequate, but I try to air them out and brush them as much as possible.

Some nights we all sleep without our clothes, just a tangle of tan and dark bodies sprawled on pallets. My hair is rarely clean although I pour water over my head and use tallow soap. My fingernails are ragged and broken, and my hands are rough and pricked from needle mishaps. Sometimes I do not care at all.

There are three rooms in the cabin, one ours, one for any of the traders who manage to slink back here after drinking all the rum they can find, and one room where transactions take place. I just know that the canoes are being filled with crates and bundles of goods to be taken up river to a French fort called Fort Chartres. There are eight additional men who were hired as pilots, for what they tell me is a terrible trip up river. I cannot tell much about them; several are very dark and may be part Indian or part Negro. Some speak a language I cannot recognize. They are very powerful-looking young men who want to go north, either to the forts or to the lake area above the Mississippi. If I were not heavy with child, I might be worried about them. Henri, however, runs a disciplined operation, so I doubt that he would tolerate misbehavior with his women, nor would the other traders. He laughs and assures me that all will be well.

Sepi smiles and takes care of my needs. I cannot wait to get out of this hot, bug-infested place. Although Henri brings us food from the port, clams, shellfish and the like, we see nothing of the notorious city. I have partaken of a soup of sorts in which everything seems to move. The local people throw anything in it including vegetables and greens. It is tasty once you get rid of the numerous shells. The French call it gumbo.

The two English women, slaves of Henri's trader friends, are here. We have spoken rarely on our long journey. As I, they have lost family members; one lost all when she was captured near where we lived in Pennsylvania. Michael was right. . . we would not have been safe there. She saw her children tomahawked and her husband scalped and is no longer sane. She cannot concentrate and often looks to the sky and sings unfamiliar songs. She laughs uncontrollably, and her owner often slaps or shakes her to silence. She cares nothing for her appearance, long greasy hair in tangles down her back, dress torn and dirty. The other woman tries to comfort her and is the only calming influence. I fear it is too late to help her.

July 1, 1758

I cannot get out of this place soon enough. There is no help for me here. The city is French, and I would have no idea where to go if I did leave. There are no English here, just French, Indians, and Negro slaves. It must be a brawling city full of all manner of people, many disreputable, I think. The sounds of the port drift to us on nights when the wind blows from the south. We can hear strange music, laughter, gunshots, and loud voices. It is better to stay with those I know than risk a worse fate. We are often sent to our room after dark while the traders argue over their prices. The smell of liquor pervades the entire cabin, along with the smoke of pipes and the smell of unwashed men.

I believe we will leave soon to head up river. The canoes are nearly full, Henri says, and men have been hired. The two English women were taken from here yesterday after a conference between their owners and a wealthy French gentleman. I think they were sold, but no one tells me, and I do not ask. Perhaps I am lucky that Henri keeps me, or perhaps he did not get the price he wanted. Perhaps it is my pregnancy that keeps me with him. I do not know and do not care as long as I am not sold.

I think of Michael rarely these days. Sometimes I cannot remember what he looks like. Perhaps it is better this way.

September 1, 1758

It is night, very late I think. The sky is black, but millions of stars appear above me, illuminating the river shore. Although I am so very tired and sore from river travel, I cannot sleep tonight. The others snore near me, but I ignore their noises and concentrate on the gentle lapping of the river against the shoreline, hoping I can forget the usual images that appear in my dreams.

Perhaps two months have passed since we left that unpleasant cabin in New Orleans. Although I was glad to depart, I had no idea of what travel up river would be like. This trip has been difficult, and it is a wonder we still survive. The paddlers fight every minute to maneuver the canoes a few miles a day against the strong river currents. I am no help, except for mending torn clothing and blankets.

The paddlers are not pleasant and hate this trip north. One is black as coal, another pox-scarred and copper colored. It is only the promise of money that keeps them moving. Henri has traveled this route many times and ignores complaints. Sepi and I simply obey his commands and do the best we can. Sepi soothes me with promises of future comfort, whatever that might be. My baby often moves within me, and, I suspect, will arrive in the fall.

October 21, 1758

After almost four months of difficult travel bucking the currents, plagued by bad weather, heavy rains and debris, the traders finally recognized a village and fort situated on the eastern shore of the great river. Anna looked in the direction Sepi pointed and delighted at the thought of stopping. Three strong paddlers had assisted Henri in paddling for hundreds of miles, back and forth, to confront the currents. The only mishap that occurred was when one of the canoes overturned, and a day was wasted trying to secure the cargo and dry it out. Unlike the trip south, barely a mile or two were made each hour.

Fearing, for her life on so many occasions each day, Anna hardly had time to think because she was so busy clutching on to the side of the canoe and held in place by the considerate Sepi. Her fingers were cut and sore from sewing, and her eyes often ached from trying to see in the twilight to perform her tasks.

Despite the danger, many nights were spent on the western shore where Anna enjoyed the sweet and tangy fall air and fell exhaustedly asleep regardless of the weather or the meager provisions that might be available. Although they passed many Indian villages, they rarely stopped and avoided the largest village, Kaskaskia, which lay not too far south from the fort that loomed on the horizon.

"What it that fort called?" Anna asked Henri as they paddled closer to the shore.

"That is Fort Chartres. It was built many years ago when the British were confined to the eastern colonies. See there, the old fort has been replaced. It now holds three hundred men and is commanded by Andrew McCarty. An Irish French man. Who has heard of an Irish French man?"

Covering four acres, the stone structure impressively overlooked the village and the river. Boasting four bastions, and built from limestone brought from upriver, the structure contained musket ports, cannon embrasures, barracks, storehouses and various other structures within the large enclosure.

"This fort. Not yet complete but enough men to protect the river and French trading routes. It is strong and allows passage to Canada to trade for furs. British have difficult time defeating us here. Indians who live close are allied with us. We protect them and trade with them."

As orange streaks spread across the sky, Anna noted the village, dwarfed by the fort, and the assortment of people, dwelling along the river in front. She suspected that they basked in their safety and the trading activities, allowing them some prominence among the poorer tribes living along the river.

"These poor savages trade with you and get gunpowder, guns and alcohol for their furs. You French encourage their dependence and warfare against the British," Anna said sarcastically. "You will see. No good will come of this, and the British will attack your forts."

Guns fired, people yelled from shore, and the newcomers were welcomed. Relieved, Henri guided the canoe to the shore and was aided by both Indians and traders who pulled the heavy canoe into a secure spot. It was with great relief and exhaustion that Anna, Sepi and the others stepped on the rocky shore and began the short walk to the village itself, complete with houses as well as a Catholic Church. The heavily pregnant Anna, tanned but thin, walked between Henri and Sepi as they greeted various traders and a few Indians in passing. Henri planned to stay at Fort Chartres long enough to trade with the soldiers and then make his way down river to Kaskaskia, where he planned to winter.

"My child, will my child be a French citizen?"

"Oui, madam. Of course, and why not? The child will live under French rule."

Anna frowned at Henri's answer but would confront the problem at a later time. In the meantime, she would enjoy being on solid ground.

For the next two nights Anna would lodge in a cabin with a soft, down-filled pallet upon which to rest. In addition, she would have bread, vegetables, and venison, along with French pastries provided by the French marines. She would have to think about French citizenship after her stomach was full and her body rested.

October 23, 1758

After two days of food and rest, Henri, Sepi, Anna, and two of the New Orleans oarsmen trudged slowly along the shore to Henri's canoe beached beyond the village, where they would board and paddle down river to the large village they had passed the week before.

"Why can we not stay longer in this fort? Why do we have to leave to go to that other village?" Anna questioned as they walked to the canoe.

"Still have goods to trade. Winter in Kaskaskia, not this fort. Find a barge to stay on during cold weather. Also, find more men to help with spring trip upriver."

"Will we go back to Logstown?" She suspected her questions often irritated the Frenchman.

"Non, not safe now. War with British now too dangerous. British may have taken Fort Duquesne by now. We take safer route, up the Illinois to Fort Pontchartrain."

"When did you hear this and why did you not tell me?"

"You my slave, not my confidant. But British try to claim all land, and their people move west continually. French have not been able to stop them. I must get one more trip in before trade routes no longer safe," he grumbled.

"Maybe I will not have to be a French citizen after all." Thoughts of home briefly entered her mind, but she pushed them away.

Anna knew her time was close and traveling in the winter with a new born was out of the question. She trusted Henri would find shelter in the large village. It would be very agreeable to stay in one place for several months, something that had not happened since she was taken months ago. Perhaps Kaskaskia would be a safe place to have her child.

After a three-hour trip back down the river, Henri and the oarsmen guided the canoe towards the waiting men on the shore who helped secure the craft while Henri, Anna and the others waited to be led into the village itself. Following an imposing Indian, the three entered a rustic cabin not far from the shore. Henri was greeted by a dark, unshaven man, obviously a man of mixed race, who seemed pleased at seeing his old friend again. He was dressed in blue pants and a white shirt, belted at his waist, and boasted silver rings in his ears and several necklaces of animal teeth, gleaming white in the dusk of the cabin.

"Greetings, Henri." He ignored the two women.

"Good to see you, Captain Jack, We need winter shelter, my friend, an old barge perhaps?"

Jack suggested an old relic that lay anchored in an inlet not far from the town.

"For a small fee," he added as he looked suspiciously at the pregnant Anna while Henri grinned. "Ah, mon ami. You have done well, I see." There was no doubt, Anna thought, that the captain believed Henri to be the prospective father, and Henri had no intention of correcting his assumption. Perhaps it was good, for he would think her to be attached to a man whose interest lay in protecting her. Briefly, Anna wondered why so many men were called Captain. Captain, of what, she wondered and decided it was a meaningless designation, for they were captains of nothing that she could determine.

Pleased at the offer of the barge, Henri did not hesitate to accept, and he contracted with the captain for the winter's lodging. Relieved, Anna could at least envision the next few months and would have her baby on this barge, whatever that meant. She soon found out.

The barge was old and decrepit, sunlight seeping through the roof of the small cabin and floor rough and uneven, stained with whatever the barge might have carried in the past. She would not speculate on that. She was not asked to help as Sepi, Henry and two Indians carried the canoe's cargo and their belongings, meager as they were, onto the barge. Sepi helped her make order, in this case, sleeping arrangements, insisting that Anna have the most secure and comfortable area. Goods were tied and stored, covered with oil cloth for protection from weather, and the canoe was brought ashore nearby so that repairs could be made over the long winter to come.

Chapter 16

November 1, 1758

Anna

We have lived on this dilapidated barge, anchored in an inlet off the great river near the French and Indian village of Kaskaskia. The town is full of others who will winter here, some French, some Indians, and some called half-breeds, half of what I do not know, but they are dark and swarthy. There are French priests here who want to baptize my child when it is born. It is French law, but I will not have it if I can help it.

I have become used to the constant movement of the barge on the water. It is monotonous, but sometimes soothing, not like the terrible trip upriver. If I were not so tired and awkward, I would take time to hate this river, this life that Henri and Sepi live. How can they stand it? But I am too exhausted to think most of the time. I am too large to climb on and off this barge, so Henri lets me be and Sepi watches over me and brings me food. I suspect she scrounges it from the natives in this village.

I have a French book to read, but it simply serves as practice for understanding French. I have an English Bible which serves the purpose of improving my English, but few here can read, so I have no help.

I still manage to mend and sew shirts, a skill much in demand here, while Sepi tans deerskins and cooks for us. Occasionally, I think, even though I try not to. I see images of my dead children and Michael and wonder what he is doing or thinking. I rarely think of Mary or Adam and wonder if it is because, deep down, I think they have adjusted to Indian life and are safe.

I suspect that my time is getting close. Sepi is truly looking forward to this child, but I remain unsure and wonder how I will care for a babe in this environment.

November 28, 1758

Anna

I cannot get comfortable and know the pains will begin soon. It is a terrible day; I hear the wind screaming, and icy rain filters through the boards, chilling me even though furs surround me on all sides. Sepi watches me closely and is prepared with towels, fresh warm water, and a soft blanket for the babe. Henri goes in and out but cannot stand the cold rain. He has been drinking French brandy, reserved for special occasions, he tells us.

I wonder if Michael suspected I was pregnant? Why, why did I not tell him? If I ever return home with a child, he may not believe that it is his. My God, what a mistake. But I pray that he knew me well enough. God knows I had enough babies, so he must have seen the signs. Perhaps not though, for he had too much to worry about since the Indian threat was upon us for so long. Mary knew, my Mary knew I was with child. But she may never return to confirm it. God, why have you made me suffer like this? The pains begin and are quick and powerful, so the ordeal will not last long, I think.

The baby comes quickly, and I ignore the pain. Sepi is very efficient and has done birthing before I know. She takes the whimpering male child from between my uncovered legs, swiftly cuts the cord and pours alcohol on the cut, wipes the baby with a clean towel, wraps him up tightly, and hands him to me, all in a matter of minutes. Henri must have heard the baby's first cry, for he enters the tiny cabin on the barge, grinning and chuckling like a new father. He opens the baby's wrap to see if it is a male child; then he efficiently rewraps the baby and pats me on the arm. "Madam," he says. "What name have you for his fine boy?" Knowing what he wants, I do not hesitate and answer, "Henry. He shall be Henry Mallow."

"Oui, madam. That is good, good name," he exclaims, smiling from ear to ear. And it is done. I have a new son named Henry, after the trader who owns me.

January 1, 1759

The new year began with little fanfare. Some residents of the village celebrated with much rum drinking, but they were mainly traders, bored with life in the village and anxiously awaiting the coming of spring when they could return to their livelihood on the rivers. Henri had decided upon his route for the year. He would travel upriver, the Illinois River, toward the great lake region where he would travel overland to the fort on the Detroit River, Fort Pontchartrain. There he would trade for furs from the Indians who came there, and he would seek a buyer for Anna and her son, perhaps someone from Montreal who desired labor.

The cold day allowed Henri to rejoice in the baby and spend much time holding the child and cooing to him in French. The baby provided amusement for all three, and Sepi could not do enough to please. Anna knew Sepi did not want Henri to sell her or Henry. She now understood enough French so she could understand their arguments. At dusk, hoping Henri would revise his decision to sell her, Anna drifted into a fitful slumber, seeing images of her family, Henri, Sepi and numerous, unsmiling Indians.

It was very late, and Anna, Sepi and the baby slept fitfully while pellets of snow fell upon the roof and droplets of water seeped through the rafters and dripped methodically in the buckets below. Anna suddenly became aware of the creaking of a door.

"Henri," she thought, "is no doubt returning from a drunken evening with his fellow traders."

She cuddled in a fur and turned on her side, only to feel movement and hot rum-laden breath upon her neck. She froze in fear as Henri whispered hoarsely, "I want you. You have had your child, and time you repaid me for your safety."

Hiding her terror, she rolled on her back and said quietly, "It is true you have taken care of me and my child. But my son, he is your namesake, is he not? Baptized in your Catholic Church. Would you take his mother by force while he lies in the same room? Would you dishonor his mother in God's presence and his presence?"

Henri paused and released his hold on her. "Ah, my namesake, your boy Henry. Yes. You win. I am too weary and drunk to argue with you."

He rose awkwardly and stumbled across the small room to Sepi who had not made a sound.

Anna's eyes remained opened, and she stared at the roof of the cabin, trying to concentrate on the wind outside and the steady drip into the buckets. "I won this time," she thought. "Will it be the last time?"

March 16, 1759

Anna rested on a log near the Mississippi shoreline just beyond the busy village. Carrying three and a half month old Henry, she had leisurely walked from the anchored barge down the path that led to the river where she nursed the baby and watched the activity. Since the day was warm, and the sun finally appeared much to the delight of everyone who found a reason to be out in its warmth, Anna emerged from the close quarters for the first time in weeks. She knew she was pale and thin and needed to revive her spirits, and it would be good for the baby to breathe fresh air for a change instead of the stale, smoke-infested air in the barge's cabin. It had become easier now to dismiss the images that still crept into her mind, and she knew that keeping busy was good medicine for both herself and Henry. She inhaled deeply and lifted her face to the wind, enjoying the fresh air. The gentle lapping of the water soothed her, and she closed her eyes in pleasure, momentarily ceding memories into the dark recesses of her mind.

The shoreline was humming with activity, traders making ready for their spring journeys, up one river or another, to the lucrative fur trade that awaited them in Canada. Warriors were haggling over wages for piloting canoes, and traders were outbidding one another for their services. Priests walked among them, enjoying the warmth and promise of spring themselves while children romped and ran along the shoreline.

Anna had avoided the Catholic priests and refused to allow her baby son to be baptized in the Catholic faith. However, Henri was dismayed and informed her that the child was doomed to purgatory, but Anna held firm. One old priest, however, completed the brief ceremony when Anna was absent from the barge, securing supplies, and Sepi, watching the child, had no choice but to obey Henri who had waited patiently for an opportunity. Furious, Anna refused to speak to either of them for days, but, in the end, Henry was a baptized Catholic, and there was nothing she could do to change it. It had happened months ago and was no longer important to her until today.

Anna's musings were interrupted by an old priest , whose wrinkled face resembled a skull quietly sat down next to her, looking admiringly at young Henry.

"Madam, you have a fine son here."

Anna ignored his meaningful gaze. "Someday, you will be grateful I baptized him, even if you did not wish it."

She sought her words carefully. "I am German of the Lutheran faith, and I forbade Henry's baptism into the Catholic faith. How dare you go against my wishes?"

"Madam, it was for his good, his soul. It is also French law. You Lutherans have taken the wrong road. You will see. The French will maintain their claims, and the British will turn back. Who is to say that you will not live the rest of your life under French rule?"

"I guess I may, but I will not embrace the Catholic faith, ever. I am Lutheran, and Henry will learn from me."

"Forgive me but you are not educated in French ways or the ways of our church. We wish to embrace you and your son to save you from eternal damnation."

That was enough for Anna, and she abruptly rose from the log. Without a backward glance, she walked away from the priest who followed her with sad, hollow eyes and a shaking head.

Anna knew it was time for Henri to leave, and she would go with him since no one had desired to buy her so far. Several men had, however, wanted her services, a night or two, but Henri would not sell her for an evening. She believed it was because of Sepi and young Henri but feared things could change, especially if enough money changed hands. Therefore, she was as anxious as he to leave this place.

Without hesitation, mood having soured, Anna, carrying Henry, returned to the barge only to be confronted by a scowling Henri.

"It is time to prepare. We leave in three days for the French Fort Pontchartrain up the Illinois River and overland. You must prepare for the journey and make sure to have supplies that you need."

"Why are we not going back to Logstown?" Anna's hopes of seeing Mary again at the Scioto village were quickly dashed.

"Non, Madame. It is not safe. Logstown is no more. British took Fort Duquesne last fall, and Logstown, now ghost town. The stupid French, not fight. They burned fort." He shook his head in disgust. "They flee north to Fort Pontchartrain. Indians too. We must take safe route and get to Pontchartrain and then, if God wills, Canada. British hold the rivers, the Allegheny and Monongahela. We traders will suffer unless the French can regain control."

"Please, Henri. I beg of you. Leave me here then. Do not take me north. I am a burden with a child." All thoughts of seeing Mary or finding a way to Virginia had vanished, and she feared the escalation of the war.

"*Non, non*, Madame. Haven't you pleaded to get out of here? I need your services. You sew good, help Sepi. Bring good price in Montreal."

"You still intend to sell me then?"

"Oui, Madame. No choice. Besides, white slaves in Montreal do not suffer. It is a much better life than here with Indians. Surely you know that, Madam. The French are civilized and treat slaves well. You will have bed and roof over your head. Your son, much better life for him."

Anna looked at him with tears in her eyes. "I am a prisoner, a prisoner chained by a baby and a trader."

"It is settled. We will leave in three days. The canoe is refurbished and ready to load. We will take the goods I packed for the trip north, I have hired two oarsmen, and Broussard and his men will accompany us. The journey will be difficult but we will do what is necessary. You will see Fort Pontchartrain instead of Logstown which is no more. From the fort you will be taken to Montreal because there is heavy trade there in slaves for the merchants in Montreal."

Chapter 17

June 20, 1759

Henri, tears in his eyes, and a crying Sepi on his arm, took his leave of Anna and young Henry in Fort Pontchartrain after a three month journey up the river and overland to the French fort on the Detroit River. The months had been long, dreary, and difficult for everyone. Anna had not thought ahead but rather took each day as it came and sewed and cared for the baby as best she could. The men were always tired and irritable, and only Sepi tried to uplift Anna's spirits.

For Anna, the trip had been a nightmare. She had hated the endless days, monotonous days, the endless paddling from one side of the river to the other, bucking the river's unpredictable current and weather. Sometimes the wind lashed out angrily and gave them no peace. She hated the wet days where the oil cloth and the furs failed to keep out the cold and dampness, the days where no one spoke except for curses at the difficulties confronting them. There were many days when the wind lashed out angrily, and the body could not be comforted. Even the trip overland was miserable, and Anna was stiff and sore from riding a packhorse.

Worried constantly about her young son, Anna rarely slept for long periods and hoped her milk would hold out, at least until they were taken to Montreal. She forced herself to eat their meager diet void of bread. Sepi did what she could to help and saw to Anna's comfort whenever she could. Even Henri had periods of remorse and looked at Anna and Henry with sympathy and regret. He had no choice because trading had become a very risky business, and he no longer wished to provide for a slave and her young son.

The arrival at Fort Pontchartrain, after days of overland riding, was a relief even though Anna knew she might be sold. The fort was impressive and lay on the Detroit River. Many well-built and solid French homes hugged the shore, and the river was active with traffic.

Sepi had become extremely melancholy at the probable loss of young Henry. She loved the child as her own, and the thought of separation was agony. The weary group dismounted and entered the west gate of the fort where Henri asked for his acquaintance Major Andre who appeared immediately, greeting Henri with affection. The major and Henry conversed for several minutes, and then the major disappeared. Time passed slowly for Anna, whose stomach churned with every second of the wait.

Anna stood back, holding her baby, while Sepi held them both, eyes wet with tears. It was not long until the major returned with another man. The men briefly conversed, and then Henri spoke. "Madam Marie, may I present Monsieur Louis Girard. He wishes for you to go with him to Montreal."

"As his slave, no doubt," she retorted but added, "I will not go without my son."

Speaking French, Girard said, "Madam Marie, I am honored to make your acquaintance." He bowed. "You will be my wife's helper, and we will treat you well. It will be our pleasure of course. And your fine son also. We will help look after him. Monsieur La Boeuf has assured me of your capabilities and loyalty. We will provide you appropriate clothes for your duties with us. My Madelaine will be pleased." Anna found that she could understand much of what he said having heard French for a year now. It would not be long until she could converse fluently in the language.

Anna hugged Sepi and tears fell upon her sunburned

face, and the two women knew they would never see each other again. Henri pulled Sepi from Anna's grasp. "Enough. We must take our leave. It is done."

Sepi could not cease her crying, and Henri became agitated. He quickly shook the men's hands, thanking the major for his help, and walked back toward the horses. Watching her companions of over a year take their leave of the fort through the front gate, Anna unhappily turned to her new master, Louis Girard, and prepared to follow his lead. Once again her future loomed as a blank slate before her.

Tall, stern, and dignified, Louis, at fifty, looked every bit the French gentleman but his appearance did not hide the gleam in his eye when he looked at Anna or any other female for that matter. Married, he had come to Fort Pontchartrain with some French soldiers from Montreal seeking a slave to take back to his long-suffering wife Madelaine. French citizens, the Girards had established a lucrative trade in a tailor shop located in the center of Montreal, their living quarters being on the second floor of a two story stone and frame house. They were prosperous by the standards of the day, and Madelaine needed help with their busy trade.

"Come. We will leave the fort and seek the bateaux to take us across the water to Montreal. We must make haste for our safety. The British may make their way to Fort Niagara, then, who knows, Quebec City. These are troubled times we live in."

He smiled at Anna, tickled the baby's chin, and took her arm. The two walked through the fort to the east gate where Louis directed them to the large canoe that would transport them north across the lake, eventually to the city of Montreal where Anna would perform her duties as Madelaine's slave.

Anna never lacked for conversation, for Louis had no patience for silence. She learned that Montreal was safe. "You have nothing to fear in Montreal. It is a safe city and well-garrisoned. We are well-protected and secure from the British. You and your son will have a good life with us. My Madelaine will take good care of you both. You will see."

Disgustedly, Anna thought, "What is the matter with this Frenchman? Has he already forgotten that I am a British citizen? That I would prefer Virginia to his French fort in nowhere? Is he so arrogant that he thinks he can offer me enough that I would choose to stay with him?"

June 22, 1759

Led by the relieved Louis Girard, Anna, holding seven month old Henry, finally entered the French city of Montreal. It was a large city with over seven hundred houses and thirty-one streets constructed by the French and occupied by mostly French citizens, traders, and a few Indians allied with French interests. Passing neat houses, many with colorful gardens showing promise of summer vegetables, Anna was briefly reminded of her homeland, her small village dotted with small gardens and flower boxes laden with colors of summer.

Observing the busy street, she noted a variety of Indians, squaws following males dressed in a mixture of deerskin and calico shirts, often tied at their waists with colorful sashes. Many French soldiers strolled in small groups down the cobblestone streets. No one expressed interest in her attire since Indians were common sights among the French. The three walked down a main street, observing two and three story wood houses, occasionally a stone one. There were no sidewalks, dust clouded the scene, and flies and mosquitoes accosted the walkers. They passed several fur-trading establishments, Catholic churches, and one monastery interspersed among numerous taverns and shops before they reached Girard's establishment in the center of the city.

Arriving at a two story building near the Rue de Notre Dame, Louis ushered Anna and Henry through a gate, then to the door of a structure where they were greeted by a middle-aged, hard looking but attractive, Madelaine Girard. Madelaine greeted the arrivals, giving Louis a quick kiss on both checks before she examined the new slave. She had desired help for two years and greatly anticipated Louis' arrival from Fort Pontchartrain, hoping he would secure her help. Dressed in a blue, full-skirted dress that swished as she walked and fitted her snugly showing her still slim figure, Madelaine was obviously a force in the household. With deliberation, she walked around Anna, appraising her new slave. Displeasure shown on her face as she examined the young woman in front of her. Two sallow-faced young girls stood in the background watching their mother and the newcomers and quietly whispered, watching reactions from both parents.

Sensing Madelaine's instant dislike, Anna kept her eyes on the wooden floor in silence, waiting for instructions from one of the Girards. Louis simply smiled and stood back, watching his wife. Anna suspected she and Henry would eventually be the target of Madelaine's fury and resolved to tread lightly in her owner's presence.

June 24, 1759

As Madelaine commanded, Anna holding Henry, having spent a sleepless, hot night in the attic room of the establishment, stood in the kitchen next to the hearth. Scrutinizing Anna's deerskin dress and moccasins, Madelaine would soon dress her appropriately. She handed Anna two worn gowns. "Marie, you will wear these. I will have no Indians confronting our customers. You must keep both yourself and baby clean. You must eat for you are pale and gaunt. And your son. You must never allow him to interfere with your duties. I will feed you and your son and keep a roof over your heads. Surely, this is better than the life you have had, is it not?"

Lowering her eyes. Anna understood most of Madelaine's French. "*Oui, Madame.*"

September 1, 1759

Heat had settled over Montreal, and the streets were covered in a haze of dust and debris while the sun beat mercilessly on the houses and their inhabitants. There had been little rain for over a month, and the foliage and gardens suffered greatly and turned brittle and brown, and the residents harvested what they could save from their once-green and productive gardens. Anna and Henry had been relegated to the attic of the Girard house where no breeze found its way and were extremely uncomfortable in the heat.

Wearing Madelaine's attire, brown dress devoid of ornamentation, Anna sat in the small kitchen while Henry dozed on a blanket at her feet. She struggled with sewing a collar onto a shirt and tried to shut out the sounds that drifted in from the main room. Her ears pricked up when she heard a customer say loudly, "Madam Girard, have you heard?" Not waiting for a response, he continued, "What will you do when the British come? Now that they have control of Fort Niagara, Quebec will be next, and then, voila, Montreal."

"Monsieur Morat, you must not worry. We are well protected here. The British will not enter our gates."

"Ah, madam, you are much too optimistic. What good will it do if this fort is under siege by the British? We will not last long, I think."

"In that case, we will keep our eyes on French ships to take us back to France."

Shortly, the door shut, and Anna heard no more. She was kept busy all day by Madelaine, who sauntered back and forth between the kitchen and the main room where she assisted various customers. Anna tried to keep Henry quiet because she knew Madelaine did not like the child's presence and constantly chided Louis for expecting her to feed another child. The dull daughters sometimes amused the baby, but their attention spans were short, and Anna could not count on them. It was difficult for Anna to manage, but she did so with the unexpected help of Girard's Negro cook, Babette, who delighted in the child and often covered for Anna during Madelaine's tirades.

Various customers entered the Girard house regularly and purchased shirts and fur trimmed capes, products of Anna's skill as a seamstress. It was a profitable business, allowing the Girards to live well in the French community. Louis did little work but was useful in a social role, amusing patrons and encouraging trade while Madelaine looked forward to contacts and social events, the center of her life. She was delighted that she no longer needed to sew and her hands began to look smooth and soft.

Anna knew the fort was on constant alert, soldiers in residence. She had not abandoned hope of rescue, but it was too painful to think of such things. Henry was growing into a handsome child, but dark and brooding. Anna attributed this behavior to their nomad existence and hoped that the stable environment of Montreal might bring about change. So far it had not, but the cook often was successful with her games with young Henry and assured Anna all would be well.

January 1, 1760

Anna
Another year begins, and I remain a slave with a fourteen month old son. Louis continues to be pleasant while Madelaine irritates me every possible way she can. I do not like how Louis looks at me, however. I see him watching me when he thinks I do not see him, and I think

Madelaine knows this too. She remains arrogant and harsh and has developed quite a hate for me, I fear. She does not like Henry either, but he amuses her two daughters who usually ignore me completely since I am only a slave. I do not mind the work because I am busy and exhausted enough to sleep soundly at night even in our very unpleasant quarters in the attic.

I hear that the British finally took Quebec last fall. Now, they are ready to mount an assault on Montreal. The French soldiers are constantly on the alert, and the city's residents are making plans…just in case. Girards are hoarding every cent they get their hands on, and others are doing the same. They inquire about French ships.

Madelaine questions me constantly, thinking I hear secret reports of the British advance. I do not, but I delight in having her think I do. I lower my eyes and say "Non," but she thinks I lie. She was on the verge of slapping me once, but Louis intervened, not that I cared.

I now speak adequate French and understand the language. Sometimes an English-speaking patron comes in the tailor shop, and I listen carefully. I fear my English language skills are poorer than they were when I was taken. I have heard no German since I left Logstown. I try to teach Henry some German and English but, since all he hears is French, his first words were of that language. It does not matter now, but what if I get the chance to return to Virginia? Poor child will only understand French, I fear.

I still see images of Michael at various moments and wonder what he is doing. Does he think me dead? What of Mary and Adam? A few Delawares have visited this city, and I have questioned some French traders about captives in their villages. No one can help me except to say that the Indian villages hold many white captives. If the British come to Montreal and manage to take it from the French, perhaps I will be sent home. Perhaps there is a small ray of hope after all.

February 2, 1760

Caught in winter's icy grip, snow blew and drifted throughout Montreal, making travel impossible and forcing all to remain huddled around raging fires, surviving as best they could on limited supplies until the weather broke. This evening was no different from those of the last two weeks. Louis stoked the fire while Madelaine paced back and forth in her heavy, full skirts, shawl clasped around her shoulders, while she complained about the absence of social gatherings. Louis ignored her and offered Anna a cup of hot tea while motioning her to move her chair closer to the warmth of the fire. Henry slept cozily in a corner with a large fur over his slight body. Louis' bored daughters had retired earlier, seeking the warmth of their beds.

As Anna complied with Louis' request, Madelaine glared at Louis. "You care more about this ignorant German woman than you care for me or our daughters. She disgusts me with her ugly German accent and her brat of a son."

Then, in anger, she hoisted her skirts and ran up the stairs to their bedroom where she removed her gown and fled under the furs that covered their bed, where she would remain until light seeped into the room the next morning.

Louis watched her with disdain and turned to Anna. "*Mon Dieu*, pay her no heed. She is upset and does not mean what she says. You are a fine, strong woman, and I do not mind that you are German. I do not think of you as a slave, not like you Virginians do of your blacks. Come closer to the fire. You are shivering." He walked towards her, arms held out, a gleaming smile on his clean-shaven face.

Anna feared him for the first time, and she knew she

must obey and not create a scene to wake Henry or summon Madelaine, who was surely capable of shooting one or both of them. She slowly rose and, before she could slide her chair closer to the fire, Louis grabbed her in a firm embrace, planting his moist lips on hers, hands moving up and down her garments. Anna silently fought his advance, but he was too strong for her. She tried to claw his face, but he held both her wrists with one hand while the other felt her thigh beneath her skirt. She smelled brandy on his hot breath as he lowered her to the floor and fell on top of her. He was not gentle and took her by force as she shut her eyes and prayed it was not happening.

"Ah, my Marie," he whispered as he rose and towered above her, pulling up his trousers and buttoning them. Anna remained prone on the floor, hands pulling her skirts over her thighs, eyes closed. Eventually opening her eyes, she glimpsed Louis departing up the stairs, and her eyes filled with tears, and she slowly forced herself into a standing position.

March 18, 1760

Anna

I am sure I am carrying Louis' child. Having had six children so far, I know the signs. I cannot, will not, have this child. Have I not suffered enough? My God, if there is one, why has this happened? It is unfair, but I will have to make a choice, and I have. I am ignorant of the ways in which women rid themselves of unwanted babies, but I will find out. I know that the natives have ways... medicines, herbs that will take care of this problem. The Ottawa woman who helps Babette will know, and she will help me. God forgive me, but I cannot have this child. I may never forgive myself for this decision, but I alone will have to live with it. No one will know, ever, and I will die with God's judgment upon me, if there is a God.

There are rumors of the British coming to take Montreal.

If so, I may be saved . . . if I live through this. Perhaps there is hope that I may be returned to Virginia with Henry. Then there is Michael whom I refuse to think about. Will he accept Henry or believe he is a son spawned by that evil Killbuck or Henri LeBoeuf who owned me for a year? Will he believe the date Henry was born? Sweet Jesus, I do not know.

Louis has not looked me in the eyes since that awful night. He suspects I would kill him if I could. He is weak without rum or brandy. Besides, Madelaine suspects, perhaps knows; she glares at me and does not speak except to issue shrill orders. Louis is afraid of her wrath. She, too, would kill him if she knew.

I overhear them talking. They want to return to France, especially Madelaine, who believes she will resume a pleasant social life there. If they have the choice, they will leave here when the British come. They will not bother with me. I shall plead with the British to be returned to Virginia... if I can.

Now, I must speak with the Ottawa woman and take care of this pregnancy. I have no doubts about it, no shame either. I am righting a wrong. This is the only way I can survive and take care of Henry.

March 20, 1760

Anna waited until the household retired, and then, secure in her attic room, she removed the pouch the Ottawa woman had given her. She gently poured the contents, dried herbs of some kind, into her cup. She then took her pot of hot water, poured it over the herbs, and stirred the now-brown, lumpy liquid. She had no idea what was in her warm drink, but she trusted the Ottawa woman and followed her instructions, drinking the murky stuff quickly. She then lay down and stared at the ceiling, watching and waiting.

The cramps began slowly, increasing in intensity until

Anna brought her knees to her chest and rolled on her side. She groaned and bit on a leather strap to keep from screaming. How long her agony continued, she did not know, but eventually the pains settled into normal menses cramps, and she waited until the blood began to flow.

Rising with difficulty, she used the rags she had piled under the bed and cleaned herself as best she could, placing the soiled cloths into a wooden bucket next to her bed. She would dispose of the evidence in the morning while the Girards still slept. She glanced at her sleeping son in the corner of the room and began to cry.

September 6, 1760

Holding her full skirts, Anna ran to the front window and watched the British troops march down the street in front of Girards' house. Louis and Madelaine had left two days before, bag and baggage, children in tow, when the news of the fall of the city was imminent. Residents were allowed to return to France, those who wished to do so, and Girards could not get ready soon enough. Anna helped them pack as ordered and knew they had no interest in her. They simply packed up and left for the ship, never looking back. Anna, Henry and the Ottawa woman remained alone in the depleted house, but all were relieved and did not fear the arrival of the British. Anna knew she was a Virginian, and there would be some help for her. Perhaps she would have the opportunity to return home.

She was startled by a knock on the front door. Peering through the window, she saw a young British officer. Opening the door a crack, she listened to the first English she had heard in quite a while.

"Madam, I am Captain Marsh of the British occupation forces. At your service." He took off his hat and bowed.

Allowing him to enter, Anna answered his questions

while he wrote down her answers. "Who owns this house?"

"Girards," Anna answered in halting English. "They left for France before the British entered the fort."

"Who are you then, Madam?"

"I am Anna Margaretha Mallow, a former slave of the Girards. I am a Virginian who was taken captive two and a half years ago by an Indian raiding party. I was sold to a French trader who later sold me to the Girards."

"I am sorry for your distress. Now it is my job to determine how many colonists have been enslaved here and make arrangements for their return home."

Although Anna had thought of this moment, she felt chills and nausea rise in her throat. "Please, I must sit down while you tell me what will happen."

She grabbed the arm of a chair and sat while the British officer continued. "You have several choices. You may stay here and become a Canadian citizen under British rule, or you may return to Virginia. If you choose to return to your former home, we can take you to Fort Pitt within the month and arrange for an escort to Virginia, or you can remain in this house until spring when you will be conducted to Fort Pitt and then home. I will assure you that Montreal is safe and you may remain in this house indefinitely."

"Sir, I am overwhelmed. This is a day I thought would never come. I have a young son."

"Ah, I see." She knew he was mentally assessing who had fathered her child.

"Will someone notify my husband of my return?"

"Of course. I will need the information from you, and we will make the necessary arrangements."

"Well then, I will choose to stay until spring. Inform my husband that I will return home in the spring, with his son."

Anna could not explain why she chose to stay in Montreal

when she could have been home within two months. She felt guilty about her decision, but she needed time, time to put her thoughts in order, time to prepare her son, time to allow Michael to adjust to her homecoming. Now, for the first time in over a year, she tried to remember every detail of her husband's face, his dark hair tied at his neck, his firm chin and olive complexion, his smile, and his deep voice. She conjured up old images but they came with fear, so she tried to shut them out.

January 1, 1761

Having made her choice to remain in Montreal until spring, Anna would have to confront her fears. Time dragged now that she had made her decision, but there was no going back. As had several others, she could have remained a citizen of Montreal and made a life for herself and Henry with the French under British rule. She had actually contemplated the idea, thinking that she could avoid more pain and loss; but in the end, she realized that it was for the good of Henry that she return. She feared that Michael might have found someone else. She had no idea, but Henry deserved the opportunity to meet his father.

Now, she had long weeks ahead of her to wait until the spring thaws when travel could begin. She concerned herself with her young son. At two and one-half, he was a moody, often sullen, child, and Anna did not like what she saw. Unlike her other children, he was not happy. She attributed this to his life so far, little stability, the Girards, her lack of time with him. But she wanted him to be raised as a Virginian. She wanted him to be a part of the new world, to speak and write English, not French. She wanted him to know his father. After all, Henry might be the only child of Michael's who now lived, and he would never know this son if she did not return.

March 22, 1761

Anna

My stomach churns as the time creeps closer to my departure from this city, now thriving with British soldiers and English-speaking families. Some French have remained, knowing their lives would not be better in France. The British commander has graciously allowed me, the Ottawa woman, and Babette to remain in this house until spring. However, the Ottawa woman has already left us to return to her people living near Fort Detroit. I shall miss her even though she rarely spoke.

Babette, on the other hand, has not stopped talking since the Girards took their hasty leave. She has told me of her life as a slave in Virginia on a large Tidewater plantation. She was captured by the Delawares when her master was killed along with his wife and baby in 1756. She and her master's surviving young sons were marched west to Fort Duquesne where she was purchased by a French trader who eventually sold her to Girard. She did not know the fate of the boys.

Babette has no idea where she will go when she is forced to leave, but I suspect she will have no difficulty finding employment. She is attractive in an exotic way, and an excellent cook. Families have already inquired for her services.

I look at myself in Madelaine's mirror but see a pale, thin-faced replica of my former self staring back at me. My hair is no longer luxuriantly thick and black, nor do my cheeks hold the healthy pink color. I try to erase the lines from my face. I am thin and wan, a ghost.

There is no turning back now. I go home for Henry, for him to know his father. I have no illusions of ever seeing my Adam and Mary again. I have little hope that Michael will love me as he did before the massacre. What happened to me was not my fault, but I know Michael would never forget a rape if I told him. Neither of us is to blame, but we cannot change what happened.

I am besieged with doubts, with questions. Will Michael insist on knowing every detail of my captivity? Or will he not ask and accept what I choose to tell him. Will he believe what I say or will he doubt me?

And what of him? Should I question what he has done these past three years? Has he sought female companionship? He is a virile man and might have thought me dead.

I shall never tell anyone of the child I aborted. It is done. Only I shall have to deal with the guilt. I will not ask Michael about other women. I do not want to know.

It is my hope that we can regain our trust, that Henry will know and love his father, and that our marriage will survive, intact, despite these terrible circumstances. I have lost all faith in God. How could a merciful God allow a person to suffer as I have? I have seen too much death to understand a merciful God. I cannot blame Michael, for he was as ignorant as I.

Chapter 18

April 1, 1761

Captain Marsh stood in the foyer of Girards' former home while Anna watched him.

"Madam, I have a letter from your husband. It did not arrive until a few weeks ago, and I apologize for not bringing it to you sooner. The winter has been bad, and mail has been very slow, I'm afraid. The letter, the letter was addressed to Commandant Rogers and is in German. We translated it, but thought you should read it."

Anna slowly reached for the letter as she thought, "Michael, a part of him after all this time."

For several minutes she stared at the paper, trying to remember German words written boldly in script. Slowly, she read her husband's letter, written last November. It was a short, formal note, and she could read nothing of Michael in it. He simply acknowledged notice of her freedom and impending return. The words blurred on the paper. "I shall await information of my wife's return and be prepared to receive her at Fort Seybert, South Branch Valley, Virginia, sometime in the spring. Please inform her that I am preparing for her return with pleasure and will meet her at the appointed time and place."

Anna held her emotions in check and returned the letter to Captain Marsh. "I need not keep this, monsieur. Thank you for your trouble. I shall await instructions."

The captain took his leave while Anna remained stone-faced. After the door closed, she was overwhelmed with emptiness and guilt. She had scant hope for her future because the letter told her nothing, and there was no joy in it.

June 18, 1761

After a grueling five-day ride, two British soldiers from Fort Pitt, with Anna aboard a borrowed horse, rode up to the newly-constructed Fort Seybert. The group halted in front of the gate as three solemn men emerged. Michael was accompanied by young Jacob Heavener and his brother Frederick, the sons of Elizabeth and Nicholas.

And so Michael Mallow came face to face with his wife after three long years of absence. Hair pulled back and tied at the nape of her neck and dressed in the doeskin dress that Sepi had made, Anna did not resemble the woman he left at the fort. Anna did not know why she discarded Madelaine's dresses and chose Indian garb for her homecoming. From her shiny black hair to her moccasin-clad feet, she could have been an Indian squaw.

Anna sought her husband's eyes and held his gaze for a second or two, interrupted as the soldiers dismounted and held her horse. Anna gave her squirming son to the soldier while she slid from the saddle and then retook the fussy child.

Between Anna and her husband there were no smiles, no tears. They would come later. The Heaveners lowered their eyes and remained silent, trying not to interfere with an emotional reunion.

Anna walked to a stone-faced Michael, who had not moved from the gate, and presented her son to his father. "Michael, meet your son, Henry. He was born in November following my captivity. He is your son." She suspected Michael would not ask about the name.

Under a bright, blue, clear sky in front of the very place where his family had been abducted three years earlier, Michael Mallow met his youngest child. Anna's face remained frozen, and she watched her husband's face, clouded with anger, love, and doubt, wrapped up into one emotion. She noted his graying, thinning hair and his full beard, still black, but interspersed with gray, wiry threads. She waited for desire to consume her, but it did not.

She saw his hands tremble as he took young Henry into his arms. She thought she saw his doubts fade as he looked at his son's dark hair and eyes, reminiscent of Michael and Georgie, his lost sons. "He cannot doubt his own son," she thought, but wariness held sway in her mind.

"Come," Michael said in a voice heavy with emotion as he clasped his wife's arm. "We will rest inside the rebuilt fort for a few minutes where you can refresh yourself and Henry. Then we will go home. Young Jacob has insisted on riding with us to the cutoff. I trust you will not mind." Jacob remained in the shadows to accompany the couple home.

Anna, Jacob and Michael made the short ride up the bridle path on South Fork Mountain leading to their cabin. The trail brought back terrible memories as Anna thought of the march where the slaughter took place three years ago.

Jacob took his leave of the couple when they reached the cutoff to return to his parents' home several miles away. The trees began to cast long shadows as the sun slid toward the tree line. Anna watched Jacob until he disappeared on the dusky trail, and then she urged her mount to follow her husband.

Within the hour, she had surveyed the cabin, now two rooms with Michael's addition of a bedroom. She noted that her small mirror rested on the table next to the bed, and she wondered if it had been placed there recently or had remained as a reminder to Michael for three years. After settling Henry on the old trundle bed in the corner, she turned quickly and returned to the main room of the cabin where she stood in front of the hearth, lying dark, memories rapidly flooding through her mind.

She pulled her rocker away from the wall and sat silently while Michael stoked up the fire to boil water for tea.

"You must be tired. You must be tired from your journey." He then sat on the stool at her feet and stared at her, his black eyes unreadable.

Anna was heady with emotion, and tears threatened to cascade down her face. "Michael, there is much I need to know. I cannot sleep until I know. I have waited over three years for answers."

"Yes, I suppose that is true. Ask me what you need to know, and I will answer as best I can." He watched the fire slowly grow and then fixed his eyes on his wife.

"When did you and the others return? Tell me that first."

Holding his head with his hands, Michael began. "It was awful, not like it was for you, I know, but I returned to nothing, nothing at all. I did not know who died, who was captured, who escaped. Twas a nightmare. We returned the day after you were taken. It was too late."

Anna lowered her eyes and wiped tears away, hoping she could maintain her composure to hear the details.

"The British finally sent help, too late, of course. Captain Brock and one hundred men arrived the day after the massacre, a few hours earlier than we did. It seems they were prepared for what they found. A man called Robertson was hiding off the trail over the mountains, and Brock found him. He had escaped from the fort." Michael's voice broke.

"Yes, I remember him all too well. He fled with the Dyer women and children. I remember him as a coward."

"I don't know about that. I only know he was found and told Brock what happened. But he did not know who died, nor did he know if you were alive or dead. He was often hysterical when questioned about the details. Guilt, I imagine. We, Nicholas Heavener and the rest of us, crossed the ford about dusk only to be stopped and held by force by Brock's men. We saw the remains of the fort, and it was gruesome, the stockade gone, embers still burning." He coughed and stopped to regain his composure.

Anna patiently waited for him to continue. "I asked what they found. Brock said they found three dead children and three adults in the fort. We had no idea who they were. I knew there were many children so I prayed ours were not among them. Brock had some pieces of cloth for identification, but I did not see anything of yours or our children's. They could not identify the bodies in the blockhouse, too burned, and the poor babies, scalped they were." He cleared his throat and wiped his eyes before continuing.

"A small search party of Brock's men had found Elizabeth and Katrina hiding in the Heavener's fruit cellar. Elizabeth said Maria, poor Maria, had been captured and did not make it. Overcome with relief, Nicholas broke away from Brock's men and rode to his wife. I did not see him again for several days. And right after that, in the dark, a man galloped across the ford to tell Brock that some women and children had been found by a family on Beaver Creek, up north. Brock determined they were the Dyers, three women and five children."

"Then I could not stand it and I had to see if our cabin still stood, so I also grabbed my horse and broke away and rode here. The cabin had not been touched so I returned to Brock, but I could not talk to those soldiers. They had no idea what it was like for me. Then, late that night, someone heard a noise. We thought it might be a savage, but it was not. It was Maria Heavener. She just came out of the woods. She tried to tell us what happened, but she was so upset and confused. She thought you and the children were still alive, but she knew some were killed. She could not tell us much . . . too upset and fearful. But she knew, she knew that it was Killbuck who had committed this savage deed."

"The dead, where are they buried? Do you know who they were?"

"We knew old Hannah Lorenz and George Moser were in the blockhouse. The third, we just thought it was a man. And the three babies, we did not know whose children they were because they could have been ours, Mauses, or the Regers. I know you will tell me who they were. Please, I need to know if they were ours?"

"No. The three babies were George and Catherine's. I cannot relate the death of those poor children although they died quickly. I need to tell you now about our children while I still can." She sat up straight and looked at the fire.

"Our three are dead. Sarah died the second day. She died quickly at a warrior's hand. I do not think she suffered. Our boys, Killbuck sent our boys to the Ohio River on horseback, the horses from the fort, Jacob's horse. Killbuck told me it was a good thing because they would live. I believed him and thought they might survive until I found out when we reached Logstown that they were both dead. Georgie drowned in that river," she paused and wiped her eyes. "Michael died of sickness in the village. I never saw him again. They are gone, our three are gone," and she sobbed.

"It is my fault, my fault." Michael raged and stood up.

"No, it is not your fault. Nor mine. Blame the British. Blame Killbuck, but do not blame yourself or me."

"And Mary and Adam? The soldiers tell me they might live as captives in Indian villages. I have to believe that."

"I do not know, but I was taken with Mary down the great Ohio to an Indian village where she was given to a chief to replace his sister. I hear that many captives survive in villages. I think she survives. And Adam, I think he too survives, but he is so young, and I fear he will be indoctrinated into their ways and may not want to return to us. The savage who took him was kind to him."

"My God. How terrible for you, for all of you. Do you know about the others?"

"The soldiers questioned me, and I told them what little I remember about the others." Anna continued in a shaky voice. "Martha Woods and her girls. Martha was such a support to me, to us. She was befriended by a savage who, I believe, took her and her girls to his village. She knew William was dead when we neared the Upper Tract Fort. She smelled the smoke. . ."

"My God, you all knew that the Upper Tract soldiers were dead?"

"Yes, we knew. Killbuck did not tell us, but we knew. We knew there was no help from there. Why, why did you, or Brock and his men, not follow us?"

"Brock's orders did not allow for tracking captives, and I could not muster enough men to follow you. Besides, it was too late; a day is too long to catch up with a raiding party."

"Ah, well, so be it. The adults, all but me, Sarah Hawes, Martha, and Eve Moser were killed. I think you know that."

"Yes, we, I, saw them. They are buried off the trail where they fell, a mass grave. There were three babies with them. I had to look at their bodies to see if you were among them. It was the hardest thing I ever had to do. To see Jacob and Maria. . ." His voice broke, and he struggled with tears.

"There were others who died. William Dyer and Wallace, their servant. We heard the shot that killed Will that morning before Jacob surrendered the fort."

"Damn him," Michael shouted.

"Stop. Jacob bears no blame. He thought it best, you know. We had so little lead and men. Do not blame him."

"Then you must blame me and the others for leaving you all there, unprotected."

"No, I do not. It is over, and there is no blame to it. We cannot change the past."

"What about the others?"

"I do not know what happened to most of the captives. I

know that Sarah Hawes was taken by Killbuck to his village. I saw our Mary taken by a chief's mother. I saw all the young men run the gauntlet and survive, even that sullen Reger boy. I believe that they all live, somewhere."

"James Dyer, he is home, Anna. He escaped last year and is here, in the South Branch Valley, on his father's land."

"How, how did he manage an escape?"

"He was smart. He let the Indians think he was trustworthy. Soon, they gave him limited freedom and took him back and forth to Fort Pitt when they went to trade. The British are not good to the savages, and many are starving so they have no choice but to deal with the fort. Anyway, he managed to get a trader's wife to hide him. The savages tried to find him but could not. Then, the next day, James left and made his way home. Took him two weeks in all to get back here. He was starving when he arrived."

"I am glad he is home. Now, I must finish. At Logstown, Killbuck sold me to a French trader who took me to New Orleans. On the return trip, Henry was born on a barge in the great Mississippi River. I was treated kindly by the trader's Indian wife who helped with the birth. Then we came north, up the Illinois River, eventually to Fort Pontchartrain, Fort Detroit now. Then I was sold to a French merchant and taken to Montreal. Did the British tell you that?"

"They told me your French owner fled to France when the British took the fort. That they would bring you home this spring. That you had a child. Oh, Anna, I am so sorry, so sorry. I do not want to hear more, not now. It is so difficult. I have had a terrible time, and I know you have too. It will be hard for us, these terrible losses. Sometimes I do not know if I can stand it. Life will never be the same for us I think."

"I know. I know, but we have Henry, you know. He is your child, and we must do the best we can for him. He is the only one, out of six, the only one. "

She did not look at her husband for fear of what she might see in his face, and she waited for him to question her. But he did not.

June 30, 1761

A graying, stouter Elizabeth Heavener walked up to the Mallow cabin door, escorted by her husband Nicholas to visit Anna, the first time they had seen her since she had been captured at Fort Seybert. Their son Jacob had escorted her home with Michael, and so they were prepared for the woman they visited today. Entering the cabin as Michael held the door open, Elizabeth was shocked and dismayed at the appearance of her dear friend Anna, but she mustered her courage, smiled profusely, and embraced the thin, pale figure before her, now dressed in brown homespun buttoned to her thin neck, hair pinned and covered by a white cap.

Anna was aware that strains of captivity showed in her face, dark circles under her eyes and new wrinkles above her prominent cheekbones. Although her dark hair had recovered its sheen, gray strands mingled among the dark ones. But she, like Elizabeth, rose to the occasion and smiled with tears in her eyes and held the embrace a few seconds longer. How she had dreaded this meeting, but the worst part was over now, and it was time to introduce Henry, who had hidden behind his father sucking his thumb. Pulling him forward, Anna looked her friend squarely in the eyes. "Elizabeth, this is Henry, our son born on the great Mississippi River. We are fortunate to have a strong, healthy son." Anna spoke in German, the language now unfamiliar on her tongue.

Nicholas, hiding his embarrassment, ruffled the child's dark hair and looked at Michael. "Ah, Mallow. You are indeed fortunate to have this fine-looking boy. And Anna, we have prayed for three years for your safe return, and God has answered our prayers."

"I no longer speak of God. I have had too many losses."
Anna looked away from both Heaveners.

"Now, Anna," said Michael. "We cannot understand
God's ways, but we must be thankful for what we have
and your return. Now, let us offer our dear friends some
refreshments and have a nice visit."

"Elizabeth," Anna said. "I want to hear about Maria.
How is she now? It is wonderful your girls were spared."

Heaveners stayed an appropriate length of time and
then took their leave of the Mallows, knowing their next
encounter with Anna would be much easier. And Elizabeth
knew she would never, never question Anna about Henry or
her captivity.

November 1, 1761

Anna

*I have been home for four and one-half months now. It
is strange to be speaking German again after three years of
hearing French, Indian, and English. My English has not
improved much; however, my French is acceptable, and Indian
words often pop into my mind. I think Michael deliberately
speaks German with me so I will forget French and become
the wife I was when I was taken, but that can never be, I know.*

*I realize how difficult it is for Michael. Although I have
suffered more than he can ever imagine, he, too, has suffered,
not physically, but emotionally. I have suffered both. Only a
mother can understand the loss of a child, and I have lost five.
It is too painful to think of Sarah, Georgie, and Michael, all
dead by the hands of the savages. Even though Georgie and
Michael were taken alive, they died, and I will always blame the
savages who took them and could not or would not save them.
I have heard that Adam and Mary still live, rumors among the
few captives who have returned from Fort Pitt, but I cannot rely
on rumors. I fear I shall never see either of them again.*

Our neighbors have questioned me. They profess sympathy but turn away if I begin to relate the details they truly do not wish to hear. Only Elizabeth offers solace. She understands my perpetual agony. Although she never asks questions, she listens and councils me for she knows my fragile state. She knows that I came close to insanity. She knows as a mother, my losses cannot be overcome, and she tries to help me cope and adjust. She knows, too, that Michael is pragmatic, that he wants things to return to normal, that he must forget or go crazy himself. That is his way, and I must learn to understand him and his ways.

What of my poor Mary and Adam? Do I dare hope they will return home someday? And if they do, will they be the children I lost? Nothing will ever be the same, I know.

During these past four months, Michael and I have not touched, and rarely have our eyes met. He plays with his son and makes every attempt to act like a devoted father. But he does not touch me, and sometimes he avoids me altogether. What can I do? He must come to me, I think. I cannot initiate affection. I fear he sees me as soiled, a wife used by Indians and Frenchmen. We lie side by side at night but might as well be in different rooms. I shall never discuss my experience with the Frenchman, never.

November 12, 1761

The fall of 1761 had quickly passed into a cold, wet, snowy November, keeping settlers inside more than normal. While the wind blew the snow and rain against the cabin walls, Anna and Michael were comfortable inside with a bedroom added to one side, affording more privacy and much-needed room. Although there were always the rumors of pending uprisings, Anna no longer feared stepping outside or seeing Henry snatched up by savages.

She lived one day at a time, trying to concentrate on her daily chores and Henry, soon to have his third birthday. She tried to anticipate Michael's moods, but as of yet, he had not needed her affection or her touch. Sometimes, her desire overwhelmed her, something she never thought would happen, and she simply tried to remember all the good times, the passionate times, but she only became more despondent in her fragile state of mind.

Tonight, Michael, hands clasped behind his back, studied Anna as she sat by the fire, knitting as was her custom. He then glanced at his sleeping son on the pallet beside the fire. Abruptly, he walked to his wife and sought her eyes. He pulled her up into his arms as tears began to flow. "Ah, Anna," he whispered. "I have missed you so much. I want you, and it has been so long."

Both held each other tightly for several minutes until the sobs ceased. He whispered his love for her, and his words touched her like a caress. Gently, he led her to the bed in the adjoining room and pulled her down upon him while kissing her passionately and hard. Anna responded equally and thought of how long she had thought of this moment.

"I love you," he murmured.

Michael undressed her tenderly while she sobbed in pleasure, anxious for his touch. He took her slowly until she could no longer stand the waiting. He finished and rolled on his back only to have Anna pull him back on top of her while covering him with wet kisses. Their pleasure continued for several hours until both lay exhausted and satisfied next to one another under the heavy fur cover. For a moment in time Anna forgot the world around her and her terrible losses.

March 21, 1762

Enjoying the last warmth of the sun as it began to settle below the trees, Anna sat on the step in front of the cabin door while she watched young Henry run in circles as he tried to catch his new mongrel puppy, a forlorn creature. The child laughed with delight every time he caught the puppy's tail, only to lose it and try again. Anna was content, not happy as she had hoped, but it would come, she kept telling herself.

Knowing she was carrying another child, she decided her condition was responsible for her occasional dark moods, certainly not Michael, for he was kind, considerate, and thrilled at the prospect of another child. Henry was thriving and seemingly happy, but he, too, had dark periods. She rarely saw in him the childish joy that she had seen in Georgie and Michael. Now, their lives were routine and difficult for money was scarce although Michael's shoe repairing helped. As long as the weather cooperated, crops and livestock would provide for their needs.

She was suddenly aroused from her sober thoughts by her husband returning from a short trip to the mill. As Michael swung the bags of flour to the ground, he joined his wife on the stoop.

"I saw James Dyer at the mill today He is extremely excited. He received word that Sarah, his sister Sarah, was seen at Fort Pitt last month. She was with a group of Indians there to trade. A soldier noticed her red hair and word got around, eventually to James. He and Matt Patton are going to Fort Pitt as soon as they can get ready for the trip. James intends to rescue her, and I do not doubt that he will. He is a very determined, clever young man, I think."

"I hope you are right. I only know she went to Killbuck's village." She did not want to remember more.

August 11, 1762

Anna

Once again I am ready to birth a child, my seventh. My God, I am only thirty-four years old. It is my duty to Michael, to give him another child to replace three losses. This child I will have, willingly, but it will take its toll, I fear, and will replace no one.

Michael has no idea, nor will he, of what I went through: the agony, the struggles, my strengths. It does not matter anymore. I am home, he accepted Henry, and I shall have this child. God, help me to survive this birth. Do not forsake me again. I have suffered too much.

The day dragged on, and a strained Elizabeth Heavener held Anna's hand as she monitored the pains, knowing it would not be long now. The baby would come very soon. Michael stood at the cabin door ready to step outside when his wife began intense labor, the habit formed during the earlier births. Anna never screamed but suffered in silence, occasionally moaning while she held onto the bedposts.

At three in the afternoon, the baby appeared, a tiny girl, but making up for it with noise. Hearing the child's cry, Michael entered the cabin and strode into the adjoining room where his wife, his new daughter, and Elizabeth were waiting for him. Cradling a worn blanket, young Henry sat in the corner, scared and uncertain, for he worried about his mother, but he ran to his father who picked him up roughly.

"We shall call her Anna Barbara," spoke Michael when he saw his new daughter for the first time.

"I want to call her Sarah." Anna cradled her newborn.

"No, I don't want daily reminders of our loss. Anna Barbara she shall be," and Michael turned away from his wife and child and sought to comfort the trembling Henry. Elizabeth squeezed Anna's hand for encouragement. "It will be fine. You have a fine new daughter. Rejoice. Her name is of little importance."

September 1, 1762

Anna held her three-week-old daughter Barbara at her breast while enjoying the warmth of the afternoon sun on her small porch overlooking the sloping valley below. She felt comforted by the familiar view, the cleared acres of mature corn waiting for harvest, the dark green forest behind, and floating white clouds chasing each other across a bright, blue sky. Henry played in the dirt a short distance away and traced paths with his stick, looking at his mother for approval. Anna smiled at the child and closed her eyes only to be jolted by the sounds of hoof beats and her husband's voice.

"Anna," Michael cried, vaulting from the saddle, barely missing stepping on a startled Henry, the bay horse rearing back in fright.

Barely catching his breath and the reins, Michael stood in front of her. "Our Mary, Mary, is coming home. She is alive and in Fort Pitt. It is a miracle, a miracle. Two French traders hid her in their canoe and smuggled her from an Indian village to Fort Pitt. I do not know the details, but she is safe and will be home in a week. Two soldiers have volunteered to bring her to us. Can you believe it? Our Mary is coming home."

Anna mustered her courage and smiled at her radiant, happy husband, hiding the feeling of dread within her, for she had just adjusted to their life, the four of them, and rarely thought of her older captive children because it was easier that way. She could not endure any more loss or disappointment and was still in fragile condition, too fragile to confront the thought of a thirteen-year-old daughter who had been indoctrinated by the Indians for four years now and certainly would not be the same child she remembered.

Chapter 19

September 11, 1762

It was late afternoon when, suffering from a hard ride on a warm day, two lathered horses trotted their way along the bridle path to the Mallow cabin. Anna watched Michael, a young girl holding onto his waist, and young Jacob Heavener, following behind. The two men halted their horses in front of the cabin, and nearly thirteen-year-old Mary slid from the rump of her father's horse and stood in front of the Mallow cabin, taking it all in with moist eyes. Her father dismounted and took the reins of both horses and led them to the nearby hitching post while Jacob simply stood quietly and watched the scene before him.

Mary halted to watch Anna standing in the open doorway, holding her baby while Henry clutched her skirt and stared at the young girl, his sister, whom he had never seen. Mary was tanned, dark hair tied at her neck, hanging half way down her back. She was dressed in Indian garb, wearing beaded moccasins, with a pouch hanging from her waist. Two silver bracelets adorned her thin, tanned arms which hung stiffly at her sides.

After observing her mother for a moment, Mary stared down at Henry, who looked at the ground and hid his head with one arm. Realizing she was watching her brother, Mary walked to him and kneeled at his feet, taking him into her open arms, murmuring in halting English, "What is your name, my little brother?"

Henry looked at his sister in surprise and awe. "Henry, Henry Mallow."

Anna saw the surge of memories in her daughter's face. "She remembers. She remembers that I was carrying a child on the trip."

Anna watched her two children and felt hope, hope that Mary would adjust, and Henry would help this process. She, however, could not yet reconcile her lost Mary with the young, tanned woman before her. Michael returned from handling the horses and walked to Anna, putting his arm around her waist.

"Mary, our daughter, is home. Do not worry. She will return to our Mary in time. She is young and will be of help to you."

It was then that Jacob spoke directly to Mary in German. "It is good that you are home Mary." With that he walked to secure his horse and, without turning back, mounted and rode the way he had come.

Mary released Henry and stood up, turning toward the sound of Jacob's words. She watched him ride down the bridle trail and a puzzled look appeared on her face. It was then Anna realized with a shock that her returned daughter was almost old enough for marriage.

May 30, 1763

Anna was terrified. Once again the settlers of Virginia, Maryland and Pennsylvania were reeling under the wrath of the disgruntled tribes who had renewed their attacks with a vengeance.

Michael explained, "A chief of the Ottawa tribe, Pontiac, is not ready to give up. He knows that the British will not keep the treaty. He sees that the English have continued to cross the mountains for more land, even into the Ohio country. He is uniting the tribes against us."

Hearing this news, Anna constantly thought of Indians

and Killbuck, and she approached Michael as he prepared to leave this rainy spring morning.

Grabbing his arm, she said, "Do not leave me today. I fear the Indians and cannot stay alone . . . too many memories. Please don't go."

Gently taking her hands and pulling them around his waist, he quietly said, "Dearest, do not despair," and he kissed her earlobe. "There are no savages in Augusta County, my love. They are too busy up north attacking British forts. Besides, the British are not treating them well, and many are starving and without weapons. Pontiac will not prevail. We are safe here, and I will not be far. I must feed our livestock and check the cows and calves. I will not be long. You will see."

"But it is Killbuck I fear. Why can I not dismiss him? How I hate him. Do you ever hear of him? Does he lead these new raids?"

A look of hate spread across his face. "Hush. That devil will not come to Augusta County again. I hear nothing of him, and some believe he is infirm or even dead. Do not think of him. I beg you."

August 30, 1763

Heat had embraced the South Fork Valley for the entire week, and showed no signs of letting up its hold. Sweating profusely and smelling of horses, Michael shoved open the cabin door to confront Anna as she removed fresh bread from the fireplace rack. She was startled by her husband's unexpected entry. The cabin was extremely hot, and beads of perspiration shown on her forehead.

"What is it? My God, is it the savages?"

"I have news. Col. Henry Bouquet, the British commander, has pushed Pontiac back and intends to march into the Ohio country. Pontiac is finished and has retreated west, and Fort Pitt and Fort Detroit are no longer in danger. Bouquet hates the Indians and will eventually subdue them. It is only a matter of time now until these ignorant savages are defeated forever. There is also the rumor that the commander of Fort Pitt gave the Indians blankets infected with the smallpox last month. I do not know if it is true, but smallpox has spread among the Ohio villages. Even settlers in the Ohio Valley have been infected. They say over two thousand settlers have died from Pontiac's warriors and the smallpox," he answered breathlessly.

"My God. Do you know what you are saying? Our Adam is in one of the villages. What if he contracts the pox?"

"I don't know. I just know I am glad Bouquet hates the savages and hope he kills them all. We do not know if Adam lives. And if he does, he may not want to return to us like other captives have. It has been five years, and he was so little, so young." His eyes became moist with the memory of his oldest son. Anna turned away to contemplate this news and also thought of her son.

February 1, 1764

Anna

A cold wind blows steadily outside, and Michael has gone out to feed our livestock including our new hogs. I hear the wolves howling, and Michael fears they will get our shoats. We are fortunate and have much to be grateful for despite our losses. I awoke feeling nauseous and know the signs. It is a curse to be this fertile I think. Now I fear I am carrying my eighth child. I will not tell Michael yet, although he knows me well and will guess.

My Mary does well now. She is very enamored by Jacob Heavener who has been so good to her and helped in returning my girl to her former self. Mary and I rarely share our captive experiences. I think she does not wish to know what might have happened to me after Henry was born. She never asks about the Frenchman or my experiences in Montreal because she does not want to know. But she has told me enough of her life in the Scioto village in Ohio to assure me she was not used by their men. It was fortunate she was rescued, for her age was advancing enough that she surely would have become a warrior's wife within the next year or so. Many captive women have returned with children by Indian warriors, and I thank God she did not.

There has been some good news, so rare in my life these days. Sarah Dyer Hawes is home now. Her brother James rescued her they say. I knew he and Matt had gone to Fort Pitt last fall to seek her among nearby Indian villages where rumors of her existence came from. She is such an attractive redhead and not hard to miss, even in Indian garb. We hear a British trader saw her with Indians who were trading at Fort Pitt and notified James who could not get to the fort soon enough. He located her in Sawtunk, Killbuck's village, and waited weeks until she appeared again in the fort where the Indians, now desperate for food and ammunition, came to trade. Somehow he managed to get her aside and hide her until the Indians gave up searching. Then the three of them came home by horseback, hiding in the day and riding at night to elude any Indians who might be hunting her. Her daughter Hannah, now almost nine years old, did not recognize her mother for weeks and refused to have anything to do with her. But finally Hannah gave in and accepted Sarah, who has now moved back to her old home with her daughter. Sarah has no shortage of suitors and will no doubt marry again I think. Besides, she is now a wealthy woman having her husband's land and land willed to her by her father, Roger Dyer, who died in the massacre.

September 1, 1764

Anna
My God, my eighth child has just been delivered. We will call him Michael. Why could we not call Barbara Sarah as I wished? After all, Michael is the name of one we lost. Why

is this different? But is does not matter. I have done my duty and presented my husband another child to replace one lost. One can never replace a lost child, however. I still see my dear Sarah, seeking my eyes, asking for nourishment. I still see Georgie's terror when he was placed on that savage's horse. I still see Michael's eyes questioning me as he was forcibly grabbed. Those images will never leave me. Never.

And now I touch the small head at my breast, covered with dark hair, reminiscent of my first Michael, but not my first of course. I shall love his child as the others. I just wish his name were Jacob or Nicholas, not Michael, for my Michael has already lived and died, and I remember his dark curls and his father's nose. Elizabeth is wrong. Names matter.

November 15, 1764

Anna knew Michael was nervous and frustrated. There was news from the Ohio Valley. Michael told her, "Colonel Henry Bouquet has continued to place fear in savages. He led his army into Ohio, deeper than any British force had been before. The Shawnees, Delawares, and Senecas are ready for peace. The tribes are to bring in all their white and Negro captives for the trip back to Fort Pitt. Adam, our Adam, may be one of them."

Michael knew Adam might be among this large group but would not know for sure for weeks or even months. Anna, too, felt the same fear, knowing that Adam would not be the same son she lost, if and when he were returned.

November 29, 1764

There was great rejoicing in Augusta County for a militia escort brought home several of their children captured at Fort Seybert. Adam Mallow was not among them, nor had his name shown up on the lists of returned captives. Several tribes had admitted to having captives still in their villages but promised to return the rest in the spring.

Jacob and Mary had joined their neighbors when the captives returned. Mary later told her parents, "Both Dorothy and Barbara Reger were returned along with Elizabeth Maus and Eve Harper Moser. Elizabeth had to be brought home bound for fear she would attempt to rejoin her Indian family."

Anna listened in silence, remembering the faces as they had been six years ago on the journey to Ohio.

"The Seybert girls have also been rescued but did not come home but were taken to Maryland to join their brothers, Nicholas, Henry, and George, the three having made their way back to friends after escaping from the Indians two years ago."

Jacob added, "They will come back here one of these days."

"Adam, any news about Adam?" Michael asked.

"No, but Eve Moser related rumors of the others. She had heard that Sarah Maus had married and would not leave her warrior husband who had hidden her from the troops. She said no one knew of Johnny Reger or Anthony Maus so they could be dead or well-indoctrinated into their Indian lives. As for Killbuck, Eve had heard he lives in Newcomerstown, a Delaware village in Ohio, but she did not know if he had joined Pontiac."

March 10, 1765

Anna

Will our troubles never cease? We suspect that Adam is alive and was returned to Col. Bouquet's forces last fall when the girls were returned. He failed to disclose his real name; perhaps he had forgotten it for he was only six and one half when we were taken. Michael knows that several captives reside in Philadelphia because no one knows who they are. Michael is obsessed with finding him. I am afraid. It may be a mixed blessing.

It has taken Mary several years to become white again. I credit Jacob Heavener, Nicholas and Elizabeth's son for helping her. He is twenty-one but has followed her since she arrived home three years ago. He adores her it seems. She is too young to marry but he wishes it of course. I fear I shall have no say in the matter. I will miss her help with Henry and Barbara and now little Michael. I believe Mary wants to leave this house for she remembers how it was before we were taken. It cannot return to that. I shall never be the same and rarely feel happy. Henry and Barbara, and little Michael cannot replace Adam, Georgie, and Michael. Barbara is a strange child, moody even at three. Henry clings to me still even though he is seven now. And Michael, their father, tries to please them, but he cannot. Too often he looks at them and sees his older sons and pain fills his eyes and heart. He will not want to lose his Mary, but he will allow the marriage for it is good for her to leave us and start her own family.

May 28, 1765

A beautiful May morning embraced the South Branch Valley when young Mary Mallow married Jacob Heavener. The Mallow cabin was the site of the marriage festivities. Elizabeth and Jacob Heavener, parents of the groom, proudly watched their son marry their dear friends' daughter, witnessed by everyone who could make the trip to the Mallow farm. Former captive Elizabeth Maus, who had made a remarkable recovery from captivity, escorted by Frederic Heavener, soon to be her husband, watched in anticipation of her own marriage. The two Heavener girls, Maria and Katrina, were present along with Michael's brother and family. Perhaps forty neighbors and family enjoyed the day while the Mallows provided food and drink to all.

It was an occasion for much happiness, and Mary glowed in her new white dress and her hair plaited with flowers.

Young Jacob was very excited and pleased with his beautiful young bride, now completely without the stain of her Indian captivity. If memories remained, Mary never spoke of them.

Anna held her youngest, Michael, who squirmed incessantly and certainly wanted to be let loose to crawl wherever he wished. He twisted in her arms and would not remain still. Barbara, at three, refused to come out of the adjoining bedroom and instead crouched in a corner with her well-worn quilt against her face while sucking her thumb. She wanted none of the festivities and did not want to share her mother. Neither her father nor brother Henry, whom she adored, could coax her into joining the others.

Michael proudly held Mary's arm as she spoke her vows to Jacob. Tears formed in his eyes as he placed his daughter's hand in Jacob's, and the itinerant preacher smiled as he pronounced them man and wife.

Anna had not wanted to lose her daughter, but she told Michael, "Mary will be happier with Jacob, you know. She will forget her life as an Indian. I fear that I remind her of that life."

Anna had been home for four years and had produced two more children. Yet she knew that she was not the same woman who was captured. She recognized that Michael did not understand her, her melancholy, her remoteness at times. She pleased him, of course, and often desired his touch. Somehow it was never quite enough to overcome the memories.

October 20, 1765

Late in September a neighbor of Mallows, Ulrick Conrad, who had lost his entire family to the Indians right before the Fort Seybert massacre, managed to locate one of his daughters in Philadelphia where she had been taken by

Bouquet's troops in 1764. His wife and a son had already been returned, and two children had died in Indian villages. A third daughter had, like many others, chosen to stay with the Indians, but this daughter had been located when Conrad placed an ad in the Philadelphia paper. At Michael's request, Conrad inquired about other missing captives including Adam Mallow, and there was reason to believe that Adam had also been returned to Philadelphia and not identified as of yet. And so Anna and Michael regained hope that Adam was not only alive, but also could be redeemed if identified.

Michael, determined to pursue his first born son, now thought to be in Philadelphia, placed his own ad in the *Philadelphia Gazette*. The ad read:

Three Pounds Reward.

Seven years ago, the wife and 5 children of Michael Mallo, living on the South branch, in Augusta County, in Virginia, were taken Prisoners by the Indians, when after, the three youngest children died, and the Wife and eldest Daughter came home again; but his Son, John Adam Mallow, was, accounting in the Report of other Prisoners, delivered up by the Indians but last Fall, when he went with the Pennsylvania Troops. His Indian Name is Wannimen; he has dark brown Hair, somewhat curled, black Eyes, a Hair lip, and is of a tawny complexion; had had, as other Prisoners say, the small pox among the Indians and is now 13 years and a half old. He was taken at Seybert's Fort, on the south forks, in the abovesaid County, and, together with a Swiss woman, detained among the Shawanese, at an Indian town called Wabeda Meine. Any person, with whom he lives, or who can give an account of him to either of the following persons, vix. Benjamin Shoemaker, at Philadelphia; Adam Moser, at Tulpehocken; Jacob Haufman, at Carlisle; George Shafer, in Conecocheague; Michael Laubinger in Winchester; or to his said father, at the above mentioned place, so that he may have him again, shall have the above reward, and reasonable charges, paid by either of the persons aforesaid or by me. Michael Mallo, shoemaker.

Shortly, Adam was identified by his disfigurement, the harelip, and Michael made arrangements to leave immediately for Philadelphia.

Anna had suggested, "Take Jacob with you. Do not go alone."

"No. It is my responsibility, and I have no idea what to expect. The stories of the returned captives are tragic, and I fear for our son."

"He may not want to return."

"You may be right, but I will have to deal with that. The trip will take at least a month. Jacob and Mary will be of help to you."

November 19, 1765

It was a gloomy day when Michael Mallow returned from Philadelphia with his oldest son Adam, now fourteen, and brought home in chains. No matter how hard Michael tried, Adam refused to speak English or German. There was no doubt he would run away if freed from restraint, an all too common action of some captives who would return to their Indians homes if possible because they remembered no other. Michael was despondent, and the entire trip home had been clouded with silence and dark looks from his slim, muscular son who refused to change his Indian dress and had to be bound by his angry, frustrated father.

It had begun to drizzle when Michael astride his old gelding, leading a mare holding bound Adam Mallow, arrived home. Anna heard the sound of horses and opened the cabin door. She noted that Michael's beard had not been trimmed for weeks, and his hair was loosely tied at his neck. Michael dismounted and held both sets of reins while motioning Adam to dismount. Both men were covered with dust, Michael's clothes disheveled and boots covered in mud from the long, unpleasant trip. Despite his chains, Adam swung his leg over his horse's withers and slid effortlessly to the muddy ground. A scowl shown on his face, and his black eyes blazed in anger, but he stood tall and straight, watching warily as his father shoved him forward toward the cabin door.

Anna waited for her son to enter the room. She looked at her oldest son and felt a knot in her stomach and fear in her heart. She was secretly afraid of this now tall, dark haired and tanned son of hers, dressed in Indian garb and muscled from physical activity. She noted small pox scars on his face and the harelip from birth. She feared for him and thought white man's clothes could not hide the Indian spirit within.

With tears in her eyes, Anna walked to him, looked into his unsmiling eyes and said in German, "Welcome home, son. I am your mother. Your sister Mary is beside me."

Mary moved to her brother, crying softly, and traced her finger across his upper lip. "Oh, Adam, it has been so long, so long." And recognition came swiftly, and Adam embraced his beloved sister.

Anna knew that it would be a long time, however, until Adam forgot his thoughts of returning to his Indian village.

Chapter 20

January 1, 1766

Snow had piled high around the Mallow cabin, and the roads were presently impassable, drifts blocking passage, and trees bowing low, heavy with snow. Anna, rocking slowly with baby Michael on her lap, observed her oldest son Adam as he sat, cross-legged on the plank floor, whittling a toy for his brother Henry who was sleeping soundly on a pallet next to the fire, a warmer place than the drafty loft where he and Adam usually slept.

Engrossed in his work, Adam did not notice his mother's intense look, which was just as well since she saw a young Indian in front of her. His black hair remained long and tied at his neck, and he insisted on wearing moccasins. Having been home only six weeks, Adam had begun to speak with his parents and help his father who no longer bound his son at night to keep him from fleeing. The heavy snow was a deterrent of course. They had done everything they could to make Adam comfortable and had made no demands except that he not run away. Michael had made it clear that he would pursue his son, even harm him, should he run away.

Although Anna saw the Indian in her son, he began to see the mother in her, and often helped her with the younger ones. Anna knew he had not forgotten his Indian family and remembered them fondly. However, Anna hoped he was smart enough to recognize that he was a white and that his future was tied with his parents and their life in

Virginia. Anna was encouraged, however, because Adam had become fond of his brother Henry in particular.

May 1, 1766

On this warm, delightful spring day, Anna and Adam rode down the side of South Fork Mountain on a leisurely trip to Mary and Jacob Heavener's, a rare time for the two to be alone. Michael had suggested they do so while he minded the three younger children for a few hours. Mary's new baby was the reason, and Anna could hardly wait to see her new grandchild, a girl called Margaretha, which pleased Anna very much.

The two did not speak much at first, instead enjoying the beautiful day and the new-greened forest surrounding them. Adam had now been home for over five months and was slowly beginning to adjust to his new life with his biological parents. Anna still doubted that he would ever forget his Indian life, but it seemed that he finally came to terms with his future, and it was not with the Indians. Initiating conversation, Adam looked at his mother. "The land in Ohio, where I lived these past years, is very beautiful. I hope to go back there someday." He spoke in English and seemed to prefer it over German, often asking his parents to speak it.

As a matter of fact, Adam had relentlessly pursued the English language as it was new to him for the most part, and he did not wish to speak German. He carried on endless conversations with his father learning words, phrases, repeating and repeating. He wanted books, and books were very rare indeed, but Michael managed to secure a few.

Anna answered in English, having made efforts to improve her speaking skills. "Ah, yes, I remember the Ohio country also as very beautiful. We have seen a lot, you and I, you know. Life has given us much pain, all of us. We all have suffered much, but perhaps you also had good times in your years with the savages."

"Do not call them savages, Mother. Most are not, and I understand their desire to protect their hunting grounds. They have great respect for the land, something which whites seem to lack. I learned much from these people, but I know that I cannot return to them. My place is here, and you need not fear that I will run away."

"I know that. I do, and I am pleased that you are home and can be a brother to your three siblings. Henry needs you and may always I fear. Promise me you will watch out for him and teach him. I am so pleased that you are learning your letters, and I only wish Henry would concentrate. I have been a poor teacher for all of you, for I have prayed that my children become literate like their father. Do not stop learning my son. It is too late for me, I think."

"Do not say that, Mother. Someday you will have more time to practice reading. You will sit in your rocker and read a book."

"Perhaps I will. Of course, we need to have books to read," she laughed. And they continued their leisurely ride south to Mary's.

August 18, 1766

Anna

I am a grandmother. I cannot believe that Mary just birthed her first child, and I am thrilled. It is very late and dark, and I cannot sleep tonight. I silently get out of bed not to disturb Michael or the children. Michael is so tired these days, and I sometimes worry about his health. I leave the room and enter the main room seeking the door for some fresh air. It is so warm tonight. I walk outside and enjoy the moonlighted area before me. It is quiet, sounds of crickets and other noises fill the air. But it is monotonous noise. I sit on the step on this moonlighted night, my shift pulled up to my thighs.

Deep in thought I am startled by hands on my shoulders and feel Michael's breath on my neck as he nuzzles my shoulder. Is this a dream or not? It is not, and I turn my face to meet my husband's hard kiss, and we embrace. He lifts me up in his arms and I am young again and experience the same passion I felt when he first touched me. We are locked in an embrace when he carries me to a plot of grass next to our cabin. Yielding to his touch, I fall on the ground, not minding its hardness as Michael makes love to me firmly, but softly, on the grass of our claim in this new land. Oh, how young I feel, and it is wonderful, and I almost forget.

February 12, 1767

Exhausted Anna fell into her rocker loosening the buttons on her gown which was now too tight even though she had just let out most of her dresses. She placed her hands over her protruding belly, feeling the child move within her, and closed her eyes. Michael watched his wife and felt exhausted himself. He found he could no longer split a cord of wood easily, and his muscles ached from exertion. Adam had kindly taken the ax from his father and completed the task quickly. Both had returned to the cabin, and Michael thanked God for this strong, healthy son who was such a help with this family of five.

Anna was finally content for the most part. For the last several years she had not worried about Indian raids although she had heard the Shawnees were raiding in Pennsylvania and the Kentucky land where settlers were exploring and making tomahawk claims, despite the fact that it was illegal. The clash was not over by any means, but she lacked the energy to worry about it.

Turning to his son, Michael quietly spoke, "I do not want to alarm you son, but I heard that settlers pay no attention to the 1763 treaty prohibiting whites from settling in the Kentucky land west of the Alleghenies. There will be trouble, and the Shawnee will fight again, I fear."

"They will. They will fight for Kentucky, the sacred hunting grounds, if the whites attempt to settle there." Adam stared straight into his father's dark eyes.

"The flood of whites is too great. They can claim four hundred acres and build a cabin. No treaty will keep them from it, and soon the government will permit settlement or simply look away when it happens. The Kentucky lands are prime lands for settlement and have already been explored."

"We will never see eye to eye about settlement, but you are right. The whites will not be turned back, and the Indians will fight to the death or until their way of life is over forever. I cannot desire their extermination."

"Son, you have seen a side of these people that I have not. You must understand my hatred for them, the murder of three of mine I will never forgive. The selling of your mother, all of it." Michael looked away from his son, eyes full of anger.

"I understand, but for seven years I lived among them and was loved and trusted. I cannot hate them as you do, but I am white and will protect my white family if necessary."

"The cultures cannot co-exist. Their way of life will be terminated, right or wrong. This land beckons thousands of whites, and they will come. The numbers are too great, and the natives will be defeated. This is a hard land. We have worked hard and persevered, and, yes, we have taken their lands and will continue to do so. It cannot be stopped. There is no fairness to it. And there is a cruelness to these savages."

Adam interrupted, "The whites are cruel also. It is human nature to protect one's land whether Indian or white. The Shawnee will fight and be pushed west, and someday the

Indian life will disappear, and white settlers will own all the land all the way to the distant sea. And few of us will remember the good things about Indian life. I will remember . . ."

Having heard enough and fearing that an argument would ensue, Anna said, "Stop, both of you. This family has suffered terrible losses, but you were returned, Adam, for which we are very grateful. We must look ahead and protect what we have. We are white, of German heritage, and cannot change that. I cannot, no will not, worry about the fate of the Shawnee."

April 28, 1767

Anna

Was it just nine years ago my children died, my three, Sarah, Georgie and Michael? Has it been that long? And now I lie in bed, waiting the birth of my ninth child, and I am not yet forty. I am afraid today. Something is not right. I feel it. The pains start, but they stop, then they begin again. I see the faces of the women attending me. They frown and talk among themselves, like I cannot see their fears. They fear the child is in the wrong position, breech they say. Elizabeth is among them, with my Mary, her daughter-in law and my beloved daughter.

Where is Adam? With his father no doubt. Neither can stand my suffering. I am thankful they are together though. It has taken two years for Adam to trust us. Still, there is tension between them, and I do not know why. Perhaps it is because Adam suspects that Michael does not believe he is Henry's father, but it is good to know Adam watches my Henry. Where are my babies, Barbara and Michael?

There is no doubt that some of our neighbors and friends, despite the passing of five years, still believe Henry is not Michael's child. Some believe Killbuck is Henry's father, which is ridiculous of course. I know Michael hates the savages and always will, understandably. We have had a workable marriage these past five years. Do I not have two babes to show for it? Am I not pregnant again?"

I do believe that Michael's love for me has never wavered. He thinks he has come to terms with Henry, but I am not certain. I just know in my heart he does not place blame on me. He tries to love Henry but is beset with doubt perhaps. . . but he has tried, so very hard he has.

I know I shall not survive this birth. I feel it. Ah, what will happen to my little Michael, now three, or poor Barbara, such an unhappy child at five. Or Henry, now nine. What kind of family are we now? Neither of us speaks what is in our hearts. We have been unable to do so since my return despite our moments of passion. I die content in what I did, had to do. I survived. God sorely tested me, but I lived. I lived for my child Henry, and I wish I could live for Barbara and Michael, but I fear I will not. What will become of them I wonder? I trust Michael will be a good father to them all. He was a good husband to me.

I try to open my eyes but cannot. The pain has ceased. I see their images, Sarah, Georgie and Michael. They are smiling, and I want to walk toward them, and I do . . .

Author's Note

During the eighteenth century and before, women rarely remained unmarried. It was expedient for the returned captive females to marry promptly for single women had few rights and could not sustain themselves. Additionally, large families required the replacement of a deceased spouse in order to maintain the family unit and complete the endless chores of both father and mother. Consequently, all of the returned females, captured at Fort Seybert, married regardless of their experiences with the Indians. Nicholas Seybert, as far as is known, was the only captive to remain single, an unusual circumstance for the time period.

Anna Margaretha Mallow's name appears only once in records, the christening of her first child Anna Maria (Mary) in Christ Lutheran Church, October 1749, in Berks County, Pennsylvania. There is no evidence to suggest that she died before the massacre or was not the mother of Michael Mallow's eight known children, five as proven by Mallow's ad in the *Philadelphia Gazette*, the child born in captivity, and two more, bound out at Mallow's death in late 1772.

Biographies of her captive son Adam refer to his mother's captivity, not his stepmother's. There is simply no concrete evidence to suggest Mallow married a Mary Miller as some believe although it is possible that Anna Margaretha's maiden name was Miller. In 1769 Michael Mallow married Mary Ingle as proven in a record of the Oley Hills Union Church, also in Berks County. The author believes Anna Margaretha died around 1768 when Mallow sold his original claim to resettle near Kline, West Virginia. It is probable that he sold the original land when Anna died, purchased new land, and took a second wife.

The 1765 ad in the *Philadelphia Gazette* for the return of Adam Mallow proves that five Mallow children were taken at Fort Seybert along with their mother who returned sometime before the birth of Barbara in 1762. It is unfortunate that the names of the three youngest captive Mallow children are unknown as are details of their deaths. One Ohio county history states that the three younger children were killed in front of their mother; however, only the youngest baby's brutal death is described in many accounts. The author believes two of the Mallow children died soon after reaching Indian villages.

It is proven that Adam Mallow was forcibly returned in fall of 1765 after being secured by Col. Henry Bouquet's troops and taken to Philadelphia. His mother died before 1769, and his father in late 1772. Adam married Sarah Bush and fought at Pt. Pleasant in 1774, perhaps against Indians he had known during his captivity. As early as 1806, Adam, his sons, Adam Jr. and William Henry, and their families moved to Fayette County, Ohio, where descendants remain to this day.

When Anna Margaretha and daughter Mary returned from captivity is not known. It is probable that Anna returned in late 1760 or early 1761 after the fall of Montreal where the author believes she was held for over a year. Mary, according to one story, was rescued by fur traders and taken to Fort Pitt around 1762 or 63. She married Jacob Heavener in May 1765 at age 16 and was not listed in Bouquet's list of returned captives in 1764.

Henry Mallow, the child born in captivity, according to his Revolutionary War Pension Application, was the son of Mallow as proven by recent DNA testing of Mallow descendants. He remained in West Virginia on a portion of his father's claim. It is said that his father Michael hated Indians the rest of his life and perhaps never came to terms with Henry's parentage. Barbara and Michael, children born after Anna's return, are proven children as recorded at Mallow's death. Both were bound out, Barbara to her sister's husband, Jacob Heavener, and Michael to John Bright. Some believe there were other children.

The brave Nicholas Seybert escaped from the Indians after little more than a year. He is thought to have rescued his two brothers and returned to friends in Maryland. Eventually the three brothers returned to the South Branch area. Nicholas never married and left his estate to his siblings. The three Seybert girls were returned to Bouquet in 1764, married, and left descendants.

Nicholas Heavener, husband of Elizabeth Seybert, and son of William Heavener who probably perished at Fort Seybert, died in 1769. His widow Elizabeth remarried Christopher Lauer, husband of her deceased sister Catherine. Their daughters, Maria and Katrina, married and left descendants. Son Jacob married Mary Mallow after her return from captivity. Details of Maria Heavener's escape are not known. Sources do not place Elizabeth Heavener at the fort during the massacre, but it is highly likely she was because her daughters were there, and her husband was likely one of the men who left for supplies.

James Dyer returned in 1760 having escaped from the Indians at Fort Pitt by hiding in a trader's cabin. Details vary, but many believe that he rescued his sister Sarah Hawes, either with the help of Mathew Patton, his brother-in-law, or by himself. According to Dyer history, Sarah was held in Killbuck's village of Sawtunk and became a wealthy widow upon her return. She married Robert Davis and left descendants. James Dyer married three times and left many children. One romantic tale suggests that James found the treasure, gold coins, and used the money to purchase land. Since it is doubtful that the settlers at Fort Seybert had much in the way of gold, the story is highly doubtful.

Barbara and Dorothy Reger were returned by Bouquet in 1764 and inherited their father's estate with the stipulation that the land go to his son should the son ever return. He never did, but a John Anthony Reger appeared in Tennessee years later, and many believe he was the Reger son.

Of the three Maus (Mouse) children taken captive, only Elizabeth was returned by Bouquet's troops. The name of her mother, killed at Fort Seybert, was not recorded. Elizabeth married Frederick Heavener, son of Nicholas and Elizabeth, a few years after her return. Her sister Sarah chose to stay with the Indians and was never heard from again. Her brother John Maus never returned; however, it is thought that he turned up later as Tankard Maus of New York state and had been purchased for a tankard of ale from the Indians by a New York trader.

Eve Harper Moser was returned by Bouquet's troops and married Jacob Peterson, once a captive himself. Some believe she had a child while in captivity. There exists a court record of Eve Elizabeth Moser, executrix of Eve Elizabeth Moser's estate in 1765. Some believe that Eve had Moser's child while captive and that the child died as the only heir to George Moser's estate. Martha Woods and her daughters all returned at some point although Magdalena was held years longer than her mother and sister. Martha did not remain in the South Branch area and may have moved to the Carolinas, but no more is known of her.

There is reason to believe that another family, the Conrads, were at Fort Seybert. It is known that the father placed a 1765 ad for the return of daughter Barbara where he states his wife and son returned from captivity, and two children had died. He does not state where they were captured. However, the Conrad land was close to the fort, and it is logical to assume the family sought protection there. If the Conrads were in the fort at the time of the massacre, there may have been as many as sixty people within its stockade, many more than most accounts suggest. The number of captive children would also be significantly higher.

Robertson is listed in most accounts as an escapee from the fort. The records are silent about who he was or why he was in the fort. Some believe that he crossed the mountain and alerted the troops about the massacre. Accounts vary, and no one knows exactly who else managed to escape the fort. It is probable that Margaret Dyer and sons did so since her husband William was killed on the day of the event. Several stories relate Hannah Keister's escape with her children, and her husband Frederick was likely with the men securing supplies. Since Roger Dyer was killed near the fort, his wife Hannah had probably been in the fort with him but was not among those who were killed. There were also reports of a Heavener girl who escaped after the captives began their march to the Ohio River.

Descriptions of the fort itself vary, some believing that the stockade contained cabins. It is highly doubtful that these settlers had the time to build individual cabins, but there was most likely a blockhouse of some sort. The fort is also described as round in shape, but no one knows for certain. The location of the fort is marked on Sweedlin Road, north of Brandywine, WV on private land. The author has visited the site as well as the area where the captives began their long trip. It is unfortunate that only a sign marks the site of this massacre. Some researchers still believe that the site of Fort Seybert is unknown because the Sweedlin Road site does not fit some of the earlier descriptions.

Killbuck, the Delaware war chief who led the raids on the forts, was responsible for several forays into Virginia from 1756 through 1758. He resided in the village of Sawtunk on the Beaver River in Pennsylvania and later moved to Newcomerstown in Ohio. He is mentioned, along with his son, in several primary account journals. During the

Revolutionary War, Killbuck became a spy for the Americans against the British. In 1781 he was held in the Fort Henry jail at Wheeling, West Virginia, for protection from the British. According to author Allan Eckert in his novel *That Dark and Bloody River* (Bantam Books 1995) notorious frontiersman Lewis Wetzel and a friend entered the jail and brutally killed Killbuck. Wetzel was never prosecuted, and Killbuck's body was thrown into the Ohio River. His son, John Killbuck, became chief of the Delawares upon the death of Netawatwees through descent from his mother in the matriarchal line of succession. He never attained the influence of his predecessor and lost power.

Barack Obama's mother descends from the Mallows through Martha Mallow Holloway, who is buried with Adam and Henry Mallow in Ohio. The immigrant Mallows had three sons, and one, the returned captive Adam, moved to Ross County, Ohio, as early as 1806 when he was over sixty years old. Adam, his sons Adam Jr. and William Henry, and their families are buried in the Mallow Cemetery in Fayette County, Ohio, along with Martha Mallow Holloway and her husband Josiah Holloway.

Finally, these people were not only courageous and resourceful but also endured hardships that people today could not imagine. The author hopes that this novel will keep the memory of these brave, independent immigrants alive.

CPSIA information can be obtained
at www.ICGtesting.com
Printed in the USA
LVOW10s1035020717
540116LV00009B/362/P

9 781619 358652